WHITE HORSE

WHITE HORSE

Erika T. Wurth

FLATIRON
BOOKS
NEW YORK

WHITE HORSE. Copyright © 2022 by Erika T. Wurth. All rights reserved. Printed in the United States of America. For information, address Flatiron Books, 120 Broadway, New York, NY 10271.

www.flatironbooks.com

Library of Congress Cataloging-in-Publication Data

Names: Wurth, Erika T., author.
Title: White horse / Erika T. Wurth.
Description: First Edition. | New York : Flatiron Books, 2022
Identifiers: LCCN 2022020897 | ISBN 9781250847652 (hardcover) |
    ISBN 9781250847669 (ebook)
Subjects: LCGFT: Novels.
Classification: LCC PS3623.U78 W48 2022 | DDC 813/.6—dc23
LC record available at https://lccn.loc.gov/2022020897

Our books may be purchased in bulk for promotional, educational, or business use. Please contact your local bookseller or the Macmillan Corporate and Premium Sales Department at 1-800-221-7945, extension 5442, or by email at MacmillanSpecialMarkets@macmillan.com.

First Edition: 2022

10 9 8 7 6 5 4 3 2 1

To the nerds who fell in love with dragons and demons, with portals and alternate worlds—and who felt that in order to grow up, had to put those things aside. And who came back.

WHITE HORSE

CHAPTER ONE

There was something strange, mysterious even, about the White Horse tonight. Normally, it was merely an Indian bar. My Indian bar. But there was a milky, dreamy quality to the red lights swinging over the pool tables, like the wind from the open doors was bringing them something new, something I'd pushed away for as long as I could remember.

"Debby, do we have to talk about her *again?*" I took another swig of my beer and slammed it back down, eyeing my cousin as I did. She would never let this subject go, no matter how much I rebuffed her. I sighed, taking in the dank, wet-wood smell of the bar, the harsh laughter of the bikers in the booth behind me.

"The thing is, I found—"

I interrupted her with a brush of my hand.

I hoped Nick, the bartender, would come by and ask if I needed a refill, but all I could see was the mirror in front of me, the words Miller High Life emblazoned in gold cursive on the front. Right next to it a sign read, FIRST FIGHT. LAST DRINK. PERMANENT 86. Besides us, the bartender, and the bikers, the White Horse was empty. It was always empty, but I loved it. I loved the long wooden bar, the cats wandering in and out; the mangy orange one was my favorite. She liked to sit on top of the bar and let me pet her while she closed her cloudy eyes and purred.

Debby shifted her weight on the stool, the plastic crackling as she did, the bar stirring around me like a bad dream.

"All I'm *saying* is that you don't know your mom's story."

"Yeah, okay, Debby. That's great," I said.

I signaled Nick when he came out of the bathroom. "Two more," I said, hoping he'd remember.

A couple of Diné came through the doors, quiet the way they were, and made their way to a pool table in the back. One of them saw me when he came over to order a beer, and he gave me the friendly nod, his black hair glistening red in the faint bar light. I nodded back and that strange feeling I'd had earlier flooded back into me.

"The thing is," Debby said, "you know how we check in on your dad?

I hung my head. "Yeah, so?"

"I went over there the other day to do that, and some cleaning, because I know the nurse is great and everything, but I like to see how he is, and I'd just come home from work, and was dropping the kids off—"

"Jesus, Debby, if you're not going to let it go, spit it out."

"Okay, okay," she said, starting again. "So, Mom had been push-ing me to clear some of the boxes in the attic. And like, we were going to haul them out and throw them in the dumpster, but Mom seemed to want to look through them. And mainly they were full of old toys, and papers and rusting appliances, but then, we found something."

"What?" I whispered, and that dreamy quality snapped back.

"Something of your mom's."

I was silent. My mother. The woman who had abandoned me when I was only two days old. The woman who my father had been so dev-astated over he began to take long drives, a bottle of Jack between his legs. The woman who had made it so that I had to care for my dad like a baby, instead of the other way around, after he'd gotten into an accident that had left his body but taken his mind. Cecilia.

"And the thing is, Kari, it was some Indian jewelry—and it's *old*."

I felt like changing my drink to something stronger.

"And, like, since your mom was Apache and Chickasaw?"

I nodded.

"I'm just saying that it might be significant," she said.

I continued to stare down at the wood of the bar, run my fingers along the rough edges.

"But the important part is, like, when she found it? When I picked it up, I felt weird."

I was silent for a long time, my heart hammering in my throat. I signaled Nick and ordered a whiskey to go with my beer, the dark brown liquid splashing a bit over the rim of the tiny paper cup as he set it down. "Want one?"

"No, I gotta drive back," Debby said, glancing at her clock. "It takes at least forty-five minutes to get from Denver to Idaho Springs, and I'm sure Jack's already wondering why I'm not home."

I rolled my eyes, and we sat in an uncomfortable silence.

"You know I don't like talking about her," I finally said, grumbling.

"I'm just going to like, give it to you, okay?"

"Fine," I said, watching as she dug into her purse.

She pulled an ancient hammered-copper bracelet out of her bag, a bit of patina around the edges. It hummed with power, with history. My history. It was the kind that Indians used to wear all the time, and it *was* old. I squinted, thinking, upon closer inspection, that it was probably turn of the century. I could see, as Debby held it out in her little pink hands, that there were different objects carved into each thick copper square, links connecting each section—symbols I recognized from Indian jewelry of the time. Stuff that was common for urban Indians, or that had been lifted from plains culture. A thunderbird. A waterbird. A spiral. A Lakota chief's headdress. Then there were others that I thought were perhaps Apache. Symbols for water. The sun and mountains. The moon and arrows. A war club—yes, that was definitely Apache. Stuff my Auntie Squeaker back in the Springs would know about, I was sure. And lastly, something that made me ill just looking at it—a stick figure that seemed to represent a monster of some sort. In the back of my mind, I could almost remember the name for it.

My thoughts wandered, unbidden, to my mother.

Debby shoved it into my bag, and I kept drinking, nodding as she went on about her husband, listening to the eerie, lonely sound of the wind whistling through the open door. But though I tried to focus on everything but that bracelet, it began burning into my mind, glowing almost, roping me to thoughts of my mother, and my painful, locked-away past.

CHAPTER TWO

looked at the clown's face, the big, red mouth with the hole at
the center for the ball, and thought about the two-odd years it
had taken Jack—Debby's obnoxious husband—and his best buddy
from high school, Carl, to build a mini putt-putt into the old, rotting
apartment complex that Jack had inherited from his father. Jack had
decided, upon his father's death, that what he really needed in his life
was an indoor mini putt-putt course. Carl had been very supportive
of this move. Debby less so.

Jack took an awkward swing with an ancient, rusty golf club,
and the ball ricocheted off the clown's face he'd built into an old
fireplace, whacking him in the leg. "Goddamnit," he said, picking
up a can of Miller Light sitting on an old end table. The ball had hit
uncomfortably close to his crotch.

Jack took another gulp of his beer and set it down.

"So, Kari—got a boyfriend yet?" Jack asked.

Carl perked up. We'd boned once in high school, and Carl had
never forgotten it.

"Yeah, actually," I responded. "I do."

Jack blanched.

"Kari!" Debby said, squealing and clapping her tiny white hands. "You didn't tell me about this! Why didn't you *tell* me about this?"

"Well," Carl said, "don't keep us in suspense. Who's the lucky guy?" He pushed the remaining dark blond wisps of his hair over his pate.

"Yeah, Kari," Jack said suspiciously.

"Your *dad*," I said, barely suppressing a cruel jag of laughter, and Jack's expression blackened.

"Kari," Debby said nervously.

"That's not funny, my dad's *dead*," he said, and I could hear Carl muffling laughter.

"Jesus, Carl, be on my side for once!" Jack said, thwacking him in the arm. "She's never gonna get on that d—"

"Hey!" Carl said. Then, "Ow." He rubbed his tricep.

"Maybe you'll stop asking me that kinda shit now," I said, lifting my eyebrows up sharply, and holding my drink out to him for a cheers.

Needless to say, he didn't clink. He grunted and took another swig. Beer ran down the side of his mouth, and he brushed his arm across his lips.

He was always after me to get a man. Thing was, Debby was too. She figured that Jack wouldn't be such a jerk about us chilling together if I had a dude, and we could double-date. But that wasn't my thing. At all.

Carl saddled up to take a shot at the clown.

Jack sighed, heavily. "Look, Kari, don't take offense," Jack said, stumbling slightly where he stood. "I don't mean to try to push you or anything it's just that . . ." he stopped, and I could almost see the gears slowly grinding in his mind.

"It's that, you know, Kari, we want you to be happy. And like, when you have a partner in life, it like, means you learn stuff about yourself—" Debby started, and I groaned.

"Exactly," Jack said, interrupting. "And it makes you more mature."

I watched Jack, clearly the pinnacle of all that is male maturity, slightly stagger once more from too many Bud Lights, and wondered if he'd ever washed a pair of his own underwear in his life.

"Baby, I can speak for myself," Debby said, giggling girlishly. But she was clearly irritated. Jack interrupted her a lot.

"I don't—I mean, I didn't," Jack started. "I'm sorry, I didn't mean to interrupt, or like, speak for you."

"Oh, you *didn't*," Debby said, and I tried to stop my eyeballs from rolling so far back in my head that they disappeared for the rest of time.

"I mean, look, Kari, you're strong and independent, and that's not a bad thing," Debby said.

Jack stared at her slack-jawed for a moment, clearly confused about where she was going with this line of thought, and Carl took a whack. The ball sailed straight into the clown's mouth, and the clown swallowed and yelled "Whooopeee!" Carl followed with a whoop of his own, walking into the bedroom to get to the ball.

"Yeah, that's right," Jack said, uneasily.

I suppressed laughter.

He knew he was being manipulated into something, and he didn't like it one bit.

"She can take care of herself," he said, hiccupping in the middle of his sentence.

"I *completely* agree with you. That's exactly why I need to hang out with her sometimes—just her and me," Debby said, pulling her club up and over her shoulder. It was Jack's turn with the clown, and he was taking his sweet time. I always went last.

"What? No. No. That's not—"

Debby rotated in my direction, sipped at her rum and Coke, and set it delicately back down on a glossy, wooden coffee table. The table was covered in stickers—mainly Care Bear.

"Because sometimes you get in trouble on your own, don't you, Kari?" She said, her voice high-pitched and sweet as a child's.

I went to open my mouth, and Debby burned holes into me. She knew goddamn well that my troublemaking days were long over. That when I hooked up with a guy, I always texted her his number and address. That I hadn't even smoked weed in years. That Bud Light was the hardest drug I downed these days. And she knew exactly why. Jaime.

"Yeah," I answered.

"Debby," Jack said, "that's on you. Sweetie, I love you, you know I do, but sometimes you're too . . . too—you know, obsessed with helping other people. Which is what I love about you," he said quickly. "But you don't need to babysit a grown woman."

I wanted to blow fire at him, but honestly? He was kind of right. I didn't need a babysitter—I needed Debby to stand up to Jack for once. He was a typical dude, but he supported his kids, he often took Debby out to eat, gave her foot massages, said nice things to her. Though he didn't like it whenever I stood up to him, he'd not only back down, he'd often see my point. So why she wouldn't tell him to chill the hell out was beyond me.

"You want to try again?" Debby asked Jack, interrupting him.

"What?" he said, backing into one of the little hedge-animals that he and Carl had scattered throughout the rooms.

"With the clown?"

"Oh, yeah," he said, disentangling himself from the hedge. After about the fourth whack, the ball went through, and Jack trailed behind Carl into the bedroom.

Debby picked up her club, and on the third attempt, got the ball in. I whacked a few times and followed.

Jack and Carl were mumbling amongst themselves, and Debby rolled her eyes and elbowed her way through them, breaking them up. This next course was her favorite, and no matter who was in what order, they always let Debby go first.

It was three cat butts, with long, wavy tails moving across the floor. You had to time your shot just right, so that the ball would enter the empty spaces between the tails, and pop up, and into, of course, a cat butthole.

"This one always makes me vaguely uncomfortable," I said, sipping my beer and standing back.

Debby had her tongue out, squeezed in between her lips.

The men guffawed at my comment, and Debby whacked, violently, and the ball rolled up and into the butthole of an orange cat. There was even a little faux-litter box that one of her cats had mistaken for real once, to Jack's consternation. Sometimes me and Debby would take lawn chairs and sit in the box during the summer, and let her kids play while we drank mai tais.

"Yes!" Debby said, plucking her drink, complete with mini umbrella, up from the floor where she'd set it, and took a celebratory sip.

Jack went next, and it took him a couple tries to get a ball up and into a gray butthole.

Despite what Jack had said in the clown room, I was hoping he was finished, and that Debby wouldn't bring it up again. But as soon as she'd finished drinking, she said, "Okay, so like I was saying," and Carl started moaning.

"Oh no, I thought we were *done* with this," Carl said, planting one hand over his eyes.

"The thing is you know what Kari's like. She needs someone patient and reasonable with her, to stop her getting into trouble." Debby's mouth creased into an expression of satisfaction, and she walked into the bedroom for the next step up. Jack had built the cat butts into an old closet that led to another bedroom. This one was my favorite.

The balls were waiting at the bottom of several old kiddie pools. There were four pools, and a bunch of fake greenery and fake flowers. To make the setup weirder, there were four plastic Ronald McDonalds in each pool, complete with vines and flowers wrapped all around them, that Carl had found in a dump in Denver—or so he claimed—in each corner of the room. Jack had spent hours drilling holes into their faces to elongate their mouths, and every mouth led to a different room. And each pool had a little fountain.

Jack frowned and walked up to one of the Ronalds. He looked ready to whack but stopped and turned to me. "You really think you need a babysitter? Cause that seems like the opposite of who you are to me."

He went to hit the ball again and stopped once more. "In fact, damn, Kari. That's something I always respected about you."

The irony.

I was in a tough spot. If I told him I didn't need a babysitter, which was true, he'd justify throwing a shit fit every time I wanted Debby to go off with me to the White Horse, or to Walmart, or wherever.

"I mean, sometimes, I guess, I just . . . look. What's wrong with just me and Debby hanging without you sometimes? I think you're the one acting like he needs a babysitter," I said, unable to help myself.

His face twisted with confusion and rage.

Jack exploded. "Why don't you find one of those men you fucking hook up with to hang out alone with then? And not my wife!"

"I don't like them for that long," I said, not missing a beat, and ending with a Nicholsonesque smile.

"Kari, oh my God! Stop it!" Debby sputtered.

"Yeah," Jack echoed.

I snorted.

"Jack, you apologize to Kari!" Debby said, turning to him, her lower lip trembling.

"I—" Jack said.

I started dancing, banging my head in celebration, one hand in the air, fingers crooked into a devil-sign.

"Kari, you're only making it worse!" She swiped a tear away from her face.

"Yeah, Kari," Jack said, his eyes narrowing.

I stopped. Sighed.

Debby's voice was quavering now. "Jack, please. I do everything for you. Why can't you let me have this? I cook. I clean. I work. And I know what you're going to say, you don't have the time to take care of the kids while I hang with Kari. But *I* find the time, all the time, while you're off with Carl talking about high school and chicks and building this—" she said, gesturing with the club and swinging it near Carl's head, who wisely ducked, "thing," she finished.

The silence in the room was palpable, and we all watched Jack take a breath.

I wondered if he'd apologize. He was as stubborn as I was, and it was always like this. Me, wanting her to myself, and Jack, wanting the same. An eternal tug-of-war.

"I'm sorry, Kari. I just . . . I guess I don't see why you have to go off alone with her, that's all," he said. "I'm sorry, baby," he finished, his eyes cutting over to Debby. "I know you do a lot for me. I'm sorry."

She sighed, heavily.

It was my turn.

"I'm sorry," I said lamely, and Jack narrowed his eyes at me again. He knew I wasn't sorry, not one bit.

What I'd wanted to say—what was on the tip of my tongue— was, I'm sorry Jack's a jerk. Or worse, a basically okay human being who, because he was a dude, because the whole world thought his kind of shit was warranted, because my sweet cousin had had kids with him too early to know what she was getting into, thought forcing Debby to make him her entire life was okay.

This is exactly why I'd never had a boyfriend. Why Jaime and I had made the pact early on. But I'd been the only one to keep it.

CHAPTER THREE

The lights of Roller City flickered pink, then green, highlighting the path in front of us, and Debby pushed ahead of me, smiled, and twirled, ending with a bow.

I clapped, and she giggled like a kid.

"Still got it!" she yelled over the sounds of "All the Way Up."

She rejoined me and we linked hands, our left feet pushing back smooth and long at the same time, then our right, to the beat of the song.

We'd come here as children, sometimes every weekend—at first, Debby lacing my skates for me, holding my hand and guiding me to the floor, catching me as I fell, showing me the way to keep my balance, then slowly, how to bring flash into something simple and beautiful, full of teenage grace. We began to dance together, to spin, and in my case, to catch the eyes of the boys in the sweaty, hormone-soaked corners of the rink.

But not in Debby's. Even then, it was Jack waiting for her. Jack with his shy eyes. Jack, who watched me grow from child to woman, who bought me ice cream, the kind that came in little cups, with built-in little spoons, handing me my favorite, chocolate—first, even before he handed Debby hers.

I remembered thinking of him as an older brother. I remembered liking him.

Debby squealed with excitement. The song she'd requested was on. I didn't think they would do it: Roller City had closed at one point, and when it reopened, like much of Denver, it was full of polish, suburban charm; its carpeting a thick neon and black, ROLLER CITY in fancy green cursive embedded into the fabric.

Though her musical tastes and mine were as far apart as humanly possible, her joy over hearing Tiffany's "I Think We're Alone Now," her flushed cheeks, her triple spin, made me feel like the past was here, was linked to us as surely as our arms were linked into one another's, as if a portal had opened and allowed us in, just for this one moment, back into the best parts of both of our adolescence.

That didn't mean I wasn't going to tease her mercilessly about it.

We skated to the song, Debby singing her middle-aged heart out, and when it finished, she pushed to the edge, and hung her head, her thin, slightly curly hair drenched in sweat. When it came back up, she asked me if we could take a break, and I agreed.

We sat down, and I plopped my skates up on the seat next to me.

"You thirsty?" she asked, and I nodded, and got us both Cokes at the concession stand. I peered hard at the menu, but the little ice creams were long gone.

She sipped, ran her hand along her brow. "It's been so long. I can't believe I remembered how to skate at all!"

"And then some," I said, "to Tiffany—because," and here I paused to close my eyes, and thrust one light brown fist up into the air, "I think we're alone noooow."

I opened my eyes and smiled.

"Don't you start. Tiffany got me through some dark times."

I laughed and took a long gulp of my soda. "That and New Kids on the Block."

"I don't care what you say," she said, pulling her hands through her hair, "I loved them."

I remembered. She'd had their poster on her wall for years, until her mother's Christianity had accelerated into evangelical, and she'd torn it down, thrown it away. I remembered Aunt Sandy had called it evidence of her unholy, lustful feelings. God, Debby had cried.

"I think we're alooone now," I sang again, and Debby whacked me on the arm until I stopped. "So, how'd you get away from Jack?" I asked, shifting on my seat.

She glared. "Kari, you make it sound like I'm in prison."

"Shit, Debby. As far as I'm concerned, you are. I don't want to tell nobody where I'm going all the time."

"That's not fair!"

"Debby, when I called you, I could hear him yelling 'Where are my shorts?' in the background."

"Well, the baby vomited all over his favorite shorts," she said, "plus, it's not only Jack—I work too, you know, and my mom can't take the kids every time you have a yen to go roller skating."

I sighed. "I know, Debby, but like sometimes, I just wish . . ." I trailed off.

"You just wish it was like when we were teenagers."

I rolled my eyes. "No."

"You just want me to have zero responsibilities, like you, and that's not my life, Kari. I'm sorry." She crossed her arms over her chest, and her brow darkened.

I knew I was in trouble, that I should probably do something to head off the oncoming storm, but I was sick of her and Jack going on at me about this shit. They'd even tried to fix me up with Carl once. I told Debby he had trouble getting it up at sixteen, and that I could only imagine how much worse that had gotten over time. She'd just gotten red in the face and told me that a *real* relationship wasn't all about sex. I'd countered with, well, that's why I ain't interested in a *real* relationship. That had shut her up.

"I have two jobs," I said defensively. What was it with married people, especially ones with kids? They always thought they had it harder than everyone else, and they always thought that having kids meant they were doing something heroic.

"But that's not the same as a family," she retorted.

I sat back. "I guess." I did love her kids. They were cute as hell, and I liked taking them around, bragging on them about their early reading skills when people asked if they were mine. And then I would laugh and say *no*.

We were quiet for some time.

"Did you and Jaime ever come here?" Debby asked tentatively.

It was as if she'd slapped me. My mouth went dry.

"I'm sorry. I know you don't like to talk about her Kari, but . . . I feel sometimes like she's why you . . . well. Why you stopped. It wasn't your fault, you know."

"I know *that*," I said sharply, too sharply. "And stopped what? Growing up? Bullshit, I call bullshit on that. Just cause I didn't hook up with some guy who wants me to wash his shorts, and pop kids out . . ." I stopped. We were going round about this, and I was just glad she had gotten away from Jack for the afternoon. And I was about to say something I couldn't take back.

"I'm sorry," she said. "I know you dealt with a lot. You're strong, Kari, you . . . cut a lot of bad stuff out of your life. You know how proud I am of you."

I grunted.

"How about we go get a drink?"

I relaxed. "That sounds great."

We yanked our skates off, Debby chattering away as she pulled the door open about where we should go, how there was a great new wine bar she'd heard about from one of her friends who had moved to Lakewood, how she was worried about her youngest—her teeth were coming in, and she was keeping her up at night, keeping them all up.

I told her I was down for the wine bar. I liked dives and cheap beer, but I also liked making Debby happy.

Debby squealed and clapped her hands. "I'm so glad! Jack will never go to places like that."

"I know."

"But I mean, he does take me out."

"I know," I repeated, pausing to pull a stone out of my boot. The parking lot was covered with them.

"I'm so psyched to try this new place," Debby said, shoving her key into her door and twisting. She hit the unlock button for me, and I got in. Her phone beeped with a text, and she frowned. "Jack's just . . . checking to see when I'm coming home."

I threw my head back and grunted.

"Kari," she said, whining.

"Give it to me." I gestured for the phone.

"Right. Like that wouldn't make it so much worse," she responded, running one hand nervously through her hair.

I sat back, hoping we'd at least get an hour at the bar before the man-fits began.

She texted furiously for a few minutes, and then put it down. "I think we're good for a while," she said.

I sighed, glad she'd put him off.

Debby turned the key, and the engine sputtered.

"Shoot," she said, "I need to take it in, or have Jack look at it."

"Sounds like you just need a new starter," I said. "You should let me do it. I can do that, at least." Jack was always promising to "get to it" and telling Debby it was a waste of money to have a professional look at the fridge, or the car—and then whatever it was would break down, cost them even more time and money.

"Jack can do it," she said.

"Okay." I rolled the manual window down and the lights snapped on in front of Roller City. It was dim, and the bulbs flickered on and off, making an electric clicking sound as they did. There was a slight, smoky mist rolling in, and I watched it roil up under the light, under the awning, and I blinked, and leaned forward. It was as if . . . no, was that . . . a person? There had been no one there a second ago, and the door hadn't opened. But I could swear . . . I felt the hair on the back of my neck spike. I was really peering now at what, at first, had seemed like a bit of movement in the shadow. And then, under the awning, like a dream, like a goddamned childhood nightmare, there she was, as if she'd never gone, standing in the shadows of the roller rink—her shy, yet defiant expression, her curly chestnut hair floating in the soft, evening wind. Her beautiful Blackness like a dream. Jaime. My Jaime.

My heart hitched, I felt a wave of shock roll over me, and the car engine came to life.

"Yes!" Debby said.

When I looked back, Jaime was gone.

CHAPTER FOUR

I am thirteen years old when my new best friend Jaime and I sneak behind the school to smoke cigarettes. I love her already. She is beautiful and she is strong, and she has big, dark eyes that are so, so sad. She is like the women in Daddy's black-and-white movies—the ones that make him cry—except she's better, because she's young and she's wild and she's free.

She's already told me some of her secrets, and they've made my mouth water for the rest. I can tell she's not holding back to seem more interesting, it's because all her secrets hurt so much that letting them out will be like dying, just a little bit.

She wants to know if I'm worth all of those tiny deaths.

We're smoking and whispering, the wind in the pines covering our voices like a dream, when the boys from math class find us. They're white boys, not that we talk that way, we don't, we pretend we're not different, but we know they know. We know it's part of why they've come for us. They've come to tell us what we can do with our bodies. Jaime cocks her head, all the secrets in the world behind her long, long lashes. One side of her mouth turns up, and she says *hey* like she knows them, and they are in thrall, they are laughing nervously, they ask if they can bum a cig and she says *yes, yes.*

I smoke and I watch, and I learn how Jaime talks to boys, to men. As if they aren't anything to fear. One of them asks her if she wants to go behind that tree, that one right there with the bright, pungent sap leaking out.

I am also in thrall of Jaime, with her soft dark curls, her eyes like a god's.

Rapt with her power, I wait to see if she will go, my heart moving hard, like the cogs in a locomotive.

She says *yes* so softly it's like a kiss, like the wings of a moth at night and they move like ghosts, talking and smoking and they disappear behind the trees like they've never existed at all.

I wait for the other boy to ask me, but he doesn't.

I ask him.

We move beyond the trees.

CHAPTER FIVE

At the White Horse, I was sitting at the bar, alone, as usual, staring into space. I'd texted Debby, asked her to join me, but she said she had to work. I told her that she should call in sick, see if her mom wouldn't take the kids, and she'd responded that she had mouths to feed. L-A-M-E, I'd texted back, and she'd gone silent.

It was just as well. Seeing Jaime in the shadows of Roller City had put me on edge. I knew it had been some trick of the brain—I was working too many late nights—but still, it had been unsettling. I hadn't felt right since that evening. I kept trying to convince myself that it had been someone else, some young girl that, in the shadows, looked just like her.

So much like her.

I took a sip of my Bud and squinted over at Nick. He was watching Fox and shaking his head.

"Nick, take a break," I said.

"Kari, this is important! You should watch and learn." He readjusted on his stool, his eyes burning into the television.

"Sure, Nick," I said, and resumed staring at the wall.

If I was honest with myself, not only was I deeply unsettled by my brain playing shitty tricks on me, but I was also still annoyed with Debby for all of that "you need a man, Kari!" and "Kids make me a real adult, Kari!" talk. And for some reason, ever since she'd given me that bracelet of my mom's, she'd been after me about Jaime—and my mom. Possibly why my mind had decided that insomnia equals seeing dead friends from the past in the shadows of Roller City.

I shook my head and sipped.

Jaime and my mother. Two people I despised talking about—hell, even thinking about, for very different reasons. The past was the past. And though I thought Debby's man was the one who needed to grow the hell up, I didn't begrudge her getting married, or having kids. It was her preaching at me about it. Imagining that my life, which was safe and good—and one in which I waitressed, read, and most of all, didn't do drugs—was meaningless only because I wasn't making crotch fruit was totally bullshit. If Jaime had to die, at least she'd sacrificed herself for something, I thought guiltily. But I'd made my peace with it—by moving on.

I was interrupted in my thoughts by my favorite cat, the orange tabby. She wove in-between my legs, and then leapt up to the bar.

"Hi baby," I said, petting her.

She purred, laid down, closed her eyes, and I focused on the big, plastic, white horse inlaid onto the black and gold cutout in the wall that held a number of bottles of hard liquor. To its right was a hand-held drum that someone had painted a white horse onto, and a black T-shirt with the bar's logo was pinned underneath both.

I blinked and sat back. Wait. That was a painting that I'd never noticed before, though I was here every week—often in this exact spot. I squinted, and leaned in, examining the symbols: what looked to be a war club, maybe a rain cloud, and a few other things.

Where had I seen those symbols before? I squinted, thinking, absentmindedly petting the tabby.

It came to me in a flash. The bracelet. I'd seen them on the bracelet, the one Debby had given to me. The one that had belonged to my mother, Cecilia. What the fuck?

I shook my head, images of Jaime, pictures I'd seen of my mother, the symbols of the bracelet and the painting swimming in front of me. For a moment, I tried to make sense of it all, puzzle it out. Why would these symbols—the exact same symbols on the bracelet I had at home—be suddenly on a painting in my favorite bar? One that I'd never seen before?

"Nick," I said.

"Yeah?"

I opened my mouth to ask him about the painting when a thunderclap hit, reverberating so loudly that the building seemed to shake.

"Shit," I said.

Nick looked worriedly at the ceiling, the walls. After a moment, he started laughing.

"What?" I asked.

"Takes a licking but keeps on ticking!"

I laughed then too. Nick and his junky, old expressions.

The rain then began to fall in earnest, the sound like a thousand little bullets overhead.

"Help me get the buckets, will you Kari?"

"Sure," I said, getting up and going around to the back. Together, we picked the gray, plastic buckets up, and one by one, put them in their usual places.

I sat back down. After a couple sips, I remembered what I was going to ask Nick, but suddenly, it didn't seem so important anymore.

I kicked the beer all the way back, and continued petting the cat in front of me, listening to the sounds of Fox News being drowned out by a hard, fresh, spring rain.

CHAPTER SIX

Wandering Broadway, flitting in and out of my favorite dusty used bookstores, I felt like a shadow was on me. I traced a finger along a beige hardcover in the Broadway Book Mall and squinted. I loved this place. Piles and piles of disorganized books, and the owners knew everything. I was hoping to find a new Stephen King.

I was just about to pluck the book that I'd been fingering out of the shelf when I felt it. Breath on my neck. Hot, and sick smelling.

Then, "Your demon rides."

I whipped around, my heart hammering.

A man on the other side of fifty stood before me, his white face sunken in with drugs and booze and sorrow, his mouth a pucker of misdirected rage. Another Broadway bum, drunk-sick and possibly not knowing where he was, who I was—hell, even who he was himself.

"Uncle," I said, trying to give him a little Indian respect, "what's wrong?"

He wavered like he was underwater.

"She ain't gonna get off your back until you look at her," he said, grumbling, his fury deflated.

"You're thirsty, ain't you?"

His lips trembled. I gave him a dollar, watched him walk away, stumbling back onto the sidewalk, merging with the crowd on his way to the dirty-ass liquor store a few blocks down.

"That was nice of you," the owner said.

I turned around. "Shit, could've been me, in another life."

He cocked his head, narrowed his eyes, taking in my tight black jeans, heavy metal T-shirt. I walked down the aisles on my way to the horror section, seeing the shadows gather in front of me like an animal, hovering, waiting, back arched. I thought again of the bracelet, the one thing I knew of it. I let the shadows pull me in, backward to tenth grade.

Jaime and I had been sitting outside Auntie Squeaker's trailer, drunk on cheap beer. I was teasing Jaime for her teen obsession with *Knight Rider*. Auntie Squeaker was a distant Apache relative—the one you went to for cures, for gossip, for everything. We called her Auntie Squeaker on account of her voice; she'd been a two-pack-a-day woman for as long as I could remember. Jaime—my best friend—was furious. She always got mad when we razzed her, and it only made it funnier. My head was full-on thrown back, something someone had said had been so funny.

The talk then turned, to Jaime's relief, to a girl whose mom had come in on her when she was with a guy. I told her I was grateful my mother wasn't around. I remember feeling simultaneously flippant and bitter.

"Shouldn't speak ill of the dead," Squeaker said, her black eyes going small. "I knew your momma."

"So," I said, feigning a casual tone, pitching my empty beer can into the trash.

Squeaker smoothed her muumuu, her gray Walmart hoodie illustrating the beginning of the end of summer.

"Listen—"

"Let it go, Auntie," Jaime said, running her hands over her black curls.

She seemed to, and the joking commenced. One tall, bearded boy turned the hose on all of us, extinguishing cigarettes, and a girl went after him, punching him in the hands until he let go of it, the rainbows from the water moving through the air like a dream. That had stayed with me, all these years. That rainbow. That water. That anger. That innocence.

"Your daddy ever show you a bracelet?" Squeaker asked.

"A what?" I'd lit myself another cig, got myself another watery beer. I'd taken my shoes off, let my feet run through the dirt, the sparse grass, the pink, plastic flamingos Squeaker had set up in the front shimmering in the distance. "My dad doesn't really talk. Which you know."

Squeaker ignored that.

"Your momma had a bracelet. Had power."

I was used to this shit from Squeaker, talk of spirits and power and politics. But she knew better than to talk about my mom.

"No," I said flatly.

"I saw it. Wish I knew what happened to it. It's been passed down in your family for generations."

I threw my head between my knees. When I looked up, Jaime was smiling at me. I smiled back. I got up, pulled her into an embrace, and we began to dance, an awkward waltz across the rocky dirt, and I sang over the jagged sounds coming from the radio, "Powerrrr! Oh! Powerrrr!"

Jaime laughed, and joined me in singing, and Auntie Squeaker let it go, settled into her ancient white and green lawn chair. But her eyes kept that knowing expression the entire night. And I forgot about it, the bracelet, or at least I thought I did.

CHAPTER SEVEN

The White Horse was lonely tonight: just me, and a Lakota who looked to be in her late fifties, her long hair pushed up around her crown, her forehead resting gently on the bar. When I first came in, she'd wanted to know my tribe, if I had a boyfriend, would I do a shot with her. I said yes to the shot. She talked then, her soft, brown hand hitting the bar with some force, about her ex-husband. How he'd never really been there for her. I nodded until she fell asleep.

"I knew her husband," Nick said, sitting on the stool next to her, on the other side of the bar.

There was a leak in the ceiling from the rain, and Nick had put one of the buckets under it, the cats coming in and out and drinking from it, my favorite orange tabby purring next to me on the bar.

"You going to fix that leak?" I asked.

"Whole building falling apart. Not even worth it," Nick said, turning back to the television. The colors on the screen were bright, the anchors blond. Nick turned to me. "You should buy this place."

I opened my mouth to laugh, then shut it. "Maybe," I said. I mean, I did want to own a bar. Someday. But the White Horse was a mess.

Luckily, Nick changed the subject. "Her husband. Cree. From Canada." Nick shook his head. "Liked to party."

I glanced at the woman. She was snoring now. She'd earned her rest. "What happen to him?"

"Went back to Canada, I guess," Nick said, scratching at his hair. "But I'll call her son when it's time to close up. She hardly drinks, but when she does . . ." he said, trailing off and gesturing to her. "He always comes and picks her up when she gets like this. Lawyer." He smiled. "Make a good boyfriend."

I rolled my eyes.

"Thanks, *Mom*," I said.

Nick went back to his land of alternative facts, and I stared at my phone. Debby had been texting me nonstop about that goddamn bracelet the last week or so, ever since I confessed that I'd seen Jaime in the parking lot of Roller City. She was sure, of course, that I had seen her ghost—and I was sure that I had not. She was also sure that it had something to do with the bracelet, which was so Debby. She loved fantasy books, with castles and fairies and shit—and she and her mom believed in all kinds of magic. Everyone in the Springs was into that happy horseshit.

Honestly, the whole thing had brought up so many bad memories that all I'd done was leave the bracelet at the bottom of my bag and try like hell to forget about it. I'd been working practically nonstop anyway.

I hadn't forgotten about it though. I'd started dreaming about it, the figures on the bracelet, especially the monster, coming to life. It had long, dark hair and yellow claws that curled up at the end, sharply. It was also surreally tall, its hot, rancid breath reeking of human meat.

The bracelet.

The spot where I'd seen the painting with the same symbols on it that I'd remembered on the bracelet was empty. I had to sit back, close my eyes, shake my head, and then open them again. What the hell?

"Nick!"

"Yeah," he answered, not even turning his head.

"What happened to that new painting you had up?"

"New painting?"

"Yeah, you know," I said, growing frustrated, "that one that was here last week." I pointed to the spot in front of me.

"Kari," Nick said, turning to look at me over his shoulder, an amused, self-aware expression on his face, "I ain't put anything new up since '94." He turned back around after shaking his head.

I was silent for a moment. I had seen it. Right there, right in front of my face. Not one week ago, not long after I'd seen the exact same symbols on the bracelet.

"It had a thunderbird, and like," I said, picking my bag up, and rifling through it, "other symbols, like . . . hold on."

I plucked my wallet out and set it on the bar. Then, pushed my hairbrush aside, tissues, and about a billion receipts. "Gotta clean this thing out," I murmured, irritated.

After a few passes, my fingers connected with metal. There was a buzz. A strange feeling came over me then. A feeling of darkness, dread. Pain even. I pulled it out against my better judgment and the temperature in the room dropped hard and fast, my breath freezing in front of me, the smell of scotch permeating the air.

And that's when I sensed something. Something unnatural.

There was a woman standing by the pool tables who hadn't been there moments before. I stood up, and stumbled into the bar, my back pressed against the wood.

"I—" I started. "Nick, I—"

Her head was down, her long, dark hair covering her face. Her skin was brown, but gray—not the color of a living person. At all.

She was just standing there, still.

"Nick," I hissed, and her muscles began to twitch unnaturally, and I felt my throat close up in terror, my mouth run dry.

A sound like bones cracking came from her limbs, and abruptly, she moved jerkily a few inches in my direction, her head still down.

My mouth opened, then closed, and my heart hammered so hard for a moment, I genuinely thought I was going to have a heart attack, or at least pass out.

She stopped, and I watched as my breath came out in an icy stream.

She raised her head up sharply, her eyes white, her mouth pouring blood, and screamed.

CHAPTER EIGHT

I was in Dad's kitchen in the Springs trying not to piss myself thinking about what I'd seen in the White Horse. I always felt better when I made food for Dad—all he'd eat, except for cereal and spaghetti, was bologna sandwiches. It had to be Wonder Bread, Miracle Whip, one thin leaf of iceberg lettuce, cut diagonally, or he wouldn't touch it.

I wasn't sure what I'd witnessed. All I knew was that it—she—had disappeared minutes after she'd appeared, screaming.

Nick hadn't seen a thing, and I'd gone home right after to hold myself, and a bottle of whiskey, all of the lights in the apartment blazing the entire night, me jumping at every sound. At one point, the refrigerator switching on nearly made me come out of my own skin.

I picked the dish up and walked into the living room listening to the metal I'd been enjoying fade and echo throughout the cramped, dim yellow kitchen on the ancient boom box I kept for when I visited Dad in Idaho Springs. I stood in the archway, the notes of the TV beginning to replace the music, and thought about my drive here. The stark difference between Denver, where I lived now, and Idaho Springs, where I'd grown up.

I glanced in at Dad and sighed. He was watching TV intently, his expression like a child's. He rarely spoke since the accident. His brain had been fried good. My poor daddy.

Outside, the town was quiet, the sun slowly fading from the western sides of the houses I'd grown up in. They were peeling, they were dim; they were white, yellow, and brick red. Across the street in front of my father's house was trailer city, where most of my friends had lived, our scabby knees crowded next to each other on American Furniture Warehouse couches. Some of my old buddies were gone, scattered, others living in the same trailers they'd grown up in, the babies crying on their laps their own now. We'd sit in double-wides drinking vodka and gin, and whatever beer we could get our hands on, and drive up and down the dirt roads, passing pink flamingos stuck into hard, rocky soil topped with beige prairie grass that had somehow taken root, the sound of the cars on I-70 droning on and on into the night.

Downtown, I knew the bars were really heating up; Tommy-knocker's, I was sure, would be hopping, the lonely old drunks having to give way to the nighttime partiers. Like zombies on the narrow, red-cobble streets, shuffling their feet, looking for a home. Beau Jo's, where I'd wiped down the nasty, sneeze-covered salad bar countless times as a teenager, would be closing down, the waiters and bussers ready to start another round of drinking and dancing and sex, the next morning nursing hangovers with weak coffee and cherry Pop-Tarts, their black aprons crisp, ready to take the orders of families from suburbs on their way to the ski resorts.

I placed the dish in front of Daddy, where he sat on the sagging couch. He lifted the sandwich, examined it briefly, and began to chew, bits of puffy white bread falling from his thin, pink lips. He stopped and smiled at me unexpectedly.

I sat down next to him and watched him eat, patted him gently on his navy sweatpants-covered leg. I bought him a new set of white

T-shirts and pants from the Walmart in Evergreen every year, where half of my graduating class worked.

We watched a rerun of *Friends,* and for the first time in a while, he laughed at one of the jokes.

"Are you in a good mood, Dad?" I asked, smoothing the last of the thin wisps of his hair and taking a sip at my drink, sighed heavily. Relaxing next to Dad was exactly what I'd needed.

He seemed to smile at me then, but I wasn't sure if it was directed toward me, or the TV—or toward something less tangible, something I couldn't see at all.

I cleaned his dish and came back. He was watching me as I did, unusual for him these days. Since he was done, I sat back down next to him and leaned on his big, soft shoulder, his shirt also soft.

He patted my arm, and I felt a surge of love for him so strong it crowded my throat.

"I love you, Dad."

We watched until the episode finished, and just as a commercial came on, the door opened and Debby walked in, wearing a white T-shirt with the phrase TRY ME in big, silver letters across the chest, a pink camo-print sweatshirt on top. I was sure that both were acquisitions from the Walmart, where she worked as a manager.

"What's up?" she asked, and I grunted. I was still mad at her for digging that bracelet out. I wasn't sure what had happened to me at the White Horse, but I knew that I never wanted to touch—or even see—that bracelet again. She plopped down beside me, her head hitting the yellow clock on the wall behind her. I reached behind to adjust it, dust coating my fingers. It had stopped working a decade ago, but none of us had bothered to put batteries in or replace it.

She watched for a while, and then asked for a drink.

Still not saying anything, I went to the kitchen for a glass, pulled the whiskey bottle off the old, wooden coffee table, and roughly poured her a finger.

She sipped and sat back, her eyes closing for a moment. When she opened them up again, her glance was sly, sidewise, and I knew she was up to something.

"Don't be mad at me for this," she said.

Shit. I was still mad at her for the bracelet thing. What could she be up to now? I sighed, drinking the rest of what was in my glass, the realization hitting me as I did.

"You *didn't*," I said, picking up the bottle of whiskey I'd opened up somewhere in the middle of *Friends*, and pouring myself another. I'd been pouring myself an extra ever since that night in the White Horse. And I wasn't sleeping.

She'd brought that goddamn bracelet, I knew it. I'd thrown it at her, after that horrible thing that had happened to me in the White Horse—making sure that my fingers didn't touch it.

"I did," she said. "I'm only saying," she said, adjusting on the old couch, "that okay, it was scary, your like, vision but—"

"Vision," I said, scoffing. I'd never seen a ghost in my life, paid no attention to the Indians in town who spoke about visions any more than the evangelicals babbling about seeing the devil.

What I didn't tell her was that my nightmares were getting more frequent. Much more visceral. Horrible, wrenching nightmares that would start with a man standing near a little boy in bed. He'd tell the boy to pray. And then he'd start touching him. Then, the boy would turn into the monster figure on the bracelet. It was familiar somehow, like it was maybe from a story Auntie Squeaker had told me. I could almost remember the name of it. But the worst part was, when I woke up, I could still smell the rotting meat stench that emanated from the creature's hair.

"I probably have a brain tumor, Debby. And for the record? I'm *still* mad at you for foisting it on me in the first place. So maybe quit while you're ahead."

She snorted derisively. Took a sip. Then, "I think we should let your dad see the bracelet."

I blinked, trying to process what she'd just said.

"*What?* Why would you say that?" I felt shock, anger. I was protective when it came to my father, and if that thing had the kind of power over him that it had over me, I didn't know what it would do to him. He was so delicate.

"Because, Kari, that ghost you saw? It means something. And you need to know exactly what. And your dad might be able—"

"He doesn't really *talk*, Debby," I said, interrupting. "And you know how he is. It could break him," I said, frowning, and rubbing Daddy's arm.

He seemed to smile, just a little.

"—in his way," she said, continuing, "to show you something important."

"Important? What the *fuck,* Debby? What do you mean by important?"

She snorted in exasperation. "Don't you get it, Kari?"

I really didn't.

"The ghost was your mother! Oh my *God,* you're so blind."

It took me a minute to process what Debby was saying. I wanted to yell at her, but the absurdity of her statement, her total need for Idaho Springs drama washed over me, and I couldn't help it. I burst into laughter.

Debby snorted in frustration. "You know you saw something real. That matters to you, to who you are. That bracelet, and your mother, were trying to show you something. You *know* you need to let your dad touch the bracelet."

I didn't know.

"And like, your dad? He won't see what you see. He'll react to it differently. And I promise, if it seems like he's responding negatively at all, I'll yank it."

Why was Debby like this? Always pushing me. Pushing me in directions I didn't want to go.

I was silent for a time, thinking back to the woman I'd seen at the White Horse. Who'd disappeared into thin air right after she'd screamed. I took another sip.

"What the fuck, Debby?"

She frowned, her lips trembling. "I just . . ."

"Jesus, Debby, what's wrong with you? Besides you, all I have is my dad. And for you to even suggest he touch something that might be able to shoot visions of ghosts into someone—even if that's probably bullshit, it's just . . . fucking selfish, Debby. All cause you want to see what it can do. I know you. You always want some kind of drama, some kind of adventure. Get your kicks somewhere else, shit."

She was silent, and then the tears began, her blue eyes filling.

I felt like trash.

"Just—put it in here," I said, opening the drawer in the wooden, '70s-style end table. She hesitated, then placed it in gently, like it was a child.

I slammed the door shut.

We were both silent then, resentment winding around my heart hard. But the comfort of having my cousin, my replacement mother, hell, just another human being—loath as I was to admit it—to watch reruns late into the night with, was nice. Debby started snoring, the booze finally working enough magic to make me relax, the sounds of *One Day at a Time* echoing gently through my childhood home.

An image of the woman in the bar flashed into my mind. I shook my head slightly, trying to rid myself of her. Debby stirred in her sleep. I focused on the television. For a moment, I was successful. And then, another flash. I squeezed my eyes shut against the memory but that only made it more vivid. Her white eyes. Her long dark hair. I tried to push her away, but she kept coming back, and I couldn't help it, I started to compare what I'd seen of mother with what I'd seen in the bar. I'd never looked upon her in real life. I glanced up. There were pictures of her on the wall. I scanned the images, and closed my eyes, letting it in this time.

My eyes split open.

I felt sick then, unsure, and though I wanted to be angry at Debby again, glancing over at her, still asleep, her long eyelashes like a doll's, I just couldn't. I had to let this go. Find a way to live my life, let that fucking bracelet rot in the drawer and do what I'd done as long as I could remember, which was push her down, down, to the furthest places until she was nothing but memory dust.

The vision of my mother and that monster faded, at least for now, into the black of the night. Outside, the predatory hoot of a Great Horned Owl pierced over the sound of the wind whistling eerily through the needles of the pine trees. Idaho Springs was asleep, or its human residents were, safe in the knowledge that at least for now, what was to be feared was far away.

CHAPTER NINE

Lucille's was bright that morning, making my eyes hurt—but it was bright every morning, with its yellow-painted walls and Creole-themed décor. Ornate, gothic, purple and white mirrors, signs that proclaimed Mardi Gras in fancy lettering, beads of all colors draped everywhere, and masks with green ribbon flowing through them.

On my way to drop off an order and get a carafe of coffee for a table, I couldn't help but think about my mother, her ghost—the childhood memories that had begun to surface. Memories I'd been so good at pushing down until now. Distracted, my Nikes hit a small divot in the floor, and I tripped—right onto Caroline, my platter smashing soundly into her chest, and sliding down to the floor. I barely recognized who it was I'd dumped Eggs Sardou all over—until she started yelling at me.

The eggs were running down her front, covering her blue plaid shirt like a yellow blanket.

She stared at me for a moment, snapping her gum.

"Sorry," I said, pulling a rag out of my apron pocket. I started to wipe at the eggs when she pushed my hands away aggressively.

"Don't *bother*," she said.

"Shit, Caroline. I said I'm sorry," I said, leaning down to pick the platter up.

I'd felt like I was half-asleep the entire morning. I'd always had insomnia, but I was beginning to dream of the monster from the bracelet every night. I'd come across it walking home, the hair on the back of my neck spiking, my stomach filling with dread. I'd stop, my heart hammering. I'd turn, slowly, peering into the shadows. Hearing something that might be the wind. Then it would step out. It would roar, it would snarl. It would leap for me.

I'd wake up.

It was getting so bad I was afraid to go to sleep. And worst of all, the rotten meat smell would linger.

"Just watch where you're going," she hissed, her red, messy bun bouncing with each word.

"Fucking chill out, Caroline," I said, bending to pick the tangle of food and plate up off the floor.

She harrumphed loudly and stalked off toward the bathroom. Caroline was always pissy though and treated her job like she was in the service. I mean, I took my job seriously too. I was a good waiter—and bartender. But I wasn't a fucking *ass*.

I sighed. Nonetheless, I'd spilled on her. I would apologize again later if she'd let me.

I took the platter over to the kitchen, dropped another order off for Eggs Sardou, telling the cook I was sorry as I did. He shrugged.

After cleaning the mess up, I went over to the folks who'd ordered the eggs. Mercifully, they were cool. After that order was filled, I did a round of refills, and walked outside, slipping my phone out of my pocket as I went. My eyes were two burnt black bulbs. I looked at my watch. 11:30. I had hours to go.

Out back, the bussers Rafael and Martín were smoking. I greeted them in my shitty Spanish. Martín had been laughing about something, the smoke coming out of his mouth in rough, ragged jets as he did.

"Could I bum one?" I said, switching over to English.

Martín ran his hands through his thick, wavy black hair and smiled. "Sure," he said, handing me one and lighting it for me.

I'd quit five years ago.

I inhaled, the sweet scent of the tobacco in my nose, the feel of the smoke in my throat velvet. The electric shock, once the substance hit my lungs, and then bloodstream.

Then, I coughed.

"Nice, yes?" Martín said.

"Yeah," I said, "it really is."

I inhaled again, and the world grew sharp, the pine trees in the near distance crisp and green. Maybe it *was* a brain tumor. Debby had a degree in business—unlike me who'd finished high school and quit there—so you'd think she wouldn't have encouraged me with this shit. But she was an Idaho Springs girl in the end, and she liked her drama, and her superstitions. If it turned out I had a brain tumor, well at least I'd know what to do about it. But these dreams, these visions, I couldn't go on like this. It was fucking up my life. I wasn't clumsy normally. In fact, quite the opposite. I was on time. Clean. Fast. People liked me even though I had an attitude, asked to sit in my section on account of my quick wit. Shit, I was one of their best workers—I'd been there for almost ten years. But it wouldn't be long before they'd get rid of me if this continued.

"I dumped eggs all over Caroline," I said, pausing, then inhaling again.

Martín gave Rafael a sideways glance, and a small smile began to creep onto his lips. They started laughing, and I couldn't help it, I joined.

"Caroline is very—" Martín started.

"Caroline's a *bitch*," I finished for him.

Rafael laughed so hard smoke shot out of his nose, and he coughed, hard.

"She is a bitch," Martín said, shaking his head. "That is a bad word, but it is the right word for Caroline."

"It really is," I said.

"I've known a lot of bitches," I added.

"Bitches," Rafael repeated, his subtle accent making it sound fancy.

Then we all broke into laughter again.

"You off?" I asked. I knew Martín had another job that he went to right after this one, and that after that, he went to school. He was training to be a dental tech.

He nodded.

They were brothers, and lived with their parents, still. Denver was rotten expensive.

I finished the cigarette, my exhaustion creeping back as I did, and thanked Martín, who smiled a sweet, genuine smile. I straightened my hair, my apron—and thought about where I could buy a pack on my way home from work.

Back inside, I washed up, trying to get the stench of cigarettes off my fingertips. Up at the ticket rack, I could see that a few orders had been put in. Plucking one, the scent of smoke on my hair and clothing wafting down and around as I did, I remembered that one of the perks of not smoking was not stinking.

I was halfway to a table when I saw her. I stopped, mid-step, the ornate, black, gothic mirrors in front of me reflecting my shock.

The ghost from the White Horse. My mother, Cecilia.

She was staring at me, hard, her body, such as it was, in front of the windows in the back, her eyes full of rage, a blurry edge to her form. Then all around me, it went dark—a spotlight just on her, and I felt my limbs weaken beneath me, my breath grow cold.

I could still see her, and faintly the patrons all around me who seemed unaware, their clatter now muffled. She couldn't have been more than twenty years old—and this time, her skin was flush, warm. She was wearing a pair of brown bell-bottoms and a gold button-up shirt with a butterfly collar. She smiled.

But then, slowly at first, and then more rapidly, her skin began to vein purple, starting in her arms and moving up to her face, eventually becoming mottled, then gray, her eyes white, and blood began to blossom from a dent in her head and pour down her shirt, staining it.

She closed her eyes, and her scream was unnatural—at first a sharp, desperate push out, then it moved backward like she was swallowing her own suffering—like a record in satanic reverse, and I felt my heart squeeze painfully like the night I'd first seen her.

I stumbled back, one hand out, afraid I'd fall right on my ass. People nearby began looking up from their tables, and slowly, I lowered my arm, my eyes still fixated on the vision before me.

She opened her eyes abruptly, and I jumped.

Please, she said. *Help,* her arm around something I couldn't see.

CHAPTER TEN

I entered the trailer still feeling shook up, and frankly, desperate, the scent of smoke clinging to it like a dying animal. It was lined with rough-hewn, woman-made shelves, each one holding vials of indefinable and multicolored substances, bundles of grasses, weeds, and shit-tons of cigarettes. Auntie Squeaker often took them as payment when someone came to her for a homemade abortion, or cure for acne. Auntie Squeaker was related to me on my mom's side—our family, according to legend, living in boxcars in northern Mexico, practicing traditional medicine, and hiding from the American government way back in the day. At some point, as America was becoming America, and Mexico becoming Mexico, my family of Chiricahuas had come through Texas, and a few had filtered out into Colorado. And Auntie Squeaker's great-grandmother, who had been rumored to cure my grandmother's grandmother—a Chickasaw relation by marriage—of cancer, was continuing the tradition in Idaho Springs in 2016.

I was here because that shit in Lucille's had been the last straw—and Auntie Squeaker was the one person in my life that might be able to help me. I hoped she had something that could kill the ghost, not that I'd believed in any of that shit before dead people started bleeding all over my place of employment.

"Look at you," she said, clenching her cig between her lips and taking both my hands, "you must be making all your white trash cousins jealous."

"Oh, shit, Auntie."

"It's true! Still so pretty. Please tell me you ain't going to go off and marry, ruin your looks and good times?" She let go of my hands.

I laughed. "Hell, no."

"That's my girl!" She ran her fingers through her short, gray, porcupine-quill-thick hair and smiled at me.

Over on the huge, ratty, beige couch, sitting in front of the TV and scrolling through their phones, or watching the soap opera, was the usual collection of Auntie's friends—mainly women, and a few men who'd come out later in life. They were always there, Auntie's groupies. Some of them were probably cousins of mine—well, distant Indian cousins at least—related through an auntie's brother's father's cousin's mother.

"Coffee?" she asked, and when I nodded, Marvin, a man I'd gone to high school with, set his phone down and poured me a cup. We settled at the small, round Formica-topped table and I sighed, deeply.

"You here about your mother, ain't you?"

"How'd you know?"

"Seen hide nor hair of you for almost a decade—"

"I'm sorry," I interrupted. Me and Squeaker had never fought, but I'd sort of faded away after Jaime died.

She brushed my apology aside with one short, brown, elegant hand, and I opened a pack, pulled one out and lit up, shoving a full pack across and over at her. She nodded, and Marvin took it and placed it on the shelves with the others.

"You never wanted to talk about your mom when you was a teenager. You and Jaime."

At Jaime's name, I drew breath.

"I'm sorry, by the way. I heard. I wanted to come to the funeral, but I was sick with the flu and wasn't going nowhere."

"I didn't go," I whispered.

"Why not?" she asked, her eyes narrowing.

"I remember when Jaime gave you that," I said softly, pointing to the tall, velvet Virgin de Guadalupe she had up over the couch. The frame was a dark wood—Jaime had found it in the thrift store before it closed.

"Yes," Squeaker responded, putting one hand on mine.

It was faded on one side where the light came in through the window above the sink. I remembered the vibrant reds and yellows and blues it had once had.

"I couldn't do it," I said, my throat growing tight. I cleared it. Squeaker patted my hand.

"You were never good at facing up to things," she said.

"No," I admitted. "I just like to live my life, one day at a time."

"But you miss her," she said.

I nodded. Sipped my coffee. "But I miss her."

"How's your daddy?"

"Same," I said, relieved she was changing the subject. "Doesn't talk much. But he's alive. He's all I got now that Jaime's gone."

"You got that cousin of yours. Debby."

"That's true," I said. "We're tighter than we used to be."

Squeaker stood up and went to the wall that was covered in a series of air plants, each one a different color. She picked up a thick amber glass container with a spritzing mechanism and watered a large, spiky pink plant, and then moved onto a light green one with thick, juicy leaves. She pulled a few dead stems off some, and sat back down, lit a smoke.

"I know you love your daddy, but this is his fault too, you know."

My stomach jolted. "What's his fault? My mom up and left me. Abandoned Daddy—and you know what he did to himself after."

She nodded. "That was his choice. He was always a little too in love with her."

"What would you do if your wife up and left you when your kid was two days old?"

She laughed.

"I'd do the same as you, hurt and move on."

I opened my mouth to protest, but almost immediately thought better of it. She was right. I was different than my daddy that way. But still.

"He's not the same as me and you—and her," I said, practically spitting out the last. "She had to know that, and still, she did what she did, up and leaving when I was barely out of the hospital. A freaking fetus practically."

"Did she?" Auntie asked.

I went to open my mouth again, but once more, clapped it shut. I wasn't sure about that anymore. In fact, I wasn't sure about anything.

One of the men crossed through the kitchen and into the bathroom, sliding the door shut, the pictures of all the children, men, women, and two-spirits that she'd taken care of tacked to it waving slightly. There were so many faces. Some had children now because of Squeaker, some didn't have cancer anymore. Some were gone, the pain of their passing a little gentler because of Squeaker's medicine, her hands.

"Tell me why you're here, girl," she said, her lips quavering just a little.

I told her about the bracelet. About the ghosts. The dreams. About surfacing memories, memories about my past that were screwing me up. I was especially disturbed by the dreams of the boy being molested by his father.

She sat back, smoking, looking at me for a while. "I tried to talk to you about the bracelet, when you were young."

I nodded. That day with Jaime, drinking beers outside of Auntie's trailer.

"You got it with you?" she asked.

I pulled it out of my bag gingerly, with an old hankie of Dad's so I didn't have to touch it.

She took it and laid it out in front of her. She shook her head. "I'd heard about it, but I never seen it." She examined it without touching skin to metal.

"Am I crazy?" I asked finally.

She laughed. "Then, I am too."

"Did touching this make me see her? Is it really her? Why? How can I make it stop?"

She sighed, her face carrying so much weight. "These are the wrong questions."

I squinted. "Wrong questions?" Shit, she sounded like a wizard in one of Debby's goofy-ass elf novels.

Her eyes scanned the bracelet again, ignoring me.

"Auntie, If I'm not sick in the head, and this thing is making me see my mom's ghost—a woman who left me and my dad—I want to know what I need to do to make her fucking stop it. To stop . . ."—it sounded so stupid in my head—"haunting me."

I was standing now, out of breath.

Auntie kept her eyes on me. Then, "You done? There's a lot you don't know. And a lot I ain't gonna tell you until you're ready."

"Just . . . help me make it *stop*."

Auntie watched me play with my lighter, her chin tilted up. "You don't want that."

I couldn't speak. Of course, I wanted that.

Her worn fingers played at the material over the silver, and she stuck her smoke in the ashtray, and lifted the bracelet with the hankie. "You ready to hear the story of this bracelet?"

I nodded curtly. If she'd help me, sure, I'd listen to one of her stories.

"Then sit back down," she said.

I took a deep, shuddering breath, and sat.

"Turn of the century, Indians were either fleeing where they were from and settling in places like Texas where they could get work—while still avoiding being hunted down for bounty—or getting shoved onto reservations. Our side, the side you got in common with me, well, I'm sure I told you they came up from Mexico."

I took a long drag and sat back. When Auntie got started, you were in for the long haul.

"New communities grew up. And they made things like this," she said, shaking the bracelet in her small, brown fist—things that not only reflected their combined heritage, but also protected them. Hid them. Healed them."

I nodded. Bored. Then I shot straight up.

"Healed?"

"That's right. This bracelet can heal." A crooked smile played about her lightly wrinkled lips.

"Heal Daddy? Get him back to normal?" My voice was small. Pained.

"I don't know honey, but I think if you're going to find out, you've got to discover what happened to your momma."

I scoffed. "Wait, what? Can't I just . . . hold it up to his face or something? Say some words like in a book, or something? Like some old Apache . . . spell?" I felt truly insane. But if there was even a possibility . . .

She laughed. "It don't work that way."

I nearly growled out of frustration. "Well, fuck. How does it work? Like, do these things on the bracelet mean something?"

She laughed. "Course they do. This here," she said, pointing to the thunderbird, "that's for protection." She took a drag, ashed. "The waterbird—that's its companion, they work together. That's to bring prayers to the creator."

I knew that. I had friends and relatives who practiced Native American Church—I'd even done a few ceremonies, a time or two, just to be a cool friend. I knew the waterbird was also the Peyote—the path to the creator, not just the drug.

"And these are plains symbols—that stuff is powerful medicine," she said, pointing to the bow and arrows, man in a headdress, and tipi. "We all looked up to the plains people—they kept strong traditions, even when they had to hide them from the government. The Inipi. The Sundance. They're helping to make a powerful circle."

"Okay, sure," I said, growing impatient. "But what does it *mean*? Can I use it to make the ghost go away?"

She laughed. "No, honey. Just—wait. You want to know this."

I crossed my arms, sat back.

"This," she said, shaking her head, pointing to the symbol that looked like a monster with one thick, yellowed nail. The one that had made me ill just looking at it the first time. "I ain't gonna say his name, give him power. And he's from your other side, so there's only so much I can tell you. But you're fighting him, have no doubt. He's the one in your dreams, getting in the way."

"Getting in the way?" I asked.

"Getting in the way of you finding out what happened to your momma."

That didn't make any sense.

She took a long drag, then put the cig out, twisting it hard in the tray until it was only smoke.

"And this," she said, "thank the creator for it. It's an Apache war club. That's power. That's what you'll need if you want to defeat that one," she said, pointing to the monster.

What she meant by needing the war club, I could only imagine. How the fuck was I going to get my hands on an actual Apache war club?

"But what about healing Daddy?" I said. I didn't know what to do with all of what Auntie Squeaker had just said. That wasn't me. I wasn't about monsters or ghosts or shit. I was about concrete results.

And if this thing could cure my dad, I wanted to know how. Now. Specifically.

"The healing only comes on when the owner of the bracelet wishes it."

It was my turn to laugh. "I'm the goddamn owner now, so—I wish it, shit!"

"No."

My mouth opened and shut.

"Your mother hasn't walked on. And she can't walk on until you find out what happened to her. Then, the bracelet will be yours. And maybe then it can heal."

I put my head in my hands, rage building behind my heart, at my mother, at Squeaker, at the world. Suddenly the smell of scotch, rich and yellow, filled the air, and the hair on my arms rose.

"Sweetie, your mom is behind you right now."

I whipped around, and sure enough, she was there. I hadn't even touched the goddamn bracelet this time.

She was weeping.

Normally, I was terrified of her. But today, all I could feel was rage.

"I hate you!" I screamed, and she disappeared.

CHAPTER ELEVEN

I was sitting at Dad's house in the Springs, my heart beating like an animal's.

Dad was content, sleepy-eyed, watching *The Jeffersons,* a show I vaguely remembered from childhood reruns. I was back from Sunday service: driving in from Denver to drink Bud and shoot empty cans off the side of a mountain with Debby and her crew in Idaho Springs. I knew what I wanted to do here, alone, in my father's place.

I watched him, his eyes closing, my heart hammering, his eyes fluttering open again. Something on the television made him smile. Finally, his eyes shut.

The pictures of my mother, of my father's family sat above—my father's family had been in Idaho Springs for generations, and they were watching me almost expectantly from their ancient frames in the walls. My father's people had been miners. Now they worked at the Walmart.

I peered into the drawer, where I'd placed it again after hanging with Squeaker, and slid it open all the way. I rifled through thread, scissors, school pictures of me as a child, blond, when I was very, very young, my eyes black and haunted. My fingers brushed a whole collection of safety pins.

Where was it?

I thought briefly about what Daddy did while I was gone. Did he ever get up, besides to use the bathroom? Left to his own devices, he would function, but not quite. And some days were more lucid than others. I had memories of days, here and there—as a child mainly, where we would have conversations, though they were limited. That hadn't happened in a good, long time, however.

I kept sifting. More safety pins. A receipt that fell apart in my hands. Old photos of uncles and aunties that I hadn't seen in years. I paused over those, looking at them closely before turning them loose. A dark hairpin—I supposed that had been my mother's, though I couldn't be sure. I must have really shoved it in there.

I stopped, finally finding what I was looking for.

The bracelet.

I hesitated. I knew what would happen the minute I touched it. Shit, it was happening now even when I wasn't.

The metal seemed almost to grow hot, fuse to my fingers this time, but before I could scream, I was gone—

I was my mother, her long, brown fingers on my neck, her neck. She was yelling at her father in the doorway of a small apartment, telling him that she was going to a friend's house to study whether he liked it or not.

She was lying. He knew it.

He came around the corner, his large, hooded brown eyes filled with anger, suspicion. My mother's body, my body, tensed at his approach. They argued fiercely. He was telling her she better not be going where he thought she was going, that there was only trouble there, that he was worried about her. Cecilia was asking him if he didn't have any pride in being Indian and his eyes were filling with black, and I felt the fear in her gut, visceral. He grabbed for her hand, and she darted, quick, like a hawk, and ran down the steps as he followed, fast, but she was faster, all the way down to her beat-up car, pulling out, moving down the road, parking in front of a place I recognized, the Indian Center.

Inside, lines of metal chairs had been set out, and in the front, there was a man with long, dark hair in two braids lecturing, his back to a flag with a Lakota in a headdress. He was talking about the American Indian Movement. Cecilia sat, and I listened with her ears, the air around me filled with promise, energy. He spoke of how it had been illegal to practice our spirituality until 1978, and Cecilia's heart filled first with rage, then a deep, wide sadness, her eyes focusing on something on the wall. An Apache war club. I wanted to process that but the wave of grief my mother felt was so visceral as she wept that I wept with her, with my mother, a woman whose face I had never seen except from the two-dimensional space of a photo. It was so hard to hate her, so fucking hard.

I went to open my eyes, but I had left.

I was back on my father's couch, and though I didn't cry anymore, I curled into a ball until the sickness subsided, trying desperately to take in what had happened to me.

My eyes flashed open. The war club—auntie had said it would protect me from the monster. I shook my head. It sounded absurd. I thought about what Squeaker had said in the trailer, and a story came to mind. One that she'd told me years ago. A story of a warrior who had won a battle with a monster. He'd won it with a war club that had been made with sacred intention, in the most secret of ways. Her face had been obscured by smoke when she'd told me that my ancestor Geronimo had held it. I'd scoffed and said, *but Auntie, those guys used shotguns.* She'd looked at me between puffs, her eyes black, and said, *they only looked like guns, daughter.*

CHAPTER TWELVE

I was alone in the White Horse, and all I wanted to do was drink.

The blue Coors Light chandelier flickered on my right, and I looked up, and stared at the B-21-BEHAVE-OR-B-GONE sign and sighed.

I went to take another sip when I realized there *were* people in the bar.

Two old Indians stood in the back: one with long hair, the sides shaved, the other, with a full head of hair, glistening in the dim, red light. They smoked, sitting back in the booths as if in their own living rooms. Looking at them, I almost felt out of time. They wore the most beautiful, old-fashioned suits, one of them with round, metal earrings—the kind I'd only seen in books fading in the backs of houses now long-abandoned; or simply, abandoned by me. The other had red cloth wrapped around his forehead. They were silent, their eyes focused on something I couldn't see. Something about them was otherworldly, strange. I couldn't put my finger on it, but I felt lit-up, light-headed.

I was about to ask Nick about them when the door opened. What I'd been looking for in the first place walked right in and settled down on the stool next to me, wrapping his short, muscular legs around the metal.

I smiled, the combination of booze and exhaustion ringing through my head like distant, constant bells.

He smiled back.

Two hours later, I was drunk.

"I mean this shit's crazy, right?" I said, taking the shot of whiskey and slamming it on the bar. This was a mistake, as the whiskey was in one of Nick's infamous paper cups, and the cup crumpled. I was glad I'd drunk the whole thing. I wiped at my full, pale purple-pink lips with the back of my hand, the Miller High Life sign wavering like it was underwater.

"Your visions?" the Ojibwe guy I'd picked up—or at least had decided I was going to pick up—asked, almost nonchalantly. He had a full head of wavy dark hair with several bright, silver-white strands woven in, and he was lean and rough from working construction all his life. I'd been happy as hell when he walked in, but goddamn if I couldn't get anything out of him.

"You 'membered!" I slurred, and he nodded.

I sighed and patted him on his hard, broad back. "Thanks for listening."

He nodded again. "S'cool."

I glanced over at the firm, round muscles in his arms.

"Another shot," I told Nick once he wandered back over. He had been watching the TV intently. He leaned over the old wooden bar, his elbows hanging off the edge, listening to me over the sound of CCR's "Fortunate Son."

"Really. Sorry," I said, sliding my fingers over the man's flat brown hand beside me. He smiled faintly, distantly. I kept forgetting his name. I knew he'd given it to me when I'd first asked him to play pool, but I'd already had a couple of beers by then. "I don't usually tell strangers all kinds of personal shit about myself."

He shrugged.

"Well, it's appreciated," I said, rubbing the worn skin below his knuckles.

He watched my hand travel toward his bicep, but then his eyes flipped over to gaze into mine. I hadn't noticed how piercing his hazel eyes were. I pulled my fingers away quick.

"Would you like a shot? It's on me," I said, smiling at him. "You deserve it, after having to listen to me go on about my personal stuff for so long."

"I pretty much stick to beer."

I nodded. "Beer then?" Damn, motherfucker couldn't recognize an easy lay if it fell in his lap.

"Okay," he said.

"Great," I said. Now I was getting somewhere.

Nick came with my shot, and I took it, glad he'd remembered, and slammed the cup down again like an idiot, watching the paper crush beneath my fingers. Nick had told me once that he'd stopped carrying glass. I wiped my mouth, the taste of the whiskey sticky and bitter. My throat had been feeling strange lately, like it was filled with something. And there was a taste, a metallic, coppery taste at the back—almost like blood.

The guy next to me—Ian, I remembered in a flash—sipped his beer.

"You from Denver?" he asked.

Shit, finally, something.

"Yeah," I said. "You're not though."

He laughed a little at my boldness.

"No, I'm from Minneapolis," he said.

"I see," I said, thinking to take a risk. Stroking the thick meat of his upper arms, I asked, "All them Nish boys from Minneapolis work construction like you do? You've got them big arms, shit."

His eyes cut quickly over at me, a small smile playing about his sweet, purple lips. "Strong," I said, moving higher.

"I am."

"I bet you are."

He laughed, took the rest of his drink in one hard gulp.

"You want to see how strong?" he asked.

"Baby, I do."

He sighed, a long, soft motion that started in his nose and ended in his chest. "You seemed pretty upset earlier. I don't want to push you."

I hung my head for a minute, then put my hand on his again, took it off. "Look, I'm having a bad time, and I thought that maybe you could give me a good one. Make me forget about shit for a while. That's how I work. I keep it simple. Drink," I said, unfolding and lifting the crushed cup briefly, smiling a sarcastic little smile and shaking it to-and-fro gently in the air for a moment, and then set it down back on the bar. "Fuck. Work. Maybe a little TV. I ain't complicated."

"If you're sure, I'm sure," he answered, getting up.

I got off the barstool and swayed a little. I felt strange then, like I was inside out, outside of time. I felt dizzy, and I turned to tell Nick that I didn't feel so good, when I spotted the old Indians in the back, and a wave of nausea hit me so intensely that I had to close my eyes. When I opened them, the bar was gone. It was an empty lot, though some buildings might've been in the distance, and trees surrounded me.

The two Indian men were still there, still smoking, sitting at the table in their beautiful old suits and metal earrings. There was a light on them, only on them—coming from the moon, highlighting their faces, the woods dark and unknowable behind them. A humming came from the distance, and a kind of metallic rattle, as if it were coming from an old heater. The sound of crunching, as if bone had been broken. One of them lifted his glass of bourbon. He winked, then the other shook his head and the wind picked up, the sound of it through the trees lonely and terrible. The lyrics to the Eagles' "Hotel California" coming from somewhere deep in the woods, though it was faint. I opened my mouth to say something when the blood came back in my mouth, and I coughed and coughed, and it felt like I was dying.

The bar was back. The men in the booths were still smoking, not looking at me, not surrounded by moonlight and woods. I stumbled backward off the stool, but this time I hadn't passed out.

"You, okay?" Ian asked.

I blinked, rapidly, and told him to call a cab.

His home was small, dingy, but clean, the sex perfunctory, his hard, calloused hands moving over me quickly, his mouth wet, and afterward, I drifted off into a fitful sleep, images of the monster, my mother, and most of all, of those two old Indians at the bar coming to me in my sleep again and again.

I sensed something in the room, at the edge of my consciousness, and my eyes began to blink open. And then I felt it. I shot up in bed.

Right dead center in his bedroom was my mother, and she was screaming, blood running out of her mouth. I scooted back rapidly against the wall, holding the blankets around me, shivering, my eyes closed. Something touched my hand, and it was my turn to scream, my eyes flying open.

It was only Ian. My mother was gone.

I had to get out of there.

"I'm sorry, but look, I gotta go," I said, scrambling up, and into my clothes. Jesus Christ, now I knew what it was like to have your mom show up when you'd just boned someone—except in my case, she was fucking dead.

"What?" He seemed confused, still half-asleep even though I'd woken him up by screaming, one hand crumpled into the blue sheets.

"I'm just going through some stuff. But thanks," I said, pulling my shirt over my head. "This was just what I needed."

"Sister?" Ian said, lighting a cigarette, and I rolled my eyes. I hated that sister shit—particularly after I'd just fucked someone. It usually meant a speech was coming, and usually by a man. I was in no mood.

"I'm on my way out," I said, a touch of venom in my voice. "But could I get a smoke?"

He laughed, softly. Kindly. "I been there, plenty. Gotta let shit go sometimes, you know?" he said, handing me a cig and the lighter.

"I'm fine. I don't need a daddy. I got one of those," I said, lighting it. Motherfucker had barely said anything all night and now he was Oprah fucking Winfrey.

He nodded, shut his trap.

I left, feeling relief flood into me as soon as I did, calling an Uber once I got out the door. Since it was the middle of the night—maybe fifteen minutes past the witching hour—I ended up waiting a good, long time in the dark, in the cold, grateful, at least, for the smoke. I felt tired, and hungover, like my whole body was buzzing so hard I might blink out of existence. I didn't drink like this anymore. I had to get it together. I wasn't going to go backward, into that bleak, wide territory I'd occupied in my teens and twenties. That same space that had pulled Jaime in and took her, and with it, my desire to be close to anyone but Debby.

I had to heal Daddy. I just had to. But I already felt so lost.

CHAPTER THIRTEEN

Driving west toward Idaho Springs from Denver, I was thinking about stopping at the Shell at the edge of town and picking up a pack of Camel Shorts, my favorite cigarettes of all
time. I frowned, and the light dimmed, becoming yellow and artifi-
cial as I entered the Twin Tunnels. I was almost home. The ride to
the Springs was only forty-five minutes in reality, but emotionally, it
was like entering another world. The city had disappeared as I'd hit
I-70, buildings giving way to long, green fields and eventually, if they
were out, to herds of buffalo on either side, right as the mountains
came into view, not long before the exit to Evergreen. Evergreen,
which had turned closed-gate housing and yoga-loving long before
Idaho Springs.

Then there was the steep climb down, the sheer drop of cliff, the
new highway that led to Central City, which had once been beautiful. Full of old turn-of-the-century houses, and long-glass-doored
businesses downtown, with ornate twists in the architecture lining
the sides. A tourist trap, but a wonderful one; rock shops and faux-
old-fashioned photography. I remembered going there with friends
countless times, hitching and drinking and laughing as we held the
newly minted black-and-whites of us dressed up like barmaids,

feather boas wrapped around our long brown and white necks. Before the casinos. They provided jobs, but, alongside the Walmart in Evergreen, they changed everything. Central City had become a ghost town, the only occupied buildings the ones where you could gamble and get a steak dinner for $12.99 in the same territory I imagined the Arapaho once defending, paying with so many of their lives.

I rolled the window down to light a smoke, and the big, old mill came up on my right. This place. Of sorrow, of cigarettes, of babies born to teenagers who lit the tip of black eyeliners in the back of their old cars so it would go on smooth, heavy, one finger holding an eyelid down, drunk and oblivious to the rest of the world.

I slowed to exit, rolling over the small bridge that linked highway to town, and then the Safeway was on my left, the gas station where I used to hang out as a kid, bumming smokes off strangers. Then it was downtown, Beau Jo's and the shiny coffee shop with the gorgeous tin roof that had come in when I was a teenager, where I'd bought coffee—and pills and weed from the local drug dealer, a kid named Margaritte, who I'd teased relentlessly in junior high.

Finally, on the other end, trailer park city on the left with its sea of pink flamingos, and my dad's and cousin's fading white houses on the right.

I parked and got out.

A few hours later, Debby was desperately trying to calm the four-year-old—Rachel—down enough to get her into bed, while the two-year-old sat next to me, propped in front of *Dora the Explorer*, one hand around her bottle like it was a Bud, the other, perched companionably on my arm. I cheers ed her with my beer, and she giggled.

"I'm out," Jack said.

Debby looked up, blinked. "Out?"

"Yeah, me and Carl are going to Tommyknocker's."

Carl was standing behind Jack, an awkward shadow.

"I thought Kari and I could go out for a change," she responded, bouncing her kid up and down.

Jack narrowed his green-blue eyes. "I don't want you running around with her."

"And I don't want you running around with Carl," Debby retorted.

In answer, Jack turned around, the sound of the screen-door slamming behind him like a bullet.

Debby started crying, and Rachel crawled up into the La-Z-Boy with her, curling into her lap, she and Rachel sobbing together until Rachel stopped and ran her small, chubby fingers down her mom's face, telling her not to cry.

I felt like hell.

"Honestly, Debby? Maybe I should just find shit out about my mom solo. Not drag you into it. He already hates it when you and I go off on our own."

We'd been discussing my talk with Squeaker, my next steps, when Jack came in. Debby had made the mistake of updating him, telling him she wanted to take me to a spiritualist she and her mom liked in Denver. He'd told her that I could go on my own, and they'd argued.

"What? No. Don't let that fool," she said, her foot flipping in the direction that he left in, "influence you."

Her kid started hiccupping, then her eyes began fluttering closed.

"Besides, I think it'll help you move forward to know what happened to your mother," Debby said.

I made a sigh of pure exasperation. "That's *not* why I'm doing it. I'm doing it for Daddy." I stopped, sipped. "Not everybody got to be like you, Debby. I don't need a boyfriend or a college degree to be happy. I've moved forward, I'm fine. Shit."

"Don't you yell at me too," she said, her voice wavering.

I sighed. "I'm sorry. I'm just . . . look at the crap it's causing between you and Jack. I don't want to make that worse," I said, glancing at her sleeping child.

"I already told you not to worry about him. Kari, your mom's ghost, she's been like, unleashed. You can't change that."

I was silent.

"And Jack and me . . . we gotta have it out sometime."

My stomach tightened. I had begged her to come live with me, countless times. But I didn't want to be the reason they split. Or had some crazy argument in front of the kids—worse than what they'd just seen. Growing up, I heard countless tales of men beating their wives in front of their kids, beating their kids. Or not coming home at all. Or staying at home, drinking and doing nothing else. There were a thousand ways to turn your life into a living hell, and though Jack and Debby weren't perfect, I'd do anything I could to not let them slide into that.

The images on the TV were strange and soupy in my sleepy, half-drunk state. I felt angry then, tired. I wished Debby had never found that bracelet. That I'd never touched it. That my mother had never left. Or that my father had never started drinking. That he'd never gotten into that accident. Ended up with brain damage. My God, what *had* happened to my mother? If she was a ghost, surely, she was long dead.

I was half-asleep when my eyes flew open.

"Debby," I said, "don't cops have records of shit?"

Her eyes sparkled. "They do."

I nodded. Debby knew a lot about cops, and records and all that— all our cousins were cops and she and Jack hung out with them, down at the Derby. And her husband worked security at the prison.

"What if I went down to the station in town—wouldn't they have records about my mom? And anything to do with her?"

"They would. And you're her kid, so they'd have to release whatever they got to you."

I nodded again. "I'm doing this tomorrow."

"You mean *we* are."

I laughed. "Jack's not going to like that," I said.

"Too bad!" she responded, and took a long, rebellious sip of her Bud, choking a bit at the end of it, her little, chubby arm coming around to block the cough.

I shrugged and went back to the blue light of the TV, my eyes closing again for real this time.

CHAPTER FOURTEEN

The police badges in front of me glinted in the buzzing, fluorescent light. I was at 1711 Miner Street, standing at the counter, waiting to see if I had to flash my tits to get any one of these old boys' attention. Debby knew me good though, and she kept telling me to *let her handle it* in tiny, scratchy whispers. I was letting her. I didn't like it much, as being nice or patient was against my nature, but I'd come to understand in life that there were times you had to shut your goddamn mouth to get what you wanted. And I had begun to want this, bad. I prayed to the heavy metal gods—and most specifically to *the* heavy metal god, Dave Mustaine—that this shit would work out in my favor, and something helpful about my mom would come up.

Finally, after Debby had smiled and said hello super brightly enough times, a short, white man with a handlebar mustache came by, his gut poking up and over his belt. He was, as Debby would put it, peak Idaho Springs.

"Help you, ladies?" he said, glancing over at me uneasily. I couldn't blame him. I always looked like trouble in my dark T-shirts and black jeans, and in my younger days, I'd been in here plenty on misdemeanors. Hell, he might've cuffed me once, and not in that good way. He was probably related to me on Debby's side too. Half the white folks in this town were second or third cousins. It was like a Rez. Though unlike a Rez—or like Indians everywhere I'd ever been—they didn't refer to each other as cousins.

"Hi, Officer! Bob, right? You remember me! Jack's wife?" Debby said.

At the mention of Jack's name, I stopped myself from rolling my eyes. He had apologized for going out and leaving her alone with the kids and taken us all out to breakfast. He did this kind of thing a lot. Debby's house was covered in thoughtful little trinkets. Cheap silver bracelets. Tiny porcelain cats.

Debby smiled brightly, like she had a pink lamé baton in one hand. She was wearing a different sparkle-themed T-shirt today. This one said, DADDY'S LIL' PRINCESS. Ironic, as Debby's dad hadn't been around since she was a kid.

The officer blinked a few times and then nodded. "Derby?"

"That's right! We've had drinks at the Derby!" she said, like she was encouraging a small child to use the toilet for the first time.

"Right," he said, one hand going to his mustache, and twisting.

Debby giggled happily, and I resisted the urge to roll my eyes again. This was why I worked at dive bars like the Hangar Bar, and places where I didn't have to be all sunshine and happiness, though I had to be at least passably nice at Lucille's. I hated this kind of shit.

Just then, Debby's phone rang—the tone a few bars from Britney's Spears's "I'm a Slave 4 U," and I knew it was Jack, wondering where she was, wondering if she was with me. He was such a douche. Couldn't he wash his own fucking boxers for once? Every time he did something nice, he just had to follow it up with some bullshit.

"My cousin here," Debby started, glancing down at her phone nervously and placing it on silent, "her mother disappeared when she was just two days old. Isn't that sad?" Officer Bob squinted in confusion, my light-brown skin contrasting brightly with Debby's white.

He just stood there, silent. I could've sworn I spied donut crumbs on the end of one side of his mustache.

"And her dad, well, he didn't take it well. Got into an accident not long after."

Nothing.

"And so, she just wants to know if there were any missing persons filed on her mom, or even," and here, Debby stopped to shake her head tragically, "any death certificates. Just so that she could know for sure."

"ID?" he said. "Phone number?"

Finally, something from Officer Bob.

I pulled my wallet out of my black, fringe faux-leather purse, and handed my ID over. Gave him my number.

"May take some time," he said.

"Any chance you can speed it up? Jack always talks about how wonderful the men in this station are."

"We'll see," he said. "Take a seat."

About thirty minutes later, after Debby had forced me to look at a bunch of mainly cat-themed memes on Facebook, to my great surprise, the all-powerful Bob came out from behind the counter and over to us.

"Got a death certificate and a few other things—she was presumed dead on account of no remains being found."

"Thank you so much, Officer! I'll tell Jack how *wonderful* you were to us," she said, nearly squealing as he walked back around to the counter.

"Could you lay it on any thicker?" I said. "Shit."

"I got us what we wanted in thirty minutes, you curmudgeon."

I supposed that was true. I sat up, and we pored over the thin file. Nothing much. Nothing helpful at all in fact. Just a certificate that presumed her death, like Bob had said—showing that she'd been born in Denver—and a missing person's report, filed by my dad.

"Dammit, I was so hoping there'd be something that could lead us somewhere," Debby said. Her phone started ringing again, and she set to texting.

I'd hoped so too. We got up to go.

Just as we were about to leave, I felt eyes on my back. I turned around. There was an older officer in plainclothes staring at me by the watercooler, his hair gray, his face showing years of dealing with the kind of shit one deals with in this small, hurt little town. He wasn't getting any water, either. Just staring, hard. I nodded. He nodded back. And I left with a strange, echoing feeling throughout my body, though I knew that might just be the heady, buzzy exhaustion I'd been living with since that first visitation.

CHAPTER FIFTEEN

Of Feather and Bone was playing at the Hi-Dive, and it was exactly what I needed. I needed their grinding, caustic, death-metal sound: their lyrics about the Aztec underworld, mortality, and their uncompromising stance on Christianity and colonization. Their sound was all-encompassing, cruel, even genre-bending, with elements of punk and grindcore; their sudden transitions an adrenaline shot straight to the heart. *Embrace the Wretched Flesh* had just been released, and the title of the album described exactly what I was feeling: a need to escape. Knowing that was impossible.

I stood in the sweaty, tattooed, and pierced crowd, screaming, head banging, one hand clasped around a Bud. I'd brought my whiskey in a small, silver flask, and was taking swigs out of that too. The sound was driving, everywhere, and for a minute I did escape, move into something cathartic, until a white girl on my right tripped into me, falling onto her knees. I helped her up with my free hand.

"Gracias," she said.

"Sure," I answered, not bothering to correct her. I got that a lot.

She looked confused for a minute, but then started banging again, her head doing a messy swiveling, up and down. I wondered if she'd gotten into something stronger than Bud. Her eyes were murky, her pink and blue hair greasy, a touch of vomit in one thin strand.

A new song had begun when I felt eyes on me and turned. It was a tall, dark-haired man watching me from a few bodies behind. He smiled. I smiled back, cheers-ed him with my Bud up in the air. A few minutes later he came over, weaving between people, and asked if I wanted a cig. I said yes, amid bangs, and we snaked our way past in-between sets.

Outside, feeling the cool air on my face, I watched the smoke shoot out of my mouth in a thin stream, feeling like I would do nearly anything to stop the ghost. At this point in time, I didn't want to touch that bracelet, ever again. Or find out what happened to my mom. And it was ridiculous to believe a stupid piece of copper jewelry could heal my daddy's brain. I shouldn't have let Debby, with all that elf and wizard garbage in her head, pull me into believing any of it. This shit was tearing my life up. I wasn't sleeping—it was worse than ever. I felt strange, out of it, in another world most days. And my boss at Lucille's had pulled me aside, asked me if I was okay. He was nice about it, but I could tell he was leaning toward letting me go. I'd been late a number of mornings, something that in my thirties I took pride in *never* doing.

I needed to get out of my head, if only for a little bit. And then I needed to call a brain doctor, find out what was really going on.

I realized the dark-haired guy had been talking to me for about five minutes, my head nodding automatically, before I recognized that I hadn't heard a word he'd been saying. I worked hard, between the drunk-haze and exhaustion, to tune in. Something about his friends, who were Indian.

I squinted. I'd been mistaken inside—his hair wasn't brown. He had long, red hair. Darker than Dave Mustaine's, and not curly. But it was similar enough to pique my interest.

"They turned me onto this band," he said.

I assumed he meant his Indian friends, and I held my flask out to him. He drank without questioning.

"Cool," I said.

A woman and a young man, both definitely Native, joined a few minutes later. We smiled, asked each other what tribes we were, talked about where we were from. Turned out, all of us had grown up in Denver. They were cool, funny. Anishinaabe and Lakota. The sort of Mustaine-a-like, ironically named Dave, thought both Metallica and Megadeth were overrated.

"You're overrated," I said, and he laughed.

Inside, I stuck with them, passing my flask around until it was empty, banging and screaming and pushing the ghost away with two calloused hands.

An hour later, back outside on Broadway, the streets were ominous, murky, dimly lit. The Hi-Dive a small respite against the promising, but dangerous, grit of the surrounding streets. My head swung back toward the Hi-Dive, admiring its smallness. Blueness. The way it looked neatly tucked into a corner of Broadway; the long, wooden bar inside. My new heavy metal buddies had convinced me to go home with them after the concert, to keep partying. They only lived a few blocks away, in a house one of them had inherited from a grandparent. They said that the band might show up after. God, I hadn't done this kind of thing in forever.

It was a cool old house. Brick and nicely maintained, if a little messy, and over the course of a few hours, several metalheads showed up with beer in their hands, cigarettes in their pockets. I felt at home. I felt solid, even if underwater.

Inside, there were loads of old couches and black end tables, poster after poster of local heavy metal bands like Glacial Tomb and Dreadnought framed on the walls, black candles, and skulls everywhere.

I sat down next to Dave, and we smoked together, and someone pulled a little weed out. Normally, these days, I stuck to booze. But it had been over a decade since I'd toked up, and I was in the mood. And it was only weed. I inhaled, and immediately regretted it, coughing like mad. It had been too long, and I was nearly instantaneously super high.

I excused myself to go to the bathroom, the zigzagging, black and white tile fucking with my head. In the mirror, I gazed into my black eyes, and wondered what I was doing. I liked to go home alone these days, except for an occasional White Horse hookup. But even that was getting rarer the past few years. I wanted to watch a horror flick on Netflix, drink a Bud or two, end the evening texting Debby and reading a novel.

I drank water from the tap, even though it tasted of minerals and dust, and washed my face. Re-did my makeup. When I came back, I felt better, but I figured Dave would have moved on, and that would be my cue to leave. But he was waiting for me on the couch, one long white arm draped along the top, asking me if I was okay, his smile quiet and beautiful.

I told him, "Yeah."

The two Natives I'd met with him earlier came by, Doria in particular striking me as someone I could be friends with. She was one of those elf-looking Natives, despite her heavy metal gear and ubiquitous silver piercings, with long, silky-straight hair, and ears that poked out in-between the strands. She was tiny, but tough. We talked a little more—she was a good ten years younger than me, so listening to me go on about heavy metal back in the day was of infinite delight to her. She wanted us to follow each other on Twitter, but I told her I wasn't on it, or Instagram, and she smiled, and shrugged, and she and her boyfriend—or friend, I wasn't quite sure—melded back into the party.

I had been standing, but felt like sitting then, taking a load off—though I also felt, simultaneously, like leaving. There was a nervous flutter playing deep in my stomach. I chose to ignore it, and sat down next to Dave on the orange, corduroy couch. He had been waiting. He smiled, pulled a long stand of hair behind his ear. The gesture was almost shy. Something came over me, a need to erase the ghost, or pull myself back into my own childhood, I'm not sure, but I bent over his lap, and we were kissing, my hands on his muscular thighs, his breath rich with cigarettes and beer. A few minutes later I pulled back, and he told me he had something special for me. My stomach turned.

He pushed his hand into his pocket and came out with a little packet of something white. Something I knew wasn't coke, not that I did that anymore either.

I closed my eyes, felt the sickness, the memories rocketing back through me like a tidal wave. I thought back to when I was twenty-four. I thought back to Jaime, the pain washing through me, tearing into my throat.

When I opened my eyes, he was lifting his head off the table, his long, dark-red hair held back by a freckled hand. He smiled.

"Your turn," he said.

I wanted it. Bad. Worse than I could remember in years and years, and it wasn't like I hadn't been around coke and H and so much more since I'd quit everything but booze. But there were things you turned your back on forever. And if it wasn't forever, it was as if time didn't exist at all, wasn't real, and you were stuck inside a private hell that you knew damn well was of your own making. So much of me didn't want to go back there. To stay suspended in a place where I'd almost lost my life. Where I'd watched someone I'd loved, probably the last person I'd loved besides Daddy and Debby, lose her life.

Jaime. I pushed her face away for another time.

Damn the ghost.

I could feel myself falling back despite myself, the beautiful stupid arc of it, my exhaustion giving way to release, to giving up. I reached and met Dave's fingers.

My phone began to buzz in my pocket. I ignored it. I held the dollar bill that I'd been given between two fingers. The phone died down. Started again.

I rolled the bill slowly, elaborately. If I was going to fall, I was going to enjoy every second of it. My phone buzzed again and this time, I worried for Debby, for the kids. Or was it something about Daddy? Sometimes his nurse called when there was something wrong.

"I gotta take this," I said.

Dave nodded hazily, and I walked outside, making my way through the crowd, most of whom were smoking. I coordinated a smoke.

Without checking to see who it was for sure, I answered.

"This Kari?"

"Yeah?" Fuck. It wasn't Debby after all. I'd stopped my good time for some motherfucking insurance salesman or some shit. I inhaled.

"Kari James?"

I spit the smoke out.

"Look. I gotta go. I'm not interested—"

"I've got information on your mother."

My throat closed up.

"Are you there?"

"Who the hell is this?"

"My name is Fredrico. I'm a retired cop. There's shit about your mom on file you didn't get to see. You want to?"

I was silent for beat. Then, "Yes."

We arranged for a time to talk, in-person.

On the way back to my apartment in Aurora, the lights of Denver spinning slowly out in front of me, reflected in the window of the car, I played Megadeth's "Sweating Bullets." It was a song I listened to a lot, to remind me of who I was, what I had to lose. What I had lost. As the Uber driver pulled closer and closer to home, I turned the volume up on my headphones, so that I could take in every syllable of my favorite lines, which were about the schizophrenic nature of one's past meeting one's present, especially when you had a past like mine.

CHAPTER SIXTEEN

The ex-cop, Debby, and I walked under the green awning above the entrance to the Mercury Café, and up the stairs. I'd wanted her to come just in case the dude turned out to be dangerous, though she'd had to give Jack an excuse, and juggle her kids' schedules. She'd told me Jack had gone silent on her when she'd said that she had a medical appointment. I knew eventually she'd run out of excuses, but I guessed that wasn't my problem. At the restaurant, there were string lights everywhere, and the inside was lit up like a fairy tale. The brick walls were painted red, the long, wooden bar inviting. Plants of various kinds were ubiquitous, ivy winding its way around furniture, trees in corners. Small, old dolls were scattered throughout, watching us with one eye. There were typewriters. Rusty phonographs. The vibe was eclectic, magical. I was glad he'd suggested meeting here.

Debby sat a distance from the two of us, letting us have our space, and I asked Fredrico what he wanted to drink, after we'd settled at the bar. It was hard to hear over the disjointed notes of the saxophone in the other room, where there was a stage and an open mic session.

"Whiskey, neat," he said to me, and to the waiting bartender.

"Same," I said.

"You live around here?" I asked.

"I do. I bought back in the day when it was cheap and danger-ous, once I'd left the Springs. Worked for a station around here for a while, then retired for good."

"Lucky that you did," I said. "I rent in Aurora, and it's even getting expensive there."

He nodded.

"So," I began, but was interrupted by a massive hoot from a saxo-phone from the other room. I started again, raising my voice, hoping to drown out the noise. "Thanks for calling. I've wondered if it's worth finding out what happened to my mom at all but . . . let's just say your call turned me back around. Got me curious all over again."

We got our whiskies and he nodded thoughtfully, scratched at his chest through a worn, white T-shirt, and took a sip. "I had to look up my old files but, I remembered the details eventually. It was a long time ago."

"Thirty-five years," I said.

He laughed, quietly. "I was about your age then."

He was in his mid- to late sixties, with thick, gray hair and large, slanted black eyes.

"Why were you at the station in the Springs, if you're retired?" I asked.

"Got a friend still there. We kept in touch, have lunch every Tues-day. And your face, well—it's your mom's."

"I see," I said, not really seeing at all.

"Let me just tell you what I got—which isn't much. But this case—for some reason, it's always stuck in my craw. Maybe because your mom looked a little like mine and I've always been a mama's boy, I don't know," he said, laughing softly, and rubbing the back of his neck.

I took a small drink of my whiskey. It was good. Strong. Smoky.

"But I do have some info that you might or might not have,

depending on your situation with your family." He leaned back, slid the whiskey off the table, sipped. Set it carefully back down.

I began to feel a little hope.

Another hoot from the saxophone in the other room stopped him from what he was going to say next, followed by a weird, seemingly unrelated string of words shouted by what I could only presume was the player, since the speaking had started precisely when the hooting had stopped.

"Go on," I said.

"Interesting that you got your mother's last name, by the way—not your dad's. Made this thing a little confusing at first."

"Yeah," I answered. I'd always thought that was weird, but now I figured maybe my dad had been trying to help my mom honor where she was coming from. Though who knew.

"Dad's last name's King," I said. Long line of Kings in Idaho Springs.

He nodded.

"In any case, the first thing is, your dad, Jim. He was convinced there was something suspicious in your mother's disappearance. But we questioned her family, friends. There was nothing. However, though there really wasn't a case, my gut said he was right."

Huh.

The saxophone started going off again then, strange, staccato notes, each one followed by the word "obscure."

What this fucker was on, only God knew.

Fredrico squinted thoughtfully. "And Michael and Nessie James—your grandparents—" he said, "had no idea what happened to her." His eyes grew distant then and came back. "Don't be impressed by my recollection of their names. My memory isn't what it used to be when I was on the job, but it was in the files."

"Gotcha," I said, feeling disappointed, and wanting a cigarette. Just the idea that there were police files that the cops in the Springs hadn't had access to on my grandparents, parents, made my stomach clench—but at the same time, the fact that he'd already said that my grandparents hadn't known what had happened to Cecilia was making me feel like I was probably wasting my time. Again.

"Did you ever have a suspect?" I asked, in between more saxophone and shouted "obscures," which abruptly shifted to "opaque." I could feel the desperation in my heart crawling around, sliding downward.

"No one was good for it. And on top of it, there was no evidence of foul play. Searched her parents' apartment in Aurora, your mom and dad's house in Idaho Springs, nothing. My partner figured Cecilia must've found another guy, run off. Told your dad as much."

Something occurred to me then. "With a newborn?"

"See, that didn't sit right with me either." Fredrico squinted, his eyes going out of focus. He shook head. "Thing was I remember the family was tight-lipped . . ." He stopped, his drink halfway to his mouth, his lips moving. "Maybe your dad would remember more."

He drank a bit of his whiskey, then wormed out of his light sweater, setting it over the cane barstool.

"He was in an accident. Brain damage," I said, looking up, and into the mirror in front of me, then down at my whiskey. I turned the glass thoughtfully, took a sip.

He frowned. "Sorry to hear that."

We were silent for a time.

He cut his eyes over at me then. "You ever have any contact with your grandparents?"

"No, didn't even know they existed."

He shook his head again. "Yeah. I don't know why, but I figured that."

"Why didn't you keep going? On the case?" I asked.

A tumescent kind of rage blossomed inside of me. I was suddenly pissed at this guy, pissed at the whole system. Fucking cops. Enough time to beat the shit out of someone trans, or Native or Black who happened to be in the wrong place at the wrong time, but not enough time to follow a lead. I took half of my whiskey in one swallow and ordered another.

"Take it easy, kid," he said, sensing my mood.

"I'm thirty-five." I looked back at myself in the mirror, then over at the bartender, who was wiping at the other end of the bar with a rag.

"You're a kid to me," he said.

I snorted.

That dark, moody, otherworldly feeling flooded into me. The lights now dimmed, became red, and there was something different to the room now, more ominous, the sounds of the saxophone lonely and strange. The hair on the back of my neck pricked up, and I wondered if my mother might make an appearance. The electric quality to the air before the ghost of your mother showed up.

My eyes cut over to Debby, but she was deep in her phone, probably busy liking cat memes.

He sighed. "You got to understand something. My district was underfunded. And no one gave a shit if—no offense, I'm Mexican and it's the same for us—some Indian ran off back to the Rez." He rubbed at his eyes, as if talking about this stuff made him as tired as he must have been during his working days.

"She wasn't from a Rez," I said, disgruntled.

"In any case, I'm telling you, there was no evidence. No one was talking. No one cared. I had to let the case go." His expression softened again into one of exhaustion, and I knew he wasn't being stubborn, he was telling me the truth. A truth he'd come to live with, over the course of many years, with what I had to assume was disappointment after disappointment.

"Okay," I said, wondering why he'd even bothered to contact me in the first place. "Anything else?"

"So, this is the part that might be helpful. Your grandfather and your father, they were convinced it had to do with all of the protests your mother went to."

"Protests?"

"Yeah, you know—AIM. American Indian Movement."

"Oh," I said, sitting back. That *was* something.

He scratched his face, at the black and gray stubble coming through. "There were files I couldn't get to. Ones that led all the way to the feds, and I didn't have the clearance."

I thought about my vision. The one I'd had where my mother had been at the Indian Center against her father's wishes. Was she trying to show me something that would tell me more about her death?

He took another sip. "I'm sorry. I wish had more," he finished, sipping at his whiskey, his hands tapping at the rim when he sat the glass down.

The hooter must have changed places with someone else, as now, a steady, noirish, jazzy sound was coming from the other room, and it was heightening the already strange mood of the place. I looked over my shoulder, sure I'd see the face of my mother right behind me. But there was nothing but the red lights, and the sounds of people laughing and talking at their tables and large booths, their glasses clinking against the wood.

"If I think about it, she was one of those, what you call it? Always on the news these days . . ." He struggled to think, snapping softly, while I finished my whiskey, gratefully receiving the next one, my hand around the warm glass. "Missing and Murdered types."

It took me a minute, but I got what he was saying. "Missing and Murdered Indigenous Women," I answered, and took a sip.

"That's it," he said. "Not that we talked about it that way back then."

We sat in silence for a moment.

"You know, same happens to Mexican women—those women murdered in factories. Though no one thinks of them as Indian because they speak Spanish," he said, his laughter cynical, dark. "And half the time, they don't speak Spanish, they speak some kind of Indian. Fucking irony."

I nodded. I felt sick. He was right. And I would've never thought about my mother in that regard, though now that he said it, it made sense. Who was going to go looking for a poor, brown woman back then? Who was going to now? I was lucky this guy remembered her. Was willing to meet. Wasn't white. Gave two shits. Not that he had much for me, though that fed stuff was interesting.

We sat for a time in an uncomfortable silence.

Fredrico broke it with a sigh. "You're your mother's near spitting image, you know that?"

"Yeah."

"It was why I recognized you. That face, well. Like I said."

Now I understood.

"She was pretty. Young," he said. "Hate when that's the case."

"Twenty years old," I said, a hint of bitterness in my voice.

"That's right. Shit." He tapped his leg with one, short, brown finger, then paused.

"I remember her eyes from the photos," he said, "haunted."

His own eyes grew distant, and he pulled his glass up to his lips, and then set it back down again without taking a drink.

I wanted to tell him then that Cecilia was haunting me. But I knew he'd think I was crazy.

"Oh, I almost forgot," he said, shaking his head. "Getting forgetful in my old age."

I laughed. He was hardly in elder territory.

I was really itching for a smoke now, and couldn't help but pack my cigarettes, one hand hitting the bottom of the box again and again, an old habit.

He smiled dimly and took a sip of his drink. "I got this for you, if you want to ask your grandparents more about it—wasn't sure you had their info. Like I said, I had a feeling that maybe you didn't. I don't know why. I don't know if it'll be any help, and you can't tell nobody I gave it to you, but here."

Curious, I watched as he dug in the pocket of his jeans, and fi-

nally, came up with a few balls of lint, and a piece of notebook paper.
I took it from his hand.

Scrawled on the front was an address and a phone number.

"Don't know if they're still there, but that was Michael and Nessie's
info. You know, your grandparents."

"Thank you," I said, appreciative, hopeful.

He tapped my pack. "I used to smoke. Had to, on the job.
Would've gone crazy otherwise. Finally quit—used the patches."

"I was quit for five years before—well, before I decided to look
into all of this. I'll quit again."

He nodded.

"I'm also gonna give you this," he said, handing me his card. "I'm
retired, but you need help, you call me."

I shuddered at a draft; someone had opened the door, and there
was a cold, spring rain outside. It shut with a loud clang.

"I remember your grandfather was a hunter. Had heads mounted
all over the place. Fact, that was his alibi, that he was out hunting."

"Really?" I asked.

"Yeah. Talking about it is spurring my memory. Your grandmother even signed an affidavit stating that he'd been out with a
friend—who also corroborated. Said that it had just been your
grandfather and him way out past Evergreen, out and about in the
mountains around Mount Evans, around the time that your father
made the call, said she'd gone missing."

He went silent then, and when he came out of his reverie, he
said, "I bet you're really jonesing for a smoke."

"Thanks. I'll be okay for a few more minutes," I said. I glanced
down at my phone. 11:47.

The music seemed to grow louder, moodier, the whisk-whisk of
the Zildjian and the sounds of a low, sad sax making that other world
bigger, so big, that it opened up and took me inside.

"Look," he said, clearing this throat. "If I were you, I'd start with
your grandparents."

My eyes narrowed.

"I think, if you want to get into this—and I never said that—but, if you do, I'd start with her—Nessie, your grandmother. It always seemed to me that she had something to say but kept quiet around your grandfather."

I told him that even if I found that they were still living at the address he'd given me, that it would probably be hard to get them to remember anything important. That maybe they hadn't contacted me years ago because there was something painful to do with my mom's disappearance. That maybe they didn't want to talk.

"You just got to find Nessie's pressure point."

"Pressure point?" I questioned.

"Yeah. The thing that'll spill her over the edge, make her feel like she's either got to die, or talk."

"I see," I answered.

I looked up at the mirror and saw myself, and then, sure enough, a visage so like my own, my mother's, right next to mine, tears streaming down her wide, brown face, her eyes closed, blood streaming out of a wound on the side of her head. I startled, but took a breath, steeled myself. Her mouth opened and she began sounding something out, her arm open, and to her side. I peered into the mirror, but just then, Fredrico said something, and she was gone.

CHAPTER SEVENTEEN

Dave Mustaine stared up into the sky, a cigarette between his lips, a black guitar between his legs, his signature in messy silver cursive at the bottom of the poster I'd slapped on the walls of my apartment in Denver the minute I'd moved in. I'd worshiped him, his long, wavy strawberry-red hair. His fuck-it-all attitude. He'd been, and still was, my idol, though I tried not to pay attention to his politics. I'd been to every Megadeth concert, for every album, since *Countdown to Extinction,* to *Super Collider* last year—starting when I was twelve years old. Everyone in the Springs listened to heavy metal, especially Metallica, often death metal—but it was Dave Mustaine who spoke to me when I was barely more than a child, sitting in someone's basement, getting high and drunk, when someone put *Countdown* on, and I was changed.

I'd made my decision. I just had to pick up the phone.

I plucked the picture of my mother up from the black coffee table—I'd lifted it from the drawer in the end table next to Daddy's bed. It was a Polaroid, and the borders were thick, white.

I turned the photo over and braced myself.

"Hello?" She had a sweet voice, subdued.

"Is this Nessie? Nessie James?"

"It is. Who is this?"

I took a deep breath, picked my cigarettes and lighter up, and went outside to smoke, making my way down the hallway, and down the stairs—I didn't want to stink my place up. As I went, I kept speaking.

"My name is Kari James."

"James?" She asked, a note of genuine curiosity in her voice, and I leaned over, pulling my hands into a cup to stop the wind at the foot of the stairs. The cigarette lit, and I inhaled, wondering, as I strode over the thick, red brick of the back alley, why I'd ever quit.

"I'm Cecilia's . . . child."

There was silence at the other end, and I thought perhaps she'd hung up. Finally, she spoke.

"My God."

"The thing is, I found your number and—"

"Found my number?"

"Or rather, well, it's hard to explain. See, she disappeared when I was two days old, and—"

"I'm sorry. I'm so sorry but," and she began to sniffle. "I can't talk to you."

"Wait—"

"I just can't," she finished, and hung up. I could hear her sniffling as she did.

I looked at the face of the phone as if it could show me answers, and then slipped it in the back pocket of my black jeans. Shit. I inhaled, feeling the nicotine work itself through my system, wondering what to do next.

I finished the cigarette, and went back up to my apartment, sat down on the couch. I looked back up at Dave, his long, muscular legs, his mouth twisted in a moment of passion and pain. He was like so many where I came from: angry, sad beyond measure, holding untold secrets of father's hands touching where they shouldn't, mother turning away, too-early sex in the corners of rotting apartments. That was why when so many in the country were turning to the more sober, morose sounds of Pearl Jam and Nirvana, in the Springs, we kept our hair long, our necks jerking to the harsh, cruel sounds of metal that satisfied the pain, the parts of us that would never completely recover.

There were things I could find out on my own, but eventually, I'd have to convince Nessie to talk to me—though maybe Auntie Squeaker might know something more. I recalled her saying something about telling me stuff when I was ready. That dang Squeaker. I never knew exactly what she was up to, or why—though she seemed to have her reasons. My mom and her were related, but they hadn't been close—though it seemed like my mother hadn't been close to anyone. But everyone knew everyone's business back in the Springs.

However, there was something I could do right now.

I walked over to the dresser in my bedroom, also black, and pulled at the first drawer, the handle clicking loudly into the wood. I pushed underwear and socks aside and found it exactly where I'd put it. I'd taken it from Daddy's place after the last vision, though I'd covered it in cloth, to prevent any accidental visions. I took it out and sat back down on the couch.

"Okay," I said, speaking into the silence. "Okay," I repeated, quieter.

I pulled the bracelet out of the cloth, feeling that same slight, electric feeling I'd felt the first time I'd touched it, and as if there was a soundless thundercrack, I left my apartment, and entered another world.

This time I was at a powwow. It was Denver March, the powwow I went to every year, and I was Cecilia and I was sitting with my friends in the wide, gray bleachers, Jim at my side, the dancers coming in for grand entry, my eyes focusing on the spiral on one of the traditional dancer's regalia. His eyes contained so much love and my heart—separate and not separate from my mother's—sang and sang with pain to see him so young. He laughed at Cecilia's jokes, his white, freckled hand in hers, asking her why she wasn't dancing. *Learning to Jingle at the Center* she said, and I could feel her anger at her father, Michael, in the back of her mind, the fact that he didn't want her there, didn't want her learning to dance, to sing, to speak her languages. But more than anything, she was frustrated with him because he kept telling her he was scared for her, scared that the men in AIM would be the death of her.

My eyes—Cecilia's eyes—turned back to the dancers, and the smell of the coliseum, sweat, leather from the dancers' regalia, the squeak of moccasins on rubber surrounded me and I felt safe, Jim's fingers squeezing mine, my mind separate and not separate from hers, curious about what her father could mean about the men in AIM. Why would the men in AIM mean her any harm?

But before I could learn more, Cecilia's mind turned, thinking about how grand entry was her favorite—the elders in their traditional regalia leading the way, the fancy dancers and jingle dress dancers following, the tiny tots at the tail, some obediently staying in line, others, already wandering, and then, I was shoved out, and into a white tunnel, and back into my own mind, back onto my old, black couch with more questions than answers.

CHAPTER EIGHTEEN

wake up. The sharp, woody tang of burning cedar strong in my apartment. The wind blowing my curtains out in ribbons, the moon bright behind them. Something stirs in the shadows, and I sit up, afraid. I'd been dreaming, intensely, of Orr's—the Indian store on Broadway. Of my mother in Orr's, picking through the brightly colored strands of beads, her expression tense, full of longing. She is tugging at a strand of red, unhooking it and pulling it flat against the palm of her hand, a finger moving down along the length of it. She smiles and moves on to the wall of pearlescent white beads, the strand of red clutched in her hand. The strand begins to move, to flow, like a river. She looks down, frowning, her expression turning quickly to one of shock, pain. The strand is now blood, blood that is flowing from her head, down to her clothes, onto this strand, that is a small river of blood. Rotting meat permeates the air, and she turns, and in the corner of my eye I can see its long hair, hear its low, guttural growl, as she screams and screams and screams, and I with her.

I blink, feeling the hair of the back of my neck rise. I glance at my clock. It's 11:47, and the smell of scotch is thick.

The curtains.

I peer into the moonlit almost-darkness and see an outline in the curtains, and the curtains began to take shape, and *it* moves forward. I scramble, my back to my headboard, my heart in my throat.

First the feet. Then her body.

Cecilia.

She walks to the foot of my bed, her clothes bloody, her head a mess of tissue, her eyes so like mine, pleading.

She stands there, looking down at me, and I shiver.

"What do you want?" I whisper.

She begins to cry, her arm around something I can't see.

"Mother," I say, the word unfamiliar in my mouth, "what do you want?"

Her mouth opens, and blood drops out, a curtain of red, and she begins to whisper something then, something faint at first, something that begins with an "L."

I shake my head. "I don't understand."

She screams then, her black eyes peering straight into mine— turning white, screaming a word over and over and I cower. I close my eyes. It finally stops. I open them, and she is gone.

"Loaf?" I say to myself, my heart beating hard, knowing I won't sleep again tonight. "She said . . . loaf . . ."

It doesn't make any sense at all.

CHAPTER NINETEEN

The sun was setting on Broadway, and the street was golden, flush with life. Teenagers with pink and green hair were out, couples and friends taking advantage of happy hour at The Hornet, drinks in their hands, laughter everywhere. The Mayan Theater was bright and colorful, folks streaming out of the doors on either side of the ticket counter.

I thought of the ghost, the bracelet, the visions. I wanted to go to Orr's, the Native shop in town where I'd seen my mother in my dream, but in passing The Hornet, I thought to stop in, sit at the bar. I'd also decided to go to the Indian Center eventually since I'd dreamt of that too—ask around to see if anyone remembered Cecilia. But I was contemplating asking Auntie Squeaker first. Confirm whether she knew if Mom went there for real, or if my head was just making shit up.

"Whiskey," I said to the bartender when she came up.

I tried to read, but I couldn't. I just couldn't. Maybe I needed a new book. Maybe after this, I would head to Mutiny Now. And then I could see whether I really wanted to go to Orr's after all.

A flash of last night's vision, then dream, came to me and I shuddered. The screaming. The white eyes. The whole, confusing, maddening mess of it.

The whiskey began working its way in, and I sighed, downed the rest of it.

I went back to reading, but after a few minutes, I realized that I was just going over the same passage, again and again, and I cashed out.

A couple of hipsters whacked into me outside of Mutiny Now, and one of them yelled "Watch it," and I narrowed my eyes. They scurried away quickly.

At the window of the bookstore, I leaned in, looking to see if there were any new Jensen paintings I couldn't pass up. I loved the tattered awning, the dust, the rare books behind glass, the way the place had never changed, not really. Loved the comics and coffee spot that proclaimed "COfFEe" in lettering like gears—the rows and rows of books, the spot in back where they held poetry readings. One of Jensen's paintings was cut in half and hung over the rare books section. Rumor had it that someone had asked to pay less—so Jensen cut it in two, told the guy he could pay half then.

I went back to the horror section, and, finding an old paperback that looked appealing, I bought it, stuck it in my bag. I wanted to feel satisfied. But I didn't. I felt anxious.

Back outside, I stopped to light a smoke, and a homeless Indian guy asked me for change, calling me sister in that musical way that made me realize that he was from the Rez.

"Where you from?" he asked, after I gave him a five.

I knew he wanted to know what tribe I was.

"I'm from here. Apache and Chickasaw. I'm urban. You from the Rez?"

"Navajo," he said, smiling, his dark eyes somewhere else, not here.

"Yá'át'ééh," I said.

He only laughed. Then, "You look Apache, know that?"

"So, I've been told."

He was a handsome guy, maybe in his early forties. I wondered how he'd gotten to this, but that was none of my business.

"Sister?" he said, pushing his shoulder-length black, greasy hair back delicately over one shoulder.

I'd already started moving away, but I turned around.

"You got a shadow on you."

I froze in place.

"You ain't trying to witch me, are you?" I asked, my heart thumping.

"No, no. I'm no skinwalker. But I can see the shadow. You have to feed it."

Normally, I would've shrugged what he had to say off. No matter how urban the Indians were back home, lots of them said this kind of stuff, whether they were Catholic or evangelical or Native American Church, and I'd always hated it.

"Thanks, brother," I said, that strange, otherworldly feeling crawling up and around my shoulders.

"I seen your ancestors down at the White Horse. They trying to help you, sister."

I was silent, the hair on the back of my neck spiking. He meant the two Indians I'd seen right before I hooked up with that Nish. I knew it.

"I . . ."

"You pay attention to what they trying to tell you."

I nodded. This was a sign. I knew where I had to go.

I walked down the dirty city streets like I was in a dream. Past the plant store. The vintage store—the other vintage store, the one that had been around before I had, and waited at the crosswalk, another crosswalk, my mind swirling with questions—trying to push the image of my mother's face back as the light changed, and I crossed, kept going.

I was only a few blocks away from Orr's now.

Inside the store, I breathed in the scent of old leather, felt consoled by the sight of multicolored Pendletons—the long, glass case containing mainly vintage turquoise, silver—and beadwork. I wasn't much for jewelry, but I always had a little turquoise ring on my ring finger, on my right hand, accompanied by a set of simple silver circles on my other fingers, all the way down to my thumb. I walked over to the wall of red, yellow, white—all colors of beads, and pieces of shell, coral—all you needed if you were a jeweler or beader, and thought again of the dream I'd had, of my mother in this section. I browsed for a moment, staring at the red beads in particular, fingering them out of curiosity, but there was nothing. I sighed. Maybe I was being too literal. I went around to the back where the prayer shells, sweetgrass, and sage were kept. Auntie Squeaker had brought me here for my first shell. She'd taught me how to pray Native American Church way, when I was twelve years old, swinging her ancient, peyote-stitched, red-and-yellow beaded fan over my head, saying prayers to the east. I still did it sometimes when I was down. I plucked a bundle from the back shelf and headed up to the counter. God, I had no idea what I was looking for, why I was here.

"Hey." The owner was a short, sandy-haired guy with a sandy-haired mustache to match. I liked him. Calm. Respectful. "This all for you?"

As he began to ring up the sage, I glanced down at the jewelry under the glass. He had a lot of cool, retro pieces—I'd learned what was what mainly from Squeaker, who'd bought me my first silver ring, asking that I clear some weeds around her trailer in exchange.

I nodded at his question and began going round the case.

I stopped.

"I—wait," I said, my heart thumping. "Could I take a look at this?"

He paused, came around to where I was standing. "This?" he asked, pointing at a ring.

I nodded again, and he pulled it out.

"Is this . . . what tribe was the artist?"

"Chickasaw."

I shivered.

"It's rare too. You don't see this on jewelry much. Shoot, you see more Chickasaw necklaces than rings, when you even see those. And silverwork? Never." He looked down at it with me, and then handed it over. "You Chickasaw?"

I shrugged. "Yeah. And Apache. Really, I'm urban."

"Got it," he said.

The figure on the ring was the same as the monster in my nightmares, my visions.

I touched the ring warily, but it didn't have the charge the bracelet did. Which made sense. The bracelet had been my mother's.

"You know much about the Lofa?" he asked. I could tell he didn't want to be a jerk, tell me shit I might already know.

Goosebumps rushed along my arms. I brushed one finger over the raised figure. That was its name.

"Chickasaw bogeyman. It's kind of a shitty version of Bigfoot. Skins people."

"Really," I said, faintly, thinking about what Auntie Squeaker had told me.

"Supposedly, they smell bad. Bones of their victims bad. Live in caves. There are stories of warriors trying to hunt them down, eliminate them. They say they like to kidnap women. Also, sometimes kind of described as, you know . . . a shapeshifter I guess? Just because some folks describe him as a hairy man, others a monster."

I thought about the lingering smell of the beast, after I'd dreamed of it. The smell of rotting meat.

"Can I . . . show you something?" I asked, feeling like I'd entered a dream.

"Sure," he answered.

I pulled the bracelet out gingerly, with a cloth. I'd figured they might know more about it at Orr's.

I put it down on the counter, and he leaned over. "Wow. Old. Hmmm." He picked it up. "Turn of the century, I'm guessing."

"That's right. It was my mother's. I think it's been in my family for a long time."

"See this," he said, pointing to the Lofa figure. "If this bracelet has been in your family, this means—well, according to some, to legend, that the Lofa and your family, well, they're intertwined— probably for some historical reason, something to do with your family history and their relationship with it."

I nodded, not wanting to interrupt him.

"And this," he said, pointing to the Apache symbols, "the war club specifically, is what protects you from it. This . . . is a rare piece. Very urban."

"My family's very urban, like I said."

He nodded, examined it again for a while. I noticed that he didn't touch it, not once. Finally, with a deep sigh, he looked up at me. "Thank you for letting me see that."

"Sure," I said, feeling nauseated.

"So! You want the ring?" he asked. "I seen you in here a lot. I'll give you a good price. Complete your Lofa collection," he said, chuckling.

"Just the sage," I said, pulling my wallet out.

He laughed again. "Can't say I blame you. Honestly, I'm surprised to see the Lofa on jewelry at all."

I put the sage and bracelet—carefully—in my bag, told the guy to have a nice day, and headed north until I hit the awning and black brick face of the Brutal Poodle—the lettering in white—the interior mainly red, with paintings of vicious-looking poodles everywhere. I sat down roughly at the bar and ordered a Bud.

I leaned into the rickety seat and sighed once my drink came, let the harsh, ragged sounds of "Reckoning Day" soothe me while I thought.

I supposed I could go see the brain doctor, when the date for my appointment finally came, since I'd finally gotten one. What could it hurt? If it was something, I'd face it, and at least it meant that the world that I'd known up until now was still the world. I wasn't religious. Superstitious. I liked my life concrete and tangible and simple. I knew Debby didn't approve of the way I lived, though you'd think she'd bear in mind what I'd put behind. She was always telling me to buy the White Horse, or get a boyfriend, or make new friends, but I felt comfortable, safe. And I was thinking about buying the White Horse.

I finished my beer and decided to have a smoke before I started another. I told the bartender I'd be back, fumbling for my pack as I went.

Outside, the sun had set, the last remnants of orange and red streaking the sky above the buildings, the mountains not quite visible in the west.

I lit a smoke. God, it felt good.

"Cool if I bum one?"

I looked up out of my reverie.

"Hey, yeah, sure," I said.

"Buy you a drink for it?" She was a pretty woman, probably in her late twenties, I figured, and looking at her made my heart ache. She resembled Jaime so much, with her gorgeous black curls, elegant wide nose, and mid-toned skin. She was even wearing a Guns N' Roses T-shirt, which sealed the deal on the resemblance. Of course, I was sure all the surfacing memories about her were part of why I was seeing so much of Jaime in this woman.

"Nah, happy to share," I said, but she insisted, and we started to talk, and the other thing, besides monsters and ghosts that had been pushing up into my consciousness, started to erupt, despite everything I did to push it down. Jaime.

The day she'd died, we'd been partying.

We'd been at a friend's house, and after three straight days of staying up to listen to music, laugh, get high as fuck, I went to the bathroom. It was a beautiful house, an old Victorian that our friend had inherited from a grandparent. There were countless bedrooms, and little reading nooks—even then, I made time for my horror novels, though Jaime never understood it. She'd been smart as hell, witty even in her soft, musical-voiced way, but unless you counted motorcycle mags, hadn't been a reader. Couches were everywhere, perfect places to rocket up, and slide back down.

Coming from the bathroom, I could see her laying on the couch where I'd left her, leaning into it, the most peaceful, beautiful look on her face, ethereal. I went to lay next to her, but as I grew closer, I could feel it.

I shook her. I screamed and I cried, and I held her head between my breasts like a mother, but she never moved, her head piling to the side, lifeless.

"You know what I mean?"

"Oh, sorry, what?" I asked. I felt bad. I'd gotten lost, and this woman who'd bummed a smoke, who'd joined me for a beer, who looked so much like my Jaime, was just trying to make conversation. I'd been thinking about how beautiful Jaime's singing voice had been. How delicate. How I'd told her she should be the lead singer in her own band. She'd said she was happy to be a groupie, that she had no taste for travel, or fame. But I had seen the doubt behind her eyes. I felt, with a hard, visceral twist in my heart, that I should've done more. Encouraged her more. That if I'd done that, maybe she'd still be alive.

"No worries. I was just complaining about my idiot boyfriend," she said, shaking her head and taking a drink of her Coors. "And you're right, you know, I should leave him."

I didn't remember telling her that, but it sounded like me. I always told them to leave their boyfriends. "Yeah, men are trash," I said, thinking about how there wasn't a man alive who'd broken

Jaime's heart. She'd been tough. Tougher than me. My model, my heart.

She sighed, and I peered into her large, dark eyes, and then into my own, the mirror across from us black and ornate.

"I just take so much shit, you know?"

"Don't," I said, almost choking up, and pushing it down. "Don't ever waste your time on anyone who doesn't deserve it."

Hearing the note of sorrow in my voice, she leaned in for a side-hug. I closed my eyes and patted her hand, felt better.

"You're cool, you know that? I'm glad I ran into you."

I smiled and bought us a round of shots for the pain, hoping she wouldn't ask for my number, that she'd just let this be what it was.

I'd thought my mother had said "Loaf" the last time she'd appeared.

She had said "Lofa." And she'd led me right to Orr's, right to someone who could explain it to me.

CHAPTER TWENTY

hit the can of Bud dead on, the metal making a crisp, tinging sound as it flung off the rocky mountainside. I felt a brief flood of pleasure and set the old .45 down on a folding table, the metal of the gun clunking against the cheap, white plastic.

We weren't far from Debby's house, a ways up Fall River Road, where I'd partied as a kid, drinking and drugging and passing out, my head at the foot of a large blue spruce, or resting on someone's old, dirty couch.

I loved Sunday service.

It was a lovely spring day, warm with a small breeze, and I could feel the wind at the back of my neck as it rifled through my hair. I pushed it back down, annoyed that I'd forgotten to bring a rubber band.

Jack had inherited this land from his dad, who'd inherited it from his—who'd squatted here back in the day. He'd come for gold, like so many. There was an old, musty cabin his grandfather had lived in, off to the side, in a clearing. We kept the guns there—the beer, whiskey. Carl had even lived here one summer, between jobs. I'd had sex in that cabin when I was fifteen with a boy, George, who'd died after drinking and driving our senior year. The cabin was leaning hard to the east, and I often wondered if we'd come up here one day to see it in a state of collapse—but not yet.

"A squirrel! Get it!" Carl said.

Debby's husband scrambled for his shitty .45. The trigger often stuck, as it was right now, to Jack's great consternation. Jack was cursing loudly while Carl laughed, Debby yelling at Jack that he better not kill the squirrel, followed by the sound of a drunken, disappointed moan from Carl.

"Like you never ate squirrel meat," Carl said, pushing away what was left of his wispy blond hair down around his scalp.

"What*ever*," Debby said.

I laughed, welcoming the distraction. Debby and I had pressed her mom about whether she thought there was anything suspicious about my mother's disappearance and death, but she said that she couldn't remember anything in particular. That my mom had been real private, even with Daddy sometimes.

I plucked a long, green stem of grass from the side of the mountain and chewed on it thoughtfully. I looked up the hill at the waves of sage growing and thought about how I could've saved my money, not bought the bundle of sage at Orr's. About how Auntie Squeaker had taught me not to pull at the root, so the sage could grow again.

Debby pulled her gun out of her little, tooled-leather holster—a .22 with a pearl handle, a pink rose etched into the white—and squinted, aimed, her feet spread, her sparkling, pink Adidas planted solidly on the ground. She shot three cans right in a row, a pleased expression on her face.

"Nice job, Annie Oakley," I said.

"Shut up. And thanks," she responded. That holster killed me.

I thought about my mom's ghost. It was clear Cecilia wanted me to find out what had happened to her—which might, just might, help Daddy. I shook my head and felt overwhelmed.

"Kari?"

"What?"

"I've been calling your name for like five minutes."

"Sorry. Got lots on my mind."

"We'll get to the bottom of it, don't worry," she said, handing me a beer.

"No, you won't," Jack said, his gun loose at his side. "From what you're telling me, this whole situation might be dangerous. I mean, the fucking feds? You do what you want, Kari, but I've already told Debby that she's to have nothing to do with this shit. No way. No how."

Debby's brow furrowed. "You can *tell* me whatever you want, but that doesn't mean I have to do what you want," she said.

"Baby, I'm just trying to keep you safe."

"But I really want to do this!"

"No, you're doing what she wants, like you always do."

Debby snorted. "I *thought* you said she wouldn't be doing what *she* was doing if it weren't—"

"Let's just talk about it later," I said, interrupting. This was going to go ballistic, fast.

Both grumbled, but Jack took a swig of his beer, and pulled the .45 back up, missing every can he shot at, and cursing, Debby pretending to scroll through social media on her phone.

At my father's house, sitting next to him after making him a bologna sandwich, I sighed. Debby pet my hand, reassuring me to go on.

"Daddy?"

He smiled a bit but continued to watch TV.

"Do you remember if there was anything weird happening when Cecilia disappeared?"

He frowned, deeply.

"Daddy?" I pressed.

His face crinkled in horror, and then it went slack.

"Daddy?" I repeated.

He was silent. Not even watching the television. It was as if he'd gone somewhere else, another dimension.

A deep flutter of nervousness washed through my body. Daddy was brittle. His mind was like a boat lost at sea. Sometimes it came close to the shore, only to push back. I didn't want to make it so it never made anchor again.

"He ever do this?" Debby asked.

"Kind of, but . . . not really, oh shit," I said. "It's almost his bedtime anyway. Let's just . . . leave him alone. Not freak out yet."

I said this more to reassure myself.

Debby nodded, and we watched TV, but it was all I could do to not let the flood of panic overwhelm me. Daddy was the only thing I had left. What if I'd given him an aneurism? What if he didn't wake up the next morning? I'd wanted to heal him, but what if I was making it so much worse? I began to sweat, but, as the minutes ticked by, he seemed to recover, and watch TV again, his lids growing heavy, his head beginning to fall to the side. I got him in bed and came back down.

"I think he'll be okay," I said, sitting down. I took a deep breath, and let my head fall onto the couch.

"You alright?" Debby said.

I nodded.

"Did you bring it?" Debby asked, and my stomach fluttered.

"Yeah."

She was talking about the bracelet.

I pulled it out of the felt and took a breath, looked at the Indian chief, complete with traditional headdress. It was funny how that old jewelry often had plains imagery on it, regardless of whether the maker was plains Indian or not.

I touched the bracelet, bracing, and—

I was floating, floating gently through a tunnel of light, my ancestors on each side, the Apache and Chickasaw, I recognized them from the White Horse just like the Navajo guy had said—and even a Cherokee waving a sheepish hello, his red turban catching the light.

"Figures," I said to myself.

I floated down to Michael and Nessie's apartment—I recognized it from my other visions.

I tensed. I could see Michael sitting in a chair. He was young, his hair black with threads of white. Nessie was there too, and she was smiling, handing me something. It was a medicine bag. She told me that her elders had made it just for me, and that after she gave it to me, only I was to touch it, though there were things I would want to place in it.

I realized that I was my mother then, and I smiled, the emotion overwhelming me, tears flowing, my sense of pride in who I was hitting me like a thousand suns. I ran my hands over the leather, the beadwork—the waterbird, the symbol for the Native American Church—for what brought prayers to the creator—in bright pink and blue.

Thank you, Mom, I said, and she looked down with tears in her eyes.

We'll go to Four Winds soon.

I nodded, my thoughts in sync with my mother's from over four decades ago. Four Winds was the place where a lot of things for urban Indians in Denver took place. Red Road meetings. Gatherings. Feasts. Small ceremonies.

I'm not sure that's a good idea. Michael was glaring from the chair.

Why? Nessie asked.

The people there are trouble.

Nessie frowned, and I could feel myself floating out of the room.

I was in Daddy's house—Jim to Cecilia, and I was pulling the bag out of a paraphernalia box. I hadn't known my mother did Native American Church. I pulled my hands over the leather lovingly, but I felt sad. I didn't know why. I felt like I'd left something behind.

Did you enjoy the ceremony?

I thought about the ceremony and smiled, told him not about

what had happened—that was private—but about the way that the others had welcomed me, guided me, the trust I'd felt. I frowned.

What's wrong?

I told him I knew my father was worried about me, was worried about the men at the Indian Center, the ones who spoke big with braids in their hair, but let the women do the work, who had wives, but eyed other women just the same. Jim held me tighter and told me he would keep me safe. But there were things I didn't tell Jim.

CHAPTER TWENTY-ONE

I knocked, and heard, after a few minutes, the sound of footsteps shuffling on carpet, my heart thudding hard in my chest as they did. Someone was home.

I could almost hear their breath at the door as they paused to look through the keyhole. My grandparents, Nessie and Michael, lived in an ancient, dilapidated, '60s-style apartment complex on the third floor in Aurora—not far from me, and I'd known in my heart that the address that the ex-cop had given me was still theirs.

The door opened, just an inch, the security chain stopping it.

I could see a shortish form in the shadow, a bit of gray hair blinking into the light. She peered at me, her breath coming heavy. "It's you."

I hadn't expected that. But then again, I looked just like my mother.

"You're Cecilia's girl, aren't you?" The form shifted, and for a moment, I couldn't see her at all.

"I am," I said. "Kari."

I heard sniffling. "I told you I can't talk to you."

She pulled back into the light, and I saw a long, dark, slanted eye, not unlike my own, in the crack. It blinked away tears. I felt simultaneously bad about bothering her, and willing to do anything now to get in that apartment behind her.

"Please," I said. "I just want to know about my mother."

More sniffling. The eye blinking. "I'm sorry."

The eye disappeared.

"Nessie. Look," I started, my hand out. I was hoping I sounded sincere, kind—that she'd feel some pity for me.

"I can't," she said, her voice breaking.

She was about to close the door.

"I know something terrible happened to my mother," I said. I knew I sounded desperate—but I was.

The door stopped, and I breathed a quick sigh of relief. I had rehearsed all of this in the car, even writing it down beforehand, but I was way off-script, winging it, and I was scared that this would be my only chance to talk to the one person I knew, down to my core, who could tell me everything I wanted to know about my mother—the woman who was haunting me now, night and day. The woman who was holding that healing bracelet hostage.

I continued. "But the thing is, as far as I know, I'm your only living relative. Or if not," I said, knowing that might not be true, and needing something else that might pull her in, "your only granddaughter."

There was a quick intake this time. I was getting somewhere.

"It's not that I don't want to talk to you, it's just . . . I *can't*," she said, and I worried I'd gone too far. But then again, maybe I needed to go further.

"Do you know what it's like to grow up without a mother?"

This was a gamble. She'd either shut me out completely, or this would motivate her to let me in. I'd thought about this a lot. Fredrico's pressure point.

A sob. The door stood, unmoving.

I was sure I'd gone too far, that she'd shut the door—leaving me without anything tangible to go on. And leaving me with my mother's ghost, her bloodstained form perpetually haunting me un-til I went completely insane, the promise of healing Daddy forever out of reach.

Finally, there was the scraping sound of the chain being removed, and the door opened. I stood frozen in shock for a moment, then quickly recovered. This woman, albeit older of course, was abso-lutely the woman from my visions, my grandmother. Nessie was in her mid-seventies, wearing a flowered house dress, her white hair in curlers, her brown skin relatively unwrinkled for a woman her age, spots of white dotting her arms. I assumed, like some of the Indians I'd grown up with, she had vitiligo. She smiled wearily.

"Come in," she said. "But only for a few minutes. Michael—your grandfather, isn't home."

"I see," I said, stepping in. But I didn't.

Though it was of course different in many ways, it was definitely the apartment I'd seen after touching the bracelet. The space was clean, well-kept, the furniture old. It reminded me of my father's place, though in the case of his house, it had a suspended in time quality. Nessie's couches were beige with orange crisscross patterns, the La-Z-Boy a burnt auburn. There was the faint smell of cigars and Febreze. A tabby that matched the furniture lounged on the chair. He glanced up when I came in, and satisfied I wasn't a threat, plopped his head back down. He immediately closed one eye, the other, sleepily keeping watch.

"Please, have a seat. I'm sorry I was so rude, it's just—this is hard. Harder than you know."

"Yes," I said, sitting down on one of the couches, the sound of Patsy Cline's "Walking After Midnight" drifting throughout. Nessie went over to an old tape player and turned it down.

"I love this song," I said, trying to put her at ease. It was true—I did adore Cline, actually. Heavy metal was my thing, but there was something about Cline, her sadness, the pure, silvery lilt of her voice. The ruggedness of her lyrics.

She smiled. That was the right move.

There was a bit of fur where I sat, and I hoped the cat would come and sit by me.

"I love Patsy. Love the Blues too," she said awkwardly. "My husband's more into country. His people—well, your people too, were ranchers back in Texas."

"Is that so?" I asked, realizing that I knew almost nothing about them beyond the bits and pieces Squeaker had told me, and she was related to Nessie, not Michael.

"My people were gangsters. Thieves," she said, laughing a little. "But some of them were singers, so there was that."

I'd remembered Squeaker talking about that, not that I'd wanted to listen. And here I was, hungry for it suddenly, all these years later. And she was beginning to open up. This was good.

"Thank you for that," I said. "And . . . I'm sorry for barging in on you like this. Let's talk a little, okay?"

She nodded.

"Would you like a cup of coffee?" she asked, rubbing at her temple.

I nodded and told her thank you. I still wasn't sleeping. My eyes carried a perpetual half-moon of blue underneath.

She asked how I liked it, and came back with a cup in a thick, brown, mug. It was the sort that still sat in old diners, the kind that I'd seen Daddy drink from, growing up—when he still left the house.

While she was gone, I looked around. There were large, framed pictures of old Indians, their robes red, their hair long and gray or white. There were also a number of animal heads, mounted. Several elk. Deer. And most intimidatingly, a mountain lion. Michael was a hunter, I remembered. Fredrico had told me.

She sat down on the La-Z-Boy, grimacing. I could see a cane propped on the right side of the couch.

I took a sip of the watery coffee and smiled.

"I like your prints," I said. I knew I didn't have much time, but I wanted to put Nessie at ease, if I could.

"R.C. Gorman," she said, "got them in Santa Fe, oh . . . twenty years ago now," she answered, smiling.

Shit, just like at Auntie Squeaker's.

"How are you related to Auntie Squeaker?" I asked.

She cocked her head. "Oh, let's see . . . we share the same great-great-grandmother, the one who came across from Mexico, into Texas."

I nodded. "She was all I really had of family—from your side," I said.

Her lip began to tremble.

"Are you okay?"

"You're the spitting image of my . . . my daughter," she said, and here, her voice did break, and she began to cry in earnest.

I felt my skin crawling, and sweat building under my pits, but after a few minutes she seemed to pull herself together. I felt torn up inside. Should I push her about what she knew about my mother? Would that shove this poor lady—my grandmother—right over the edge? She knew I was here to find shit out, no matter what I said to reassure her. But if I brought up that my mother was missing, and almost certainly dead—that she was haunting me, would she tell me to leave?

"I didn't know you even existed until you called," she said. She had pulled a tissue from her robe and had wiped at her eyes.

I was stunned. "I didn't know that. But how?"

She sighed. "It's a long story. But we hadn't talked to my daughter much. Hadn't seen her in years. When she disappeared," she said, her eyes skirting over to her cat, and back at me.

It took me a minute to take this in. I had so many questions.

"I wish you had talked to her. I spent my life hating my mother. Dad—Jim, if you remember—he never got over her disappearance. He got into an accident. Has brain damage."

I guess now she knew if she hadn't before.

She took a quick breath. "I'm sorry."

"He couldn't tell me anything, and my aunt, well, she doesn't know much but what he told her before that happened—on account of my mom being the private type. So, I just figured she abandoned me. Went off to party."

"No, she wasn't like that," Nessie responded, then took a sip of her coffee.

Nessie closed her eyes, one small, brown hand running over the other, smoothing the skin. After a few minutes, she opened her eyes again. "When our daughter vanished, it was very hard on us. There had been, well, I guess you could say, conflict. Cecilia was very strong-willed."

Was. She referred to her in the past tense, even though as far as anyone knew, my mother had disappeared. She'd been presumed dead though. Perhaps Nessie knew that? There was so much here, so much I didn't know.

"My husband felt it best that we leave all of that behind. Completely," she continued.

I nodded, and we were silent for a while. I wanted more out of her, but it was obvious that if I was ever going to get any additional information, it wouldn't be now. But this was a start. It was clear she was conflicted. Wanted to tell me more but felt she couldn't. Why?

"Do you have any pictures of my mother?"

She nodded. "Just a second." She got back up, and after a few minutes, came back with a yellowed envelope. "That's most of them," she said, handing it to me. "But they're yours."

"Thank you," I said, wanting to open the envelope, but keeping steady.

She sighed. "Michael was a drinker, once. But he's come to God. He's sober, now."

I nodded. What did that mean? Maybe she was opening up after all? Perhaps I could press her, get her to tell me more.

"But my mother—"

She tensed, and that's when I could hear the door opening behind me. I closed my eyes.

"Nessie, I—"

I stood up, turned around.

He was of average height, wiry, his still partially black hair cropped close to his scalp, almost in a military cut, his dark eyes burning into me. And once again, my vision was confirmed—this was Cecilia's father.

"Nessie," he said, "is this who I think it is?"

I wasn't surprised he recognized me.

"Michael, she just showed up—"

He sighed, heavily.

"She just wants to know more about her mother, Michael—"

He stared at me for a long time, a mixture of sadness and exhausted rage behind his eyes.

"Nessie didn't call me. I knocked."

"I see," he said, moving into the apartment, putting his keys and leather wallet into a silver dish on an end table. He then turned around to face me again, one hand in the pocket of his Levi's.

"I'm sorry. We don't mean to be rude. It's just that, as Nessie and I have agreed, there are things best left to the past."

Nessie was silent, but I could feel waves of nervousness flowing out from behind me from her.

"I understand, it's just that . . . I know my mother disappeared, and I guess I want to understand better why."

He sat down across from me, put his hands on his knees. He smiled, his eyes crinkling. "We didn't know about you until you called. And . . . maybe someday we'll want to get to know you better. But her disappearance was painful. It nearly killed my Nessie." He patted her arm and she smiled a tight smile.

"More coffee?" Nessie asked.

I nodded.

She got up, went into the kitchen with my mug, and came back with a refill.

I sipped.

"There's not much to know about her that your dad can't tell you."

I told him what had happened to him, and Michael told me he was sorry.

"She was smart. Strong. Willful. Did exactly what she wanted. Always at that Indian Center, where she mixed with those political Indians. Up to no good. That's how she met her end, you ask me."

I perked up. "Do you know anything about that?"

He shook his head. "Only that I begged her not to go, time and time again. She met your dad and moved out early. Didn't really speak to us much after. I guess she thought we disapproved of her activities."

I looked over at Nessie. She gave me a short, tight smile.

Michael looked over to Nessie and squinted sympathetically. "Nessie, you tired?"

"I'm just fine," she answered, squirming.

"Nessie's got a heart condition."

Sympathy, guilt, flooded my heart. I stood up. "I'm sorry to have bothered you," I said.

"It . . . it was so lovely to meet you, Kari," Nessie said, her lip quivering. "I'm sorry I was so rude. Maybe another time."

"Nessie," Michael said. "Let's talk about that later. You don't look so good."

She did look beat, and as Michael shut the door behind me, I felt a sinking feeling in my stomach. I had come so far—only to learn nothing.

CHAPTER TWENTY-TWO

I had *Rust in Peace* screaming through the speakers at the Hangar Bar where I worked nights, and since it was the late crowd, they were enjoying Mustaine's progressive, angry take on Ireland, the Cold War, drug addiction, Marvel superhero The Punisher—and UFOs. I remember reading that Mustaine and his band had to ride home in a bulletproof bus after playing for Northern Ireland, but that Mustaine had forgiven the Irish for selling bootleg copies of Megadeth T-shirts for the cause. I was about two whiskies in, and enjoying a stenosis-inducing head bang, specifically to "Hangar 18." Mustaine was a genius at guitar, but this album was a particular favorite of mine. It was so ambitious, so clean, so quick, each wild riff culminating in a chainsaw reaction leading to—for my money—one of the best acoustic climaxes of all time.

The only one not listening was Ed, a gentle schizophrenic who sat at the bar all day long, as soon as we opened, every day, all day, drinking watery Coors after watery Coors until we closed. Sometimes he would converse, sometimes he would sit, comatose, staring at the giant beer can airplane that had hung on the ceiling of the bar for as long as I could remember.

"Shatter! Shatter!" Ed yelled, barely making a dint in the music, and I stopped banging long enough to pat him on the hand. He took medication, but medication wasn't magic.

I turned to a patron who I knew was due for another and got him a Bud, the tap foaming over as I did. He grinned wickedly as I handed him the beer, and I gave him a wink and the sign of the devil and laughed. He laughed back and we enjoyed a mutual bang.

The door opened, and I smiled. It was Debby.

"Red wine?" I asked as she settled onto a cracked, red stool.

"Yasss," she said, and I went and got her a glass. I didn't know how she'd gotten away from Jack, and I didn't want to. For a while there, he'd seemed to be backing down—doing dishes, staying home nights with her and the kids. But the last couple of days, she said he'd gone right back to going out with Carl every night, complaining whenever she left the house.

She sipped, and I leaned forward.

"Your outfit is peak Springs," Debby said, giggling.

I was wearing my faded gray jeans, black spiked belt, and my tattered Metallica T-shirt. Tattered, to symbolize when Mustaine was kicked out of the band.

"Shatter! Shatter!" Ed said, fixated on Debby, his green eyes piercing over his heavy, black eyebrows. I pet his hand again and he quieted. I turned the volume down just enough so I could update Debby on what had happened at Nessie's.

By the time I'd given her the full scoop, she'd finished her glass. She slid it over the wood back toward me.

I gave her a captain's salute and poured her another. Took another shot for myself.

"Shoot," she said.

"Shit's right," I responded.

"Okay, like, what's the game plan?"

"The game plan?"

"Yeah, like what are you going to do from here?" She asked.

I straightened. "Well, I'm going to go back over to Squeaker's and ask if my mom ever went to the Indian Center—if she says yes, well—maybe someone will know something over there, if I'm really lucky. But honestly? That seems unlikely. I'm probably fucked."

"Can you just take it one day at a time? Dang!" Debby responded.

"I'm not saying I'm giving up," I said, and seeing someone with an empty cup, I went over for a refill.

When I came back, Debby was cradling her glass thoughtfully in both hands. "Let's start with what we want."

"Well, I want to know what happened to my mother. That's pretty obvious."

"Right. Now let's get to what's in the way."

"This is stupid," I said.

"Just indulge me, okay?"

"Fine. The federal government?"

"Right—" Debby started.

"I knew it," Jack said.

I hadn't seen him even come in.

"Jack!" Debby said, like she'd been shot. She turned around to face him. He was a few feet behind her, swaying drunkenly on his feet, his eyes blood-red, hair up in spikes. I had to assume he'd been drinking all day.

"You said you were at your mom's. You fucking liar."

"Okay, Jack, cool it. What's going on—" I asked.

"You shut up!"

"Jack," I said in a low voice, as people were starting to turn their heads. The Hangar Bar saw plenty of fights, but folks understood the bartenders knew how to deal with trouble. "You're in my place of business."

"I don't give a shit! You're a bad influence on *my wife*!"

Debby stood up. "Look Jack, I'll go with you right now. We can talk about it on the way."

"Oh no, he's not driving—at least not anymore. And you're certainly not getting in a car with him at the wheel," I said, shaking my head.

Jack's face turned red, and he took several steps toward me. "Don't you dare tell my wife what to do."

I shook my head. "You don't want to do that, Jack."

"Hell, I don't!"

He started wobbling toward me as rapidly as he could, and I moved. I came up, and around him, and locked my arms behind his back, and twisted, bringing him to the ground.

"Fuck!" He yelled, bucking. He was strong.

I almost lost my grip on him, but then I laid one knee solidly in the middle of his back, where I knew it would hurt. Old construction injury.

He yelled in pain, and Debby cried behind me, begging me not to hurt him.

"I ain't gonna hurt him. I'm gonna give him some decisions to make," I said, panting as he struggled like a seal beneath me.

"Jack," I said.

"Fuck . . . you!"

"Jack, you got two choices. One'll give you a little bit of dignity. The other, not so much."

"Dumb bitch!" he said, twisting again, and almost getting free.

"Why do I get the feeling that you're angling for the non-dignity option," I said, pulling up with my knee, and slamming down once more.

He grunted in pain.

"Kari!" Debby said, a hysterical note to her voice.

"I'd let him go, but he'd just come after me, Debby. What you want me to do?"

"Get offa me!" he screamed.

"I will, but here's the thing. When I do, we're going to walk to Debby's car, and you're going to get in the back, and she's going to put your stupid, animal, drunk ass to bed. Or I'm calling the cops, and you're going to the drunk tank, if you make another move toward me.

"You got it?"

He squirmed.

I sprung up, got behind the bar. He wobbled in place, and then focused on my face. "You fucking *bitch*," he said, and started coming toward me. I'd never seen him like this.

I sighed. I pulled the shotgun up from under the bar, took dead aim at his chest.

"Kari, no!" Debby squealed.

"You stand right there while my friend Ed here calls the cops."

"I'll call 'em," he said. He had them on speed dial.

"Kari, no!"

"He was coming for me, and you know it."

Jack was staring with venom in his eyes, his look so black it was about to rot and fall off. I hated doing this. Mainly, for Debby's sake. She was fully sobbing now, and it pained me to hurt her. Jack wasn't a bad guy. But he had some stupid ideas when it came to his wife, and Debby was my best friend in the world. And no one, especially not a man, *especially* not where I worked, was gonna come for me.

"I'll make you regret this," he said.

"I know," I said.

"Kari, just let him go. Let him go and we'll walk to the car and I'll take him home and let him sleep it off."

"Fuck that!" Jack said.

I nodded at Jack. "That sound like he's gonna sleep it off?"

"Why, Jack?" she asked, wailing, a sound which was joined by the blaring of a police siren in the distance.

"Why'd you have to come here? I told you not to hang out with her anymore. I told you!" Jack screamed. "I just want to protect you," he wailed. "I need you, Debby."

Debby's only response was to cry harder as two tired-looking cops came in. Specifically, Jerry and Tyrell.

I put the shotgun down slowly, then my hands up.

We spoke, and they put Jack in cuffs, who didn't go easy at first.

"It didn't have to be like that," I said, and Debby just sniffled.

I turned the music back up, pulled the good shit out, the Bulleit Bourbon, sat, and poured myself a shot.

"Look, Debby, before you get angry at me, just listen."

She was silent, her lip trembling.

"First of all, not only is the gun empty of bullets, it hasn't worked since . . . fuck, I don't know. The 1800s?"

She seemed to relax a little then.

"Secondly, the cops know the drill. That's why they didn't put a gun on me. That's why it wasn't a big deal. They know that when Ed calls from here, that someone just needs the drunk tank. I'm lucky they're cool."

"I'm still mad at you, Kari," she said, her eyes red.

"Just . . . pick him up tomorrow morning. Here's the address."

She left, and I sat down, wondering if my best, my only friend in the world, would ever talk to me again. Ed pet my hand, and I thought about when Jack and Debby started dating. She had still been babysitting me. I had disliked him immensely, hated the goofy way he'd look at her, my only real friend, my replacement mother. I'd hated that she'd bring him when she sat for me, the way they'd laugh at jokes I didn't understand. But then I saw how Jack would treat my father. He was shy around him, confused at first as to how to deal with someone whose life had been broken down into such simple parts, someone who sat in front of the TV all day and ate bologna sandwiches, and almost never left the house, who cried, to my great humiliation, sometimes for no reason, in front of anyone. But after a while, Jack would make the sandwiches Debby would ask him for just the way Daddy liked them, setting them down in front of him on the coffee table, saying, "Here you go, Mr. Jim."

I slammed my fist into the wood. I hated this. And most of all, I hated Jack.

CHAPTER TWENTY-THREE

am fifteen years old when I tell Jaime to get the fuck out of my house.

I'd gleefully popped my cherry earlier that year in the basement of a house on an old mattress, wine-sick but ready to get this part of my life over with. I remember there had been a toy truck underneath me as he came. I flung it into the darkness, listening to a child crying somewhere in the distance, sounding lost.

Jaime and I were drunk on the whiskey and Cokes conned from men we'd chatted up in a bar in Denver. We'd hitched one Saturday night, ready for adventures of the kind that could not be had in a small town that sat at the bottom of a mountain, the trees swaying above our trailers, our dingy houses, our wild, furious hearts.

We had told the men at the bar that we were *in our twenties* and they had laughed and said they'd love to buy us drinks, love to take us home. I'd been drawn to the taller one because he'd been wearing a Guns N' Roses T-shirt. I thought that band had gone a little soft, but they were Jaime's favorite band, and I still liked what this minor metalhead, and his friend, who laughed like a donkey, seemed to be offering.

What they were offering: experience.

Even at that age, I'd learned that I liked to work my way in slow, though I was never what you would call subtle. I knew what I wanted, and they had it. A little cash, enough for drinks. Packs of cigarettes poking out of their tight, slightly dirty jeans. The hint of an adventure that held just a little bit of danger.

If I was honest with myself, it was especially the last thing. This was the time that I learned to test myself, test my limits, find out what I could do and come back from, what I could do and survive.

I had decided that we would go home with them, when one of them asked me what it was like to live in Idaho Springs.

There was something about his tone. Mocking. Superior. Cruel even.

Up until then we'd been having a great time. Bonding over metal. Arguing, my long, brown hand slamming playfully down on the arm of the man who'd been supplying us with cigarettes all night. I'd been wondering what his thighs looked like under those tight jeans. What it would be like to get on top of them.

What do you mean by that? I asked, my eyes going flat as a cat's.

He blinked rapidly. He was dark-eyed, tall, longhaired. I remember thinking when we first let them approach us that he was the kind of man I would've wanted as a boyfriend, if I was the kind of person who would ever want that. Even then, I knew that wasn't for me. That there were some things better left untouched.

He said, *well, it's just, Idaho Springs is full of white trash, sorry. You're cool though.*

I had closed my eyes then, and when I opened them, he was looking at me like he'd just handed me something beautiful, like a dime bag or roses.

Do I look like trash to you? I asked.

He stammered. Shit, I wasn't even white.

I lit a smoke and squinted up at him, Jaime babbling nervously in the background, my hand fluttering behind me, trying to shut her up.

His friend told me I looked like a *hot piece of ass.*

I am a hot piece of ass, I said.

He laughed his donkey laugh.

You laugh like a donkey, I said.

His mouth clapped shut, then a minute later, opened again with *you trash bitch.*

I smiled, and his friend told us both to *cool it, cool it.* He said that's *not what I meant.* And that there was *good shit at his place,* that we *should just forget about what he said.*

I told him I couldn't forget. But that he should remember that trash rejected him.

He shrugged, knowing it was over.

I grabbed Jaime's hand, and pulled.

She was angry with me, told me to *calm down Kari,* said the guy said they *hadn't meant it,* that we should *go home with them and have some fun.*

I told her dead-eyed that she'd be going home with them on her own then, and then stalked toward the exit, smoking as I did.

A few minutes later, she was beside me, pouting.

I started walking, my thumb out. I told her to *have some fucking dignity.*

She was silent.

We found a ride, a truck that was going west. It dropped us off at the outskirts of the city, the place where the grasslands began to meet the mountains. And eventually, we found a ride going all the way to the Springs. But it took a while, our thumbs out in the dark, not far from the mountains where a boy had been killed by a lioness, worried for her cubs when he went jogging past, too close.

I didn't speak to her the whole way, just smoked and smoked, glad I'd pulled the pack off the table before I'd left.

When we got back, she told me that we should just forget about it, go back to my place, stay drunk. She had some tequila in her bag that she'd lifted from a liquor store.

We walked down the empty streets, next to the beat-up Victorians, the shacks; the shadows long, the kids asleep who went to sleep, the others, like us, just maybe getting started. There was something sad and small and yet, almost otherworldly about Idaho Springs, like there were secrets in the cold, rocky ground that might spring up at any time. And take you down with them into the dark.

At my house, Dad was slumped over on the couch, the light of the TV playing over his face. I felt bad. I hadn't been there to get him up the stairs, make him brush his teeth, tuck him into bed.

Jaime took one look at him and started laughing.

I'd never let her come in. I'd never let anyone come in.

But she was my best friend.

She was there the first time I'd had sex. The first time I'd smoked cigarettes. The first time I'd given a blow job, throwing up after, Jaime comforting me and saying that she'd done that too, her first time.

I asked her what was so *fucking funny.* Would it be my dad, who got into an accident and had brain damage, was that it? Was that what was *so funny?*

She just shrugged.

When I told her she was a *piece of fucking shit,* and to *get out and never call me again,* she looked like I'd slapped her, which I told her I would if she didn't leave, now.

On her way out, she said my dad was a *fucking retard* and said I would grow up to be one too. Thank God, she'd called me the next day and apologized, profusely.

I slammed the door closed with my foot.

I woke my dad up, and got him to bed, tucking him in as he moaned my mother's name, *Cecilia Cecilia. . . .*

God help me, I resented him so much in that moment.

I resented his weakness.

I also promised myself something. I promised myself that this was the last time I'd ever feel weak.

CHAPTER TWENTY-FOUR

Auntie Squeaker was standing in her tiny kitchen, one of her men—or perhaps he was something else, perhaps a spirit-person—pulling a purplish jar of herbs down from one of her small but well-made shelves and handing it to her. She plucked it from his hands, popped the cork, and sniffed, her flinty dark eyes going small.

"Still good," she said. "Though we need to go to the lavender fields for more."

"What's it for, Auntie?" I asked, sitting in one of the chairs around the table. "And can I help?"

"Shoo," she said, moving her hand in a whooshing motion, "I know you don't know nothing about nature's medicine. Probably end up making this cure for depression and insomnia, which you could use by the way, into something that makes hair fall off. Every-where."

I laughed.

Auntie sat down at the table with me, groaning a bit as she did.

"So," she said, her eyes narrowing thoughtfully, playfully, "you're back."

I nodded, and she continued to examine me.

"I think you're further along now, ain't you? More committed."

"I want to help Daddy, but . . ."

She laughed, the sound rough and full. "You actually ready to hear something different when it comes to your momma too. Maybe decided you don't know everything after all."

"Well, I don't know about that," I said, crossing my hands over my chest and smiling.

"Well, you got that sweet little white cousin of yours to humble you," she said, pulling a pack of playing cards out from the edge of the table, where it had been sitting against the wall.

At the mention of Debby, I squirmed a little internally. She was still mad at me. No, fucking furious. I was worried we wouldn't ever talk again. That I'd be on my own with this thing. Alone with my memories of Jaime too, which were surfacing more each day, making me relive that guilt. That feeling that I should've done something to prevent her death.

"Like the kicks, by the way," Auntie said, pointing with her lips down at my black motorcycle boots.

Squeaker split the pack, the edges of the cards worn, smudged, from years of use.

"Auntie, I got something to ask you. Something urgent."

"You need a reading."

I sat back.

"And while the spirits are reading you, go ahead. Ask. I think I know what you gonna ask me, anyway. The answer's yes."

I opened my mouth and then shut it.

She pulled the first card out, placed it on the table between us. "Ask."

"Did my mom hang out at the Indian Center?"

Auntie closed her eyes, opened them, laid another card down, and pulled her smoke out of the ashtray for a drag.

"I got a real history lesson for you," she said, pulling another card out, blowing smoke out the side of her mouth.

"You too young to remember, but when Reagan was elected, he did all kinds of shit to Indians. Took land. Reduced monies going to reservations. Denver's been a hub for Indians for forever. But in '81 this place was flooded with Indians from every Rez, and they were hopping mad—joined forces with us urban Indians. Your mom and all them Natives at the Indian Center in the city, they organized a bunch of Columbus Day protests."

At this, I sat up straight.

"All that lasted to the '90s, with academic Indians pouring blood on statues and all that. But your mom, she got into some deep shit with Indians at the Center."

"Do you think they'd know more at the Indian Center?"

"Maybe," she said, "if folks from that time still around. Denver's expensive these days. A lot of folks have up and left, had to. Even the Springs getting pricy. Never thought I'd live to see that happen. Glad I bought this rusting box thirty years ago," she said, pulling out the last cards, and smoothing them.

She was silent for a time, examining her cards. "Well."

"What?" She knew I didn't believe in this shit. Course, I hadn't believed in ghosts either until recently.

"Well," she repeated.

I sighed.

She tapped the first card. "See here? This the Ace of Diamonds. That's your invitation. To your journey."

"Okay," I said, plucking a stone out from the bottom of my boot.

"And here, right by it?" she paused to light a new cigarette. "Eight of Clubs. Tells you it's going to be a meaningful journey."

I supposed she was right there. Still. Pretty generic.

"Ah," she nodded, like a roadmap had appeared right before her eyes. "The Ten of Diamonds. Delays. And right by the Three of Diamonds—secret wish come true," she said, waggling her eyebrows up and down.

"I don't have any secret wishes," I said.

"Sure, you do. Auntie can see them riding you."

"Only thing riding me—" I started, and she interrupted me with a snort.

"Now it gets real interesting," she said. "This is the beast. The one in your dreams."

"Yes," I said, feeling sick. Feeling like I wanted her to stop.

"He'll keep coming, and if you're not careful, he'll eat you up from inside your dreams."

I felt cold. That's exactly how it was in my nightmares. He'd be chasing me. Most times I'd get away. But when I didn't, he'd pull the skin right from me, stick it in his horrible, black maw.

"He's not real," I said, more for me than her.

She stared at me. "He's not? Who's to say he's not."

"I fucking *hope* not."

"Here's the good news," she said, "you got a Queen—that's you—surrounded by two Jacks. Those are your protectors."

I didn't know who that could be. Daddy couldn't protect himself, and Debby hated me now.

She saw my expression, asked me if there wasn't more I wanted to tell her.

"No. Let's just . . . finish your cards."

"If you sure," she said. "Last one." She sat back. "Mmm. Four of Spades—decision against one's will."

"Well, I didn't want to be on this whole journey," I said, slapping my knees conclusively, "so that solves that."

"Does it?"

She cocked her head and squinted, her eyes moving to my left, over my shoulder.

"What?" I asked, uneasily.

"She's still following you, ain't she? In fact," she said, her eyes moving again, "no doubt about it."

I whipped around, and sure enough, I could see her, but faintly. She wasn't bleeding though. Just standing there, her face full of sorrow, her hands at her side, her eyes black canyons containing worlds upon worlds.

"She's strong, that one. She loves you though, Kari, I can feel it," she said, closing her eyes. "Pray with me," she said, and though the hair on the back of my neck was standing straight up, I held Auntie's hands and, silently, we prayed while one of her women lit sage.

When we were done, Cecilia was gone. Waiting in that twilight world. And I was left with more questions than answers.

CHAPTER TWENTY-FIVE

'd called and called and called again. Most times, no one picked up at the Indian Center. Then when they did, they said they'd take a message, ask around to see if anyone had known a Cecilia James, but weeks later, no one had gotten back to me.

I was starting to lose hope. Wonder why I'd ever given a shit about all of this. And that's when my mother would show again, first in my dreams, then when I'd wake up, in the shadows—then at the foot of my bead, screaming. I'd decide to keep going, call the center again, then the monster would materialize once more in my nightmares. He'd appear in the shadows first, just a hint. Then the smell of rotting meat floating out from behind a building or a cluster of trees. His roar. My heart palpitating violently. I would begin running, hearing him behind me, catching up. The feel of his long claws reaching into my flesh, pulling, ripping. The pain. My mouth opening in a scream, my lips bubbling over with blood. The overwhelming feeling that I should give all of this up, allow my mother to float, somehow, back into the ether. And then someone at the Center picked the phone up.

· · ·

"Cecilia James? Heck yes, I knew her. Poor girl. You her daughter, you say?"

My heart was beating like a rabbit's. It was a Saturday. I had a day off, and I'd been reading when I thought, why not try a call?

"Yeah. I'm trying to find out what happened to her. She just—disappeared."

"Why don't you come down tomorrow? I'd like to meet you. I was close to Cecilia. Shoot, we got in a lot of trouble together, eh?" He laughed hard, coughing at the end of it.

I agreed and hung up.

I was more of a work at the bar, go to the bar, thrash at a heavy metal concert kind of Indian than a powwow Indian. But the Indian Center, I had to admit, had its charms. I'd gone there a few times for different events—every summer they had a little daycare workshop on plants that I'd told Debby about, and she'd taken her kids. Sometimes I went for lectures, or to see children practice traditional dancing. Mainly because Debby had dragged me, but I had to admit they were cute as hell, and I loved to see the flags from every Native nation hung along the walls, the long foldout tables, the one against the wall perpetually holding a carafe of weak coffee.

Debby. I couldn't help but wish that she were with me. But there had been nothing from her, and I was too stubborn to call her first.

The man who'd asked me to come down looked Lakota, or one of the plains tribes—tall, big, his hair thinned from age but still kept in a long ponytail. As soon as I came in, I'd walked to the small series of offices, and knocked when I saw his name, Dr. Hank Goodbear.

He'd asked me to sit with him at one of the folding tables, got us both a cup of watery coffee, told me he'd met her here, forty years ago. They'd both been attending an AIM rally, and it was after that they'd organized the protests.

"You think there'd be some record of her with the Chickasaw?" I asked. I knew my Apache family had been originally from northern Mexico and had made their way into Texas and then Colorado, like Auntie Squeaker said. There was a group of Chiricahua with state recognition, I'd found when I googled—but I wasn't sure I was related to them. The Chickasaw though, they were a smaller, federally recognized group.

He shook his head. "I'm sorry, but no. Your mom—her family—your family—they went straight from Arkansas to Texas. No Trail of Tears. We checked for your mom, but your family's not on the rolls."

That surprised me.

"Don't get me wrong. All of us accepted her. Well. Except for one. But we all thought she was an asshole," he said, laughing. "Insecure on account of growing up in Ohio. Sad when they're disconnected like that."

I nodded.

"And dang," he continued, "not that it's all about blood but," and here he stopped to laugh gently again, "there was nothing that girl could be but Indian. Some might take issue with that, but shoot. This is a country that experienced genocide—some families had their own path. I'm Cheyenne, but from what I understand, a lot of those tribes in the Southeast, before they were removed to Oklahoma, some of the communities lived on the outskirts of those cities. And though they sure did remove them eventually, the government told them they were gonna do it—I have to assume some of them took that threat seriously and took off on their own—or even before that, for other reasons. At that time, those nations were fully sovereign, unlike mine and most others—they could leave when and if they wanted, even if they'd experience racism other places. And it also depended on what state you were in. Arkansas? They had a choice to become a citizen of Arkansas. Georgia? They had to get out—or die."

I sat back.

"And you know those tribes were slave owning—if you were

Black and Indian, instead of white and Indian, well, the rules weren't the same. I know. My grandfather was Black, and though my tribe's different, they got crapping on Black folks in common with the rest of Indian Country."

I nodded. I had Black-Indian cousins. I'd seen it. And I'd been told by Squeaker that was in my family line too. So much history, so much fucked up history.

"Complicated," he said, and smiled a wry smile.

"No one on the rolls, though?" I asked, thinking about all the folks I'd grown up with, the ones who claimed, like Debby's mom, that their great-great-infinity Cherokee princess grandmother had escaped the Trail of Tears. The ones who'd asked if I was Mexican, and when I'd said I was Indian, had countered, with a look of disgust in their eyes, that they were Cherokee, and I was plainly Mexican. The irony was that some of my family were originally from what is now Mexico.

He could tell exactly where my mind was going. He laughed. "You ain't no Generokee honey," he said, patting my hand respectfully. "Your family has been powwowing, going to Native American Church—protesting, for generations. Hell. You know your grandmother's grandmother spoke three Native languages? And your last name? Common—very—with Chickasaw. And Choctaw for that matter. Don't you worry about what some folks might say."

I was glad to know that.

"You a historian?" I asked. It had been a while since I had visited the center, and in all honesty, my visits had always been scattershot. I was sure I had seen him at some event at some point, but we had never talked, to my recollection.

He laughed. "I'm a professor of Native American studies at the University of Denver."

"Bet your parents are proud of you, Dr. Goodbear."

"They were," he said, "and just call me Hank."

He and I paused to drink from our Styrofoam cups, and I thought about how much I didn't know about being Native—about my own family. I remembered the half a page history lesson I had received in high school, in the rotting trailer they had set up for supposedly temporary purposes, and which had become permanent. Our teacher carried a cattle prod. His truck had a TO HELL WITH THE WHALE, SAVE THE COWBOY, sticker on it. He'd whacked the prod down on our desks as he walked in-between them, stating that if we wanted to feel sorry for the Indians, we could. There had been four or five Natives in that class. We'd looked up, and at each other.

When it had come time for him to whack the prod down on my desk, I'd caught it, stared that skinny white man dead in the eye. His lips trembled, and he slid it out of my hand. Later that year I'd pulled his parking brake, had the other Natives from my class help me push that truck down the hill, right into the ravine near the lot where we all went to smoke and get high. I'd felt better after that.

"Here's what's important, though. You really want to find out what happened to your mother? This is what you do. During those protests, we got on lists alright. Government lists. Some of us disappeared. Permanent. You file yourself a Freedom of Information Act request with the FBI. I can tell you how to do that. And the fact is, your momma knew some Indians who got into big trouble. The FBI won't admit if they killed her, but let's just say that they're not so pleased with some of the things that their predecessors done, and sometimes when you get the paperwork you can read between the lines."

"Thank you," I said. I was stunned.

"It's no problem. Just promise me that you're going to come back here."

I told him I would. And I meant it.

"We got lots going on, and I'd love to see Cecilia's girl at the Indian Center—shoot, you don't have to be some super-tradish, powwow Indian to hang with us," he said. "We got movie nights. And if you're interested, sometimes folks come in and do a language workshop."

"Okay," I answered.

"Don't want to pressure you. I can tell you're a loner. But even lone wolves got a pack."

I stood up, shook his hand, and thanked him for his time.

As I got back into my car, my mind swirled with everything I'd learned. Had my mother really gotten herself in the kind of trouble that gets you killed by the FBI?

CHAPTER TWENTY-SIX

n my dream, I am my mother.

I'm laughing, walking around with my friends, candy apples in our hands. I bite into the apple, my teeth penetrating the candy to the fruit, sweet and crisp, the juice running down my hand.

We're walking past the kiddie rides, the shrieks of small children echoing throughout, the sun setting over Lakeside. All of the colors so much brighter than in my youth.

There is a snap in perspective, and we're closer to our goal, further along the dusty path. Another snap, and we're standing at the foot of a giant roller coaster. Michael, my mother's father, is at the foot of the coaster, pulling the gears. Another, and we're on it, laughing as it pulls away.

My mother screams in pleasure as it turns, twists, and I watch, anxious for some reason, the smell of rotting meat beginning to pervade. My mother's screams change to shrieks of outright terror as I watch the man behind her, whose face was at first a blur, turn into the Lofa. It begins to tear into her, its long hair caressing her like a lover as it pulls wet, meaty chunks up and out of her neck, her shoulder, her dark hair coated in blood and viscera.

I wake up from the dream, my mother above my bed.
Her eyes turn dead white, and she screams.
I scream with her.

CHAPTER TWENTY-SEVEN

I rolled the car window down in front of Aunt Sandy's house and let the sharp tang of pine sap enter my nose through the wind, the sound of children screaming, hopefully in play, nearby. The steps leading to Sandy's house were concrete, the third step cracked all the way through. I rapped on the wood and let myself in the way I had my whole life. There was a hole in the flimsy door where Jack had knocked too hard one night, looking for Debby.

Aunt Sandy was standing in the kitchen, leaning against the gold-speckled, white counter, a Pall Mall between her stained fingers.

"Hey, Sandy."

She cocked her head at me, squinted.

"What?"

"Pretty as ever. But . . ." She cocked her head again. "You look tired."

I nodded. "Not sleeping."

I was curious about why she'd asked me to come by, especially after what had happened with her daughter. Sandy was funny; she wouldn't tell me on the phone. Though like most folks in the Springs, she liked her secrets and enjoyed her drama.

"Come here," she said, opening one short, white, wrinkled arm.

I let myself be enfolded, the scent of cigarettes and sweat and warm milk enveloping me, smells I associated with the idea of motherhood.

"Coffee?" she asked, and I nodded.

She pulled a mug with a faded I ♥ MOMMY on the face from the cracked, wooden cupboard, stickers that kids had pushed onto the wood peeling on the front. She poured the coffee in, dressed it up the way she knew I liked it, handed it to me, and we moved to the living room to sit. I migrated to my usual spot, the chair under the metallic "End of the Trail" piece—which was a metal cutout of a Native man bending over his horse, riding toward the sunset in defeat.

I was about to ask her what this was all about, when I heard the front door swing open and closed my eyes.

"Mom, really?" It was Debby.

"You two need to—"

"I had to bail my husband out of jail because of her!"

I turned around and glared at her. "He's the reason you had to bail him out of jail. And it wasn't *jail*, it was detox."

"Who—" Debby started, her arms crossed tightly over her chest.

"I don't want to hear one more word out of you two," Sandy interrupted, sounding exactly like she had when she'd split up our arguments when we'd been kids. "I've got something important for Kari, and the pair of you need to remember that you are family."

I could hear Debby breathing heavily behind me, and I rolled my eyes. I turned. She was wearing one of her sparkly T-shirts. This one said, YOU GO GIRL in gold lamé. I fought the urge to make fun of her shirt, curious now as to what Sandy had for me. Both of us went silent.

"Jack does drink too much, and you know it, Debby," Sandy said finally.

Debby kept her silence for a few moments more, and then she started sniffling. "He really is a good guy."

Damn, was I tired of that good guy shit. I loved Debby, but I just couldn't understand how she, or any other woman for that matter, put up with what she put up with, and defended her man's indefensible behavior.

I got up out of the plaid monstrosity of a La-Z-Boy and went over to Debby and put one hand on her arm. The sniffling increased.

"I'm sorry, Debby. I didn't know what else to do."

She started crying. "He . . . he's a good *guy*," she finally said, and though I wanted to snort at her repetition, I didn't.

"I know," I said, patting her arm again awkwardly.

I knew that Jack loved Debby and he loved his kids, and he was a hard worker. I'd seen him bust his ass for his wife. But he was also insecure as hell, and selfish, and if he wasn't careful, he was going to lose his family.

"I just wish . . ." I trailed off. She knew what I wished. I wished she'd leave him, or the impossible, that he'd get it together, stop drinking for a while. Realize that the way he thought he owned Debby wasn't protection, or love—it was control. Fear.

"Good girls," Sandy said, patting her frosted hair. It was sweet to hear Debby and I referred to as girls. I was thirty-five. Debby, almost forty. "Now sit down."

Sandy lit a smoke and leaned back.

Debby got herself a cup, then plopped onto the matching plaid couch. Sandy loved plaid, and deeply—it was all over the house.

"I got something strange in the mail, and I knew both of you," she said, tipping her cigarette into the ashtray, and getting up, "would want to see it. Though it's for Kari."

Debby and I exchanged curious glances waiting for Sandy to come back.

When Sandy returned, she bent over my chair, handing me a little cardboard box, one that was already opened, and addressed to me. The return address was for a Nessie James. I shivered.

"Who is it from?" Debby asked.

"Nessie," I said, starting to pull through the tissue.

"Wait—" Debby said.

I cocked my head at her.

"Think about what happens when you touch the bracelet."

"But the bracelet's special," I responded.

"But it opened you, somehow. Now you're vulnerable."

I paused, and I could tell Debby had told Sandy about my experiences, as she didn't ask her daughter to clarify. Sandy was, like most in Idaho Springs, more than willing to believe in anything to do with other worlds leaking into ours. Psychic powers. Demons. Devil worship. You name it, someone in a rotting Victorian or faded ranch-style blue house believed in it.

They were also big fans of government conspiracy theories. *The X-Files* had done well here.

I handed it over to Debby, and she pulled through the tissue, uncovering a small, white, leather medicine bag—just like the one in my vision. It was beaded in pink and blue along the edges, with a waterbird design on the front, silver cones lining the bottom. I guessed it had been made in the '60s or '70s, and the leather was quite desiccated.

The waterbird. The primary symbol for the Native American Church.

A kind of black outline surrounded the bag, something that didn't go away when I blinked. Like a tiny black hole, an opening into another world. I felt strange looking at it. I closed my eyes, thinking of my mother, and of Michael, her father. It was hard to imagine him participating in anything traditional.

I opened my eyes to see Debby carefully caressing the beads with her fingertips.

"Beautiful," Aunt Sandy said.

"This feels strange too, Kari," Debby said. "It is beautiful, though."

I sighed thoughtfully.

"Don't Indians get medicine bags? Maybe this one was meant for you, honey? Or maybe it was your mother's?" Sandy asked.

I wondered. I knew what Sandy was saying was true, Indians often did get medicine bags, and it's possible that it had been my mother's, or, that it had been meant for me. I had no way of knowing unless Nessie would tell me. I'd known Native American Church Indians, and I'd remembered them talking about that. That and Peyote Ceremonies. I briefly mused about whether my mom had done one of those, and then, realizing that had also been a part of my vision, focused on what was in front of me.

"It's too bad you can't ask Nessie about it," Debby said.

I sighed.

"You ever go and visit Auntie Squeaker?" Aunt Sandy asked, and I filled the both of them in on what I'd learned.

"So now you gotta just wait for that paperwork," Debby said, "that what do you call it?"

"Freedom of Information Act request," I answered.

"Let me see it," I whispered, gesturing to the bag like it was a sleeping child.

Debby wrapped the tissue around it and handed it to me.

There *was* something about it, I could feel it as soon as the pale leather hit my fingertips through the tissue. I was tempted to touch it then and there, but this wasn't the time or place.

"Kari?" Debby asked. "You okay?"

"Sorry. Just . . . in my last vision, the monster . . . it was tearing my mother apart."

"Jesus."

"Your poor mother," Sandy said, shaking her head. "I knew she held secrets. She had a way about her. Quiet. Mysterious. I thought it was just that she was Indian at first—"

"Mooom," Debby said, indignant.

"They're a spiritual people, Debby. That's why we are, honey," she said, sitting back.

"Oh my *God*, Mom," Debby said.

Sandy had regaled me many times with the story of the great-great-great-great-grandmother of hers who was a Cherokee princess and had escaped the Trail of Tears—and I couldn't help but think about my conversation with Hank. Debby of course told me that she'd taken a DNA test, and that they'd come out as of some African descent—but no Native American. She'd never told her mother this.

"Well, they *are*," Sandy said.

"Anyway," Debby said, rolling her eyes.

"I just need a minute to think about all of this," I said, putting the bag away, into mine.

I sat back, and sipped at the watery coffee, wishing for something stronger.

"I tell you, that Michael—my grandfather, he's convinced that it was some men involved with the AIM that might've been the death of her." I sipped again.

"You think the men killed her for some reason? Or being around them is what got her killed by the FBI?" Debby asked.

Shit. That was a good question. "I don't know," I answered. There was so much here, and everyone I'd talked to knew so little.

"You want to do something fun this weekend?" I asked Debby. Maybe my mother was trying to lead me to something again—that last dream, of Lakeside. It had been . . . persuasive. If confusing.

"What? Sunday Service?"

I laughed. "No, like something else. Something we haven't done in forever. Thing is, I got an idea."

Besides, I figured that Sunday Service was off-limits for me for a while. Debby may have forgiven me, but Jack would hold on to his anger for a good, long time.

"Pedicures!" Debby said, clapping her hands.

I rolled my eyes. "Debby, you know I hate that shit."

"Well, I'm not going to the Brutal Poodle, that's for sure," Debby said, her tone grumpy.

"No, not the Brutal Poodle."

"Well, it has to be around here. Jack will throw a fit if you and I wander off on our own," Debby said nervously.

I sighed in exasperation. "Jack will throw a fit if he knows you and I are hanging out at all."

"Kari—"

"You could actually go to real Sunday Service," Sandy said, interrupting. She never really gave up on trying to convert me. I guess that's what she meant by spiritual.

The conversation rolled over to church, and I let my mind wander.

This Sunday, whether Debby was coming with me or not, I was heading to Lakeside.

CHAPTER TWENTY-EIGHT

The roller coaster shrieked above us, the sound of rusty metal making contact with more rusty metal simultaneously exciting and terrifying, the screams of the people in the coaster joining the teeth-jattering screech as it came to a pinnacle and plunged, only feet from our heads. It was the coaster from my dream—The Cyclone. It was right next to the other coaster—the beltless, the bruising Wild Chipmunk.

Walking through Lakeside was like moving into a bygone era. The faded yellow entrance with "Lakeside" in cursive—yellow and orange sunbeams shooting out of the lettering—was peeling, and the building hadn't been the bright white of the past for many, many years. But my past was still there, a past that belonged in a city that, in ways, no longer existed. In the dream I'd had with my mother, Lakeside had been young, bright, beautiful.

I had come here as a teenager, my lithe, angry body caught between iron parts, moving up and down in different directions, pinching my arms, legs—my mind swirling with alcohol and promise. Debby and I had spent the '80s as young girls eating cotton candy and throwing balls at impossible targets shaped like spirals or clowns, flirting with boys with our eyes, lying to Sandy about where we'd been, who we'd talked to. But it was places like these that had shown the divide between my life and Debby's.

When I hit thirteen, I was already a woman, in body and mind. I was a parking lot kid, ditching and getting high with Jaime not far from the school in some metalhead's car, not giving a fuck about my grades in math or English. But Debby, only five years my senior, was studious. She was in her last year of high school for my first year of junior high, and though she loved me, she didn't approve of my lifestyle, and in her quiet way, she made it known. There were many years in which she was just my cousin, and what furthered the divide was the fact that we looked nothing alike. Her shy, quiet *hellos* in the shadows of the hallways, my *oh, she's my cousin* to confused looks from my friends, were our only interaction for years.

The screams from the big, white coaster above started again, as it came back for another round, the expressions of fear and delight above us amping me up.

"This was such a good idea," Debby said, squinting fearfully up at the coaster. She'd always been afraid of them. I'd tried to drag her on them time and time again, starting from when we were kids. I knew today I'd try once more. After all, that's what we were here for. And if I wasn't successful, the next time that I got her here—or more likely, to Elitch's, there was no way I'd quit attempting to persuade her. Of course, the one time I'd been successful, Debby *had* hurled, though she'd waited until we'd gotten off the coaster. She'd even been able to unsteadily walk a line to a trash can and yack directly into it. In a way, I'd been impressed.

"We're kind of in the line of fire, though," I said.

Debby's forehead creased in confusion.

"People on this thing often barf. And we're directly under one of the curls—which, is where I'd be most likely to barf, that is, if I—"

Getting it, Debby looked up, shuddered, and pulled us both away from the coaster.

"Ewww," she said.

I laughed.

"I know," I said. "Let's get cotton candy."

"And a Slurpee!"

"I haven't had a Slurpee in ten years," I said, shaking my head.

"That's just flat-out wrong," Debby said.

"It's fucking immoral, is what it is."

Debby giggled. Just because we were here to learn more about what I'd seen in my vision, didn't mean we couldn't have fun.

I squinted at Debby as she yipped and clapped her tiny white hands, remembering the girl she'd been, the girl I'd been too.

"It smells exactly the same here," I said, lighting a cigarette to Debby's disapproval. I was sure I'd get caught at Elitch's—but at Lakeside, they were just glad we were here.

"It does. Like sweat and burning peanuts," she responded, giggling.

Jack was furious with me, but Debby had told him that she was visiting a friend in the hospital, and that she'd gotten some time off at Walmart. I'd told her that she needed to confront him, give him an ultimatum, but she'd only said I didn't understand.

She was right. I didn't understand.

We strolled leisurely down the alleyways, past the buildings, taking it all in, its faded glory, the overgrown fountains, both gothic and '70s retro. The white Ferris wheel that someone had taken their last ride on possibly forty years ago, the gears sinking into the dust. The Labyrinth, which must have once been a hall of mirrors, but was now just a small building with planks of wood scattered, abandoned throughout. There were teenagers there, and though their hair wasn't sprayed into spikes, or frosted—though their jackets weren't acid wash, like when I was a teenager—the smell of booze and weed was emanating off them, and I smiled, their mocking laughter echoing after me.

I took the last, few, dying drags of my smoke, and stubbed the cigarette out, throwing it in the ash- and gum-covered trash can on my left.

We wandered until we found the cotton candy stand. It was a little red-and-white-striped platform, complete with wheels. We'd seen the guy moving a few feet ahead and worked to catch up. He'd stopped in front of the bumper cars.

There were layers of cotton candy in plastic: fuchsia, dusty rose, and lavender and white. Lollipops of all colors were for sale too, and Debby plucked two, round pink pops, making sure they were exactly the same for her girls, and stuck them in her pocket. Debby then deliberated about the color, as if there was any choice beyond pink, and we walked away with our treats, me making a joke about how it looked, after a few bites, as if we'd been making out with the prom queen.

"Gross," Debby said.

I laughed. I still got a good shock of pleasure teasing her.

I bit into the candy, enjoying the way it instantaneously shrunk under my teeth. I pulled at the fibrous material, until it came out in a long string, and then plucked the string from my mouth, and pushed the whole thing into my maw.

Debby was doing the same.

"I feel guilty for not taking the girls," she said, frowning in-between bites.

I stopped in my tracks. "You're a great mother. And to be a great mother, you need some time without them. It's not natural to be a parent 24/7. Don't do that to yourself."

She took a rapid breath, but didn't say anything, and I started us going again. Damn Jack for making her feel like she was a giant, walking womb.

"Do you want to get on the coaster?" Debby asked.

I sighed. I wasn't ready. "Let's play some games." I knew that was Debby's favorite thing to do at places like this. I liked the rides the best, the illicit thrills.

"They're all scams," Debby said, pulling some candy off her swirl, and tucking it into her mouth.

"Who cares?" I said, and she shrugged, but I could see her smile in my periphery.

She ran, like a kid, over to a neighboring game. The wall was a white panel with pink and blue balloons tacked to it. You had to throw a dart, try to pop the balloon. She loved this game, and I suddenly recalled her playing it here when we were kids, right before our friendship had broken off. It was nice to see Debby happy for once, caring for herself. Not minding a kid, worried if it was stuffing something it shouldn't into its mouth, or if Jack was too drunk.

She threw dart after colorful dart, missing each time and snorting in disappointment when she did.

"You want to try?" she asked, and I told her I was almost out of tickets. She went to get more, and the dude who was running the stand smiled. I was checking my phone to see if there were any calls when I thought I saw something, someone large and hulking reflected in the guy's sunglasses as I was looking back up. I turned around. Nothing. My mind went to my dream, and I felt a violent, nervous edge of excitement move through my veins.

Debby shoved a gigantic roll of blue tickets into my hands, and I could see the excitement in her eyes. I shook my head. It took her half the roll before she gave up, and moved onto the next, a game that, to my mind, was even more futile. There were little, bright green frogs sticking up above water on plastic lily pads, the goal was to swing a ring over the head of the frog, all while the whole thing spun lightly, each frog floating past in a circle.

We split the tickets, and I swung, and she swung until most of them were gone, Debby finally ringing a frog at the end, and acting like she'd won a car on a game show, jumping up and down and shouting once they gave her a choice between a roll of candy and a keychain. She chose a Power Puff keychain.

Debby wanted to get on the carousel next, which, I had to admit, held a lot of charm with its chipped, painted horses moving up and down to the broken-down sounds of carnival music, playing out disjointedly into the air, the mirror beside me reflecting my own wild laughter—and something else, that thing I'd sworn I'd seen reflected in the worker's sunglasses an hour before. I snapped my head around, hoping to catch whatever it was, but we'd moved around the bend already, and the only thing I could see was a family with twin girls with grubby faces, red hair, and soft blue dresses. I tried to shake the feeling off, not spoil the day. But the reason I'd wanted to come here moved anxiously in the back of my mind. This had to be a sign. God how I hated people who thought everything was a sign, and now I'd become one of them.

We got lunch inside the park after the carousel had lost its shine—a couple of sandwiches and some lemonades, and watched the people go by. I couldn't help but give special attention to the teenagers. It wasn't that I wanted to go back—though parts of my life had been wildly fun, many parts had been sad, tragic even. But they were a reminder of who I was.

"I love spring," Debby said. "Like, fall is my favorite, you know that. The falling leaves, the crisp air, the pumpkin spice lattes. But spring is so great."

I nodded. I did too, but my head was somewhere else.

"Do you miss being a kid?" I asked.

She sighed thoughtfully. "Sometimes. But I get to feel all that stuff again, through my children. Like Christmas. Remember how magical it was?"

I remembered. But it was shadowed by my father's inability to really celebrate it with me. To even get him next door, where I would migrate after settling Daddy in every Christmas morning, feeling bad as I shut the door on him, the glow of the television lighting his face. Even though I knew he really didn't understand that Christmas wasn't like any other day, I always felt like I was abandoning him. But he cried hysterically when we tried to get him out of the house. The last time we'd tried was almost ten years ago. He'd gone down on his knees at the door, frenzied, calling Cecilia's name over and over, like a religious chant.

"Yeah," I responded, not wanting to kill Debby's mood. Really, I should've said teenager. I didn't miss being a kid, I missed being a teenager. I missed being free, and wild, and most of all, I missed Jaime.

"I feel that magic again, when I see their eyes Christmas morning," she said. "The little one especially. Her eyes get so big." Debby was near tears.

I smiled indulgently.

Big, black clouds were gathering. I wondered if it would rain.

After an hour of Skee-Ball, hit the clown, and finally, my favorite, wheel of chance, I persuaded Debby to step it up.

The Round-Up was a ride that you stood on, strapping yourself to the circle as it spun, the bottom eventually dropping out beneath you. I loved it. Debby closed her eyes the whole time, stumbling off afterward to my riotous laughter.

I couldn't help it, teasing her was so easy.

"Shut *up*," she said, and though I laughed some more, I pulled a bottle of water out of my bag, and waited while she sipped, before we moved on—further along toward my final goal.

"I think . . . I think I'm ready," I said.

The Cyclone—one of the few authentic wooden roller coasters left in the country, was the first coaster I'd ever ridden, and it was beautiful. I'd been drunk on it, high on it, I'd given a hand job on this thing, to great consternation of the older, married couple behind me. I'd been fifteen years old, the boy climaxing right as we hit the peak, the couple tattling on us once we hit the ground, the workers laughing like hell. And now I really had a reason to ride it again.

"You getting on it with me?" I asked.

"You know they scare me," she said, her forehead creasing.

"We've come all the way here. We haven't in a decade. Who

knows how long this thing will even be open, Debby? You really
want to die knowing you didn't ride *the* Cyclone?" I asked, walking
backward toward the coaster, and shaking my head, urging her forward.

"I don't know, Kari . . ."

"I need you on this, Debby. I mean, what if I have some weird-ass
vision or experience in the middle of the ride, and end up in danger
in some way? I didn't want to tell you this, but the whole time we've
been here, I swear—I've been seeing something. I don't know what,
but it's been in my periphery the whole time."

She craned her neck, her eyes hitting the very top of the coaster,
and then sighed anxiously.

"I guess you're right," she said.

I couldn't believe it.

After a long wait in line, we buckled into the cars. I could see
The Chipmunk from my perch, the cars resembling white bullets
with blue insides, the front marked with numbers and names. The
Cyclone on the other hand, at least offered traditional coaster seats,
and most impressively, belts.

"WHOO," I said as we took off.

"Don't make it worse," Debby said. I could see her visibly
sweating.

The sky began making noises, thundercracks.

As we pulled forward, I could feel fear radiating off Debby in
waves, the sun beginning to set. We went sharply around a corner,
and Debby screeched—God, it was high-pitched, and I tried to reassure her by patting her on the back. The entrance was lit up now, and
it was beautiful, the bright white burning into the night. I urged her
to look, but she kept her eyes squeezed shut, sweat pouring down
her forehead.

I really regretted making Debby do this. But I had to. I didn't
want to do it alone.

As we hit peak after peak, corner after corner, Debby yelling like each shout was her last, my eyes flitted over to the entrance again, and I thought of its little, strange, pink doppelgänger, Casa Bonita, yet another nearly faded part of Denver's past; one that, like Lakeside, hung on, despite everything. With its terrible "Mexican" food and cheap Disney-style Yucatán-ish insides, complete with faux-waterfalls, caves and even cliff divers, it was a Denver institution, even winning a spot in an episode of *South Park*, and a place in a novel by a famous crime writer.

"Doesn't the entrance kind of look like Casa Bonita?" I asked, elbowing Debby, and trying to get her to open her eyes.

"I hate you," she said.

I sighed.

It began pouring rain.

We were near the end of the ride when I thought I saw what had been in my periphery all evening, what had been bothering me, and what seemed illuminated in the searing amusement park lights through the sheets of rain in a moment of lightning, its long hair wet and plastered to its sides, its mouth pulled up in a snarl. It was the Lofa. The big, hulking monster from my nightmares. I felt my throat swell up, and my mind fill with fear, but when we rounded the corner, it was gone.

I blinked. The thing was, I could've *sworn* that I'd seen the monster behind a brightly lit popcorn ball stand, watching us. I didn't want to make the ride any worse for Debby, who was barely hanging on as it was, so I kept my mouth shut. Then my mind went to a darker, even more irrational place. I couldn't help but wonder if it was hoping to get us alone.

That was crazy. Or was it?

As the coaster hit the final bend, and Debby squealed weakly, I pictured it in the darkened parking lot, Debby and I rounding an abandoned corner, distracted by our own laughter and maybe a drink or two, the business of finding our keys. Its hairy back. Its teeth that ripped flesh right off the muscle, off bone. I felt sick.

When the ride came to a stop, I steeled myself, and took Debby's hand.

"What the hell, Kari?" Debby said, panting. "Where are we going? It's raining like crazy!"

"Just . . . follow me."

We ran down the steps together, people angry as I jostled them out of the way, my shoes splashing in the gathering puddles. I let go of Debby's hand when we reached the bottom, confident that she'd follow me, and kept going, my breath heavy, the thud of my footfalls echoing in my ears.

But at the popcorn stand, there was nothing there, except the lingering smell of something rotten—something like old meat, permeating through the smell of rain on cement.

"I thought I saw something, is all," I said, running my hand through my wet hair and leading us to shelter. Under the awning for a small pizza restaurant, I felt insane—like someone with a fucking brain tumor. Like someone who was slowly coming apart. Had my mother meant for me to come here? Why? I didn't understand.

CHAPTER TWENTY-NINE

lay on my black velvet couch, my phone on my stomach. I'd been texting with Debby about what had happened at Lakeside the entire evening, putting Netflix on pause as I did. I was watching *The Shining,* and it was bringing me comfort.

I paused the TV again. I'd thought I'd heard something at the window, but it was just the wind moaning through the trees, a branch hitting the glass. I took a deep breath, turned the movie back on, but the feeling of unease didn't quite leave me.

Until now, I'd never thought about the other world except as something on the silver screen or the page, though I had to admit, horror had always been my favorite, which had to say something. I didn't believe in an afterlife, had never let Aunt Sandy drag me to church, even when I was a little girl. Though *Jesus* she'd tried, hard. And though some of my best friends growing up were more tradish Natives, from NAC to old school Diné lifeways, I wasn't interested in their stuff either. Whenever we'd be walking off in the woods, trying to find a place to get high, and a coyote would cross our paths and they'd shudder, tell me we had to turn around, I'd tell them to go right ahead. I was going to move forward and get baked.

The branch hit the glass even harder, faster, the wind coming up strong, and I wondered if we were in for a storm. God, that tapping—like a skeletal hand on a mirror.

I turned back to the television, and my mind wandered. The thing was, I was firmly rooted in this world. In fact, I'd been known for it. It was something that annoyed Debby and Sandy to no end, when they'd get to telling their ghost stories, about how they'd got a "feeling" in a graveyard or an old house. How certain rooms in their own homes, they just knew, were haunted, as they'd seen a reflection of a child's face in the mirror, or how they could've sworn an object had moved. Then there were my Native friends who wouldn't go to graveyards at all, or into a house where someone had died. Who told me that the thing moving something in your periphery were the Little People. I'd done nothing but yuck it up, scoff, do a little leprechaun dance around them when they said it—their eyes narrowing in irritation.

Until recently.

The phone dinged, and I jumped. I sighed, annoyed with myself. It was Debby, and she was worried.

I paused the TV to text her back, and then put it back on. It was approaching the classic scene with Jack hacking through the doorframe. Shelley Duvall's scream pierced through the night, and I laughed, feeling better. Damn—that woman had a face made of rubber. Someone pounded on the wall next to me.

I'd made my apartment my nest when I'd left high school with my GED, with black furniture and black, gothic-style mirrors, and Megadeth posters, framed of course, in black—around every corner, but the walls were thin.

"Alright, alright," I said, turning it down. But just a little.

The phone dinged again, and I hit pause once more.

Debby was really pushing for me to call the cops now. And I did have Fredrico's number. But what would I tell him? The only thing outside of my visions, visitations, was what Nessie and Michael, and Hank at the Indian Center had told me. Which was a whole lot of nothing.

I told Debby to cool it, that I needed a break from all of this, and reluctantly, she let it go when I reassured her that the doors and windows were locked, and that I'd text her first thing tomorrow morning, as usual.

I turned *The Shining* back on, thinking about how I could relate to Danny more than ever now, with my newfound "powers." If only I had a Hallorann to tell me what to do with all the shit that got in my head when I had these visions. If I only knew where any of it came from.

I flipped over, unable to settle, and decided to get myself a Bud, stopping in front of the refrigerator with the door open, my mind wandering for a while before I realized what I was doing, and got my beer, shut the door. I finished the movie, drinking the rest of my beer as I watched Danny run to his mother, his mother scooping him up, placing him safely in the snowcat, driving away.

I had to cut this pussy shit out.

I listened to a few tracks from *Countdown to Extinction*, psyching myself up, then turned the music off, the lights in the kitchen on. I went to my dresser, and rifling through my underwear, found my newest acquisition. The medicine bag really was beautiful. I wondered if there was some sort of oil I could put on it, to restore it. I was afraid the cones were going to drop off, it was so dry.

Back down on the couch, I sighed heavily. Was I sure I wanted to do this?

I pulled the bag out of the tissue and touched it. At first, I thought nothing was happening. But then—

I was at a protest outside the capital, and cops were everywhere. It was cold, a few flurries spinning through the air. A man named Russell Means was speaking at the top of the huge, stone steps and I was Cecilia. I was listening, I was shouting along with everyone else. It was a large crowd, Natives of all kinds spreading out on either side of me, some of them wearing feathers in their hair, some of them holding hand drums cradled in their arms. Though Means was a good distance from all of us, his voice was strong, and I could hear every word. Jim was at my side, and he was nervous. He kept telling me that maybe we should leave, that the police had been looking in our direction, and that he knew, that unlike him, I was brown, that I would be arrested first—or worse, I could be killed, and that he couldn't live without me, he couldn't. I put my hand on his arm and told him: *Jim, I'm already on a list. If they're going to come for me, they're going to come for me. But I have to do this. I'm sorry, Jim. I love you.*

I dimly remembered—separating my thoughts from Cecilia's for a moment, that a woman who had been involved with Means, involved with AIM, Anna Mae Aquash, had disappeared. And in that moment, as myself, as Kari, I knew what my mother had been trying to tell me all this time: they had come for her—whether that had been the men in AIM, or the FBI. There was still a mystery about that surrounding Aquash. Her body had been found in a ravine, and not long after, an autopsy revealed that she'd been murdered by gunshot, execution style.

I felt myself merging again with my mother as Means began to speak—of genocide, of colonization—and for a brief moment I separated once more, remembering someone at the Indian Center lecturing on the history of the American Indian Movement. How Means had separated from AIM at one point. Of his work in Denver in the late '90s, tying things back to Aquash—he had been here again, trying to get people to pay attention to what had been done to her. Had the same people who killed Aquash killed my mother?

I leaned in to hear more.

He was saying that "For America to live, Europe must die." That though he had wanted to be a leader, he wasn't really interested in leading anyone toward anything. Not capitalism. Or communism. That all that he was, was an Oglala Lakota, and that all of us should take strength from who we were.

My God, this was it. This was what my mother had been trying to show me.

Means was wearing a large, beaded thunderbird, the symbol of protection, and I focused on that, and the feeling all around me—of anger, yes, but of hope, hope that things would be different for their children, and their children's children, a feeling that felt so alien to everything I'd ever experienced. My life was so separate from this, this kind of passion, this feeling that something I participated in could change things. Something overwhelming began to swell up in my chest and then there was noise and then there was gunfire and screaming—

CHAPTER THIRTY

n my dream, I walk in the aisles of the Tattered Cover, the sound of whispering coming from the shelves all around, Jim behind me.

Cecilia, wait.

I laugh and turn, and fall into his sweet, pale arms. He smells like talcum powder, clean and safe and warm.

When I pull back, Jim is gone, and I am myself, alone.

A book flies out from a shelf, and lands square in front of me. I lean down. The title of the book is *Sharon*. I examine the leather cover. There are ornate designs circling the front, and I pick it up.

A feeling of deep, overwhelming curiosity—and sadness—runs through me, as if I am about to uncover something tragic, something that's going to expose the whole mystery of this thing, but just as I'm about to flip it open, I can hear the monster growling somewhere behind me. As I begin to run, the books flying out en masse, my panic growing, the books burying me, I scream as the monster approaches, the dead meat smell cloying, heavy, everywhere as it tears and tears and tears. First pages, then flesh. Mine.

I wake up.

My mother is in the window, in front of the curtains, staring at me.

"Cecilia," I whisper.

She's crying, the moonlight highlighting her face, her arm around something I can't see. "Sharon," she says, her voice breaking. "Sharon."

I stare at her as she cries, wondering.

Something made me glance over at the clock. 11:47.

I look back, but she's gone.

CHAPTER THIRTY-ONE

My fingertips flitted absently between the dusty albums in the rack at one of Denver's coolest spots, Twist & Shout, on East Colfax. It was right next door to the Tattered Cover, and I didn't think there was any harm in chilling here before I plunged in. I mean, I wanted to go. I was going to go. But the whole thing still made me feel like I was fucking crazy—and beyond that, these dreams, these visits, were so intense. Besides, I was always searching, here and on eBay, for some cool, random LPs that I didn't own.

My fingers stopped on an album I already had. *Youthanasia*.

I'd nearly lost my mind during Megadeth's *Youthanasia* tour. I was thirteen, and deeply in love with the band, Mustaine, and everything metal. I'd hitched with Jaime in the back of a rusty truck from the Springs, drinking the strawberry Boones Farm we'd lifted from the local liquor store the whole way, laughing wildly, barely staying in the bed of the truck as it sped down I-70 and high on pills some random chicks handed us outside of the store once we got there.

I shook my head and moved on. I was, of course, in the metal section. My fingers ran over the orange and black cover, featuring a kid writing in a notebook. Guns N' Roses' *Use Your Illusion I*—I already had *II*. I'd seen them in concert too, and though no one could take the throne from Mustaine, I had to admit, there were tracks I loved and listened to on the regular. There was a deeper reason for this. Jaime. That had been her band.

"Fuck yes," I whispered to myself.

"Kari," Debby said. She hated when I cussed in public, which was always.

"Debby, Jesus," I said, rolling my eyes. "Go over to the NSYNC section if you're going to piss on my parade."

Debby laughed hard. "NSYNC? Oh Kari, they haven't been together since . . . I don't even know. Since forever."

"Whatever," I said. I was just glad she had agreed to come with me. "You still love them."

She turned red.

"What did you find?" Debby asked, desperately trying to change the subject.

I showed her.

"Ah," she said. I was lucky to have someone in my life who understood me so deeply.

I sat down on a zebra-print barstool and gingerly opened the album up, splitting the thick paper open with two fingers and plucking the black, plastic disc out. I wanted to check for damage. I was a stickler for perfection. As I inspected the album for any flaws, I thought about the dream again, and tried to refocus, carefully turning the record around and around, holding it up into the light. It looked good.

"You gonna get it?" Debby asked.

I nodded, and took my album to the front, the clerk looking like Kurt Cobain had thrown up all over him, his flannel tied around his Nirvana T-shirt, his hair Gen-X greasy, though to my eye, he was almost certainly a millennial. I was a metal guy, but I appreciated the commitment.

Debby's phone rang, and she headed outside to take the call. I was sure it was Jack.

"Retro," the Cobain-alike said, and I snorted.

Outside, it was nice—there were a few clouds in the sky, a light breeze, and Debby was going on and on, reassuring Jack that she was okay, that she wouldn't be home too late, that there were plenty of leftovers for him and the kids.

Finally, she put the phone down. "You ready?" she asked.

I sighed heavily. "Yes."

If there was a place that might have information about my mother, I was glad it was the Tattered Cover. I'd spent hours there, or rather, at the old location—as a kid, scanning the shelves for anything that involved demons or ghosts, anything that would give me a nice, healthy scare. I missed that location—it was huge, glamorous. I loved the tall shelves lined with books, the stairway leading down to more, the old velvet and corduroy chairs stuffed into the corners in case you wanted to sit and read a few pages before you bought.

Inside, I took a deep breath and began walking toward the horror section, Debby close behind.

"So, you're sure this was where she was in the dream?" Debby asked.

I nodded.

Debby's phone began dinging with texts.

"Debby, just ignore it for a second," I said.

"But what if it's about the kids?"

I rolled my eyes.

I began browsing, pulling out title after title, hoping to see something with the name "Sharon" on the front. Ghosts. Castles. Vampires. I got excited for a second, seeing a "Sharon"—but it was just the author's first name. I was pretty sure a book about an ancient vampire in Scotland had nothing to do with my mother.

I closed my eyes, feeling stupid. Conjured up the dream. Tried to really feel what I was feeling in that dream. Let it guide me. I opened my eyes, and I couldn't help it, I started laughing.

Debby squinted at me inquisitively, and then went back to her texting.

Shit. There was nothing—at least here anyway—with Sharon in the title. This was so frustrating. The dream I'd had of Orr's had led me straight to something, even if I still didn't quite understand how it fit in. But this seemed like a waste of goddamn time.

Debby was still texting rapidly.

I had a thought.

I walked up to the service desk, Debby behind me, her face still deep in her phone, and waited for the hip, fifty-ish woman to finish with the last customer. Debby had barely avoided a stand full of books, an old white guy, and a goth dude in his thirties during our walk up.

"I've got kind of a weird request," I said.

She lifted her eyebrows. She had short, dark bangs and red cat-eye glasses.

"I'm wondering if you could look up any books with the title, *Sharon.*"

"Okay," she said, smiling.

She started typing into the computer, and when she was done, she swung it around.

We leaned in.

There was a biography of Sharon Stone. A book called *Sharon's Journal: A Notebook for Her Whose Name is Sharon.* Titles with Sharon as the first name of the author. I looked, briefly, at *Sharon's Journal,* as it was the only one that seemed even vaguely promising, but it was literally an empty notebook—presumably for Sharons who wanted to journal.

"Thanks," I said, "guess I'm not going to find what I'm looking for."

"Any more info you can give me?" she asked. She seemed nice.

"Not really. But again, thanks."

Debby was still texting when I finished.

"Debby?"

"Hold on."

"Really, Debby?"

She looked at me briefly before she went back in, her expression one of irritation. "Kari, one of the kids is sick, okay?"

I let out an exasperated sigh. Waited.

Finally, she stopped.

"What did you find?"

"Nothing," I said. "Absolutely nothing."

"I'm sorry."

"I just don't understand. Why the name Sharon? Why did I dream of the Tattered Cover? Nothing I learned here was any different than what I'd get from fucking Amazon. Maybe the Tattered Cover was just some random part of my dream?"

Debby shook her head. "I don't think so."

"Then—"

My phone began ringing. I picked it up. It was Nessie. My stomach tightened.

"It's Nessie," I said, and Debby followed me as we walked outside the store, Debby plopping down on the metal bench outside.

"Nessie?" I answered.

"Kari," she said. She sounded worried. Upset. "I'm sorry I couldn't tell you more."

I was silent for a moment.

"It's okay, Nessie. It's not your fault."

She sighed.

I needed a smoke.

"There are just things that I want to tell you. I do. But I can't. I just can't."

What did that mean? Why couldn't she tell me? And what things?

"Nessie, are you alright?"

I swung through the doors and sat on the bench beside Debby, struggling for my pack and lighter.

"I'm okay. I just wanted to let you know that I want to be a part of your life—it's just, like I said, there are things that I can't tell you. Things I made a promise on, and I keep my promises."

I was silent, hoping she'd continue.

"Did you get the medicine bag I sent you? I only have your aunt's address."

"I did. Thank you."

"I really felt you should have it."

I was able to successfully light my cigarette despite the breeze and took a deep puff. Then I took another and steeled myself.

I drew breath. "Can't you tell me a *little* bit more about what happened to my mother? Was she involved in things my grandfather—Michael—was scared for her to be involved in?"

I felt bad for asking her, I really did. I didn't want to worsen her health condition. Or cause her psychological pain.

She started crying.

"Nessie?"

"Kari, I shouldn't even be talking to you."

"Is there more about AIM or the FBI that you know?" I asked. I had to hope she wouldn't hang up on me. Should I tell her about my visions? Would she think I was crazy? But then again, what did I have to lose?

"Look. I've been having visions, Nessie. Dreams."

I'd been raised around, and practically by Navajos and Lakotas. They had different bogeymen—but that thing, it was otherworldly. Just talking about it gave me the creeps, the smell of it from my memory wafting in the air around me.

She was silent, and I wished I hadn't said anything.

"My grandmother was like you. Saw things," she said finally.

I breathed a sigh of relief.

"I really want to know what happened to her, Nessie. And I don't think the men in AIM, or the FBI are going to be after you if you tell me. Not anymore."

I took another hit, leaned back.

"Nessie, you can trust me. I won't say anything, to anyone. I promise."

"I don't know . . ."

I took several quick puffs before I started in on my next statement. Here was where she'd either align with me—or where she'd decide I was absolutely, completely, out of my fucking head.

"I'm seeing something else too. My mother. I've seen her ghost."

She was silent for a long time, and I thought she'd hung up.

"My God," she said, finally. "Me too."

I sighed in relief. I wasn't crazy. Or we both were. Either way, she believed me.

"I'm not like my grandmother," Nessie said. "I wanted to see things, but though I did Native American Church as a girl—I never saw anything like that. But it was . . . maybe a few weeks ago. I felt something. I told myself it was a breeze, as I was doing dishes at the window, but I knew it wasn't. When I turned around, she was there."

She paused, and I figured she was pulling herself together.

"The first time I saw her, I thought I was losing my mind," she said, quietly.

That's exactly how I'd felt.

"God, she looked just like the day she died," Nessie said. That's when she lost it. I listened to her cry, not wanting to interrupt, letting her do what she needed to do. I never knew what to do when others cried, but I knew enough to know that she just needed to get it out.

The sun was starting to set, and bright, white lights were coming on. That, and the laughter of the passersby should've been a cheerful thing, but it wasn't making a dent in my mood.

"I'm sorry," I finally said, when she quieted. "I don't mean to make it worse. It's just . . . that now I *need* to find out what happened to her. Before, I hated her. Didn't give a shit. I feel bad for that now, but I didn't know any better."

I figured the bit about the bracelet healing Daddy was too complicated to bring up now. And I was hoping that Nessie would break, tell me more about what my mother had been up to, in the time leading up to her death. I felt guilty for being that mercenary, but there it was. And shit, she was haunting Nessie too.

"When she visits, she's always asking for my help," I said.

"Yes," Nessie said, whispering, "that's what she says to me too. But she ends it with momma." Her voice went soft, close to breaking.

I lit cigarette number two.

"I was so glad when your mother married Jim. He was such a nice man. I'm sorry to hear about what happened to him."

It made me sad to talk about Daddy before his accident. He'd lost so much. I'd lost so much.

Here she stopped to blow her nose.

"I had hope for her then."

"I see," I said, but I didn't see. Not at all.

We were both silent for a time.

"Nessie, would you be willing to meet up with me?"

"Oh, Kari, I . . ."

I felt my heart speed up. Maybe I was getting to her after all.

"I promise. I'll tell no one."

"Maybe . . ."

I was getting somewhere!

I shook my head. "Nessie, Michael said that he thought that Cecilia was hanging with the wrong people at the Indian Center. And a friend at the Indian Center told me that the FBI might've disappeared her. But the only way I'll find out what really happened, is if you tell me more about what was going on then. Really, I don't think anyone who might've killed my mom is even still alive. Or if they are, they've moved on."

She was quiet, and the frustration I felt was unnameable, it was so large. I closed my eyes, tried to think about what I could say to persuade her to come and talk to me.

"I want you to know the truth. I do," Nessie said.

I withheld a snort.

But my God, she knew something.

Telling her what I wanted to tell her next was the real risk. I knew that she had a health condition. She'd mentioned that back at her apartment. I didn't want to scare her into a heart attack—or seem like I was manipulating her. I took a drag off the cigarette. Watched the smoke pile out like steam.

I supposed I'd gone this far. I took a deep breath.

"Nessie, I don't think Cecilia's going away until we figure out—or I figure out—what happened to her."

I could hear her take a strangling breath.

"Hardly a day goes by that she doesn't appear. She wants me to do something. She wants . . . I know she wants me to find out what happened to her for sure, but she also wants something else, something I can't put my finger on—"

The phone went dead.

"Nessie? Nessie?" I said, but there was no answer.

CHAPTER THIRTY-TWO

Oh shit, oh shit," I said, putting my phone back in my bag.

"What?" Debby asked.

I heard the doors to Twist & Shout open and saw that it was the Cobain-alike. He found a corner and lit up a hand-rolled American Spirit, giving me a smoker's head nod. I gave him one back.

"Fuck me," I said, and told Debby about what Nessie had said.

"Do you still want to go to The Hornet? I know we'd talked about that earlier, and I'm sure you could really use a drink now, but, if you're not in the mood . . ."

"You sure Jack would be okay with that? He seemed pretty anxious for you to get home, from what I could hear," I said.

She sighed. "Kari, one of the kids was sick. I was worried. He was worried. He's taking care of them so I can do this with you, even though he doesn't like it one bit."

"Okay," I said. "So . . . you think he'll be cool with you hanging more or not?"

"Yes, Kari."

I shrugged. "Okay. See you there."

The traffic was shitty this time of day, and as I turned left onto

York Street I almost swerved into a red Honda, its horn blowing at me, me waving in apology, the white dude behind the wheel flipping me off in response.

After parking behind the brightly colored Mayan Theater, Debby's car just a few spots away, we were sitting at the long wooden bar at The Hornet, a Bud in my hand, a glass of merlot in Debby's. Debby was scrolling away on her phone, her sparkle-shirt with BIRTHDAY GIRL glinting in the light.

"You know what, Kari, you've got to handle this carefully," she said, setting her phone down.

"You think?"

"Enough with the sarcasm, okay? What I'm saying is that of course I think you should push Nessie—but, like, she does have a heart condition. And like, Michael's probably only trying to protect her. You don't want to piss him off and get in-between a couple."

"I've noticed that," I said, and she turned red.

"Look—it's just, you've never had a boyfriend. Or husband. So, you don't know what it's like—"

"To have someone tell you what to do?" I interrupted.

"That's so you, Kari. It's more than that. It's like, when you're part of a family, you make agreements. You compromise. You make promises. And it matters if you keep them. It can make or break a relationship. And maybe not talking about something really, really, painful, was a promise they made to each other, long ago. Heck, maybe Nessie had a heart attack, and he's trying to keep her alive."

"So, you're telling me to let this go?"

"No!"

"What then, shit!"

"I'm just saying, what you should do, is—"

Her phone dinged, and I closed my eyes.

"Party's over," I said moodily. I couldn't help it.

"Cut it out," she said, but I could see from her expression that she knew I was right.

She started texting furiously, but to no avail. The phone began ringing, and she took it.

I watched her gesture wildly through the window, trying to reason, I was sure, with a whiskey-drunk Jack. His buddy Carl probably sat on the couch behind him, watching TV with his mouth open and drooling.

Finally, she walked back in, tears pouring down her face.

She took the rest of her glass in one gulp.

"Jack's threatening me."

"What?" I was ready to drop everything, run over there, kick his *fucking* ass.

"No-no, not like that. Not . . ." She stopped to sob, and then continued, "he's threatening like, to leave me."

It took me a minute to process this. "I thought he was cool with us hanging today, tonight. So, why?"

"Because he says I don't prioritize him, that I care more about you than I do my own children." Now she was really wailing. "He says that even when I knew Rachel was sick, I decided to go out with you, like I was still single."

"You need to tell him," I said, real venom entering my voice, "that if he doesn't put the *goddamn* whiskey bottle down, and get his head out of his stinking *ass,* that you're going to leave him, and take the kids."

She merely sniffled.

"Did you hear what I said?"

"Yes, I heard you. Kari, you don't understand. Like I said, in relationships there are compromises. And he's their father. I love him. He's a good guy—"

"He's *not* a good guy, if he says stuff like this to you," I said. Jesus Christ this was so frustrating. She was impenetrable.

"It's just, he's mad that I've been spending so much time with you, trying to help you with your mom stuff," she said. "And that, like, I don't even care that this situation is potentially dangerous."

She sipped at her wine. "I mean he's right. I mean, that is true."

I rolled my eyes. "You've helped me here and there, but you're not giving your life up for it or anything. And it seems to me that he's the one acting dangerous. And you're a great mother. Don't let him pull that shit on you."

I needed a smoke.

Debby was silent. There was nothing to say, really, that we hadn't said a million times before. He was such gigantic fuck-up baby.

"He always does this, Debby. Always! We're driving somewhere and he calls you up because he can't find the diapers. Or the kids are crying. Or he's bored because Carl is sleeping one off, and he wants you to entertain him."

"That's not fair," she said, her tears drying up. "He let me come even though you got him thrown in detox."

"*Let* you? Do you hear yourself? He constantly sabotages us whenever you're having fun." I couldn't help it, I was on a roll, and there was no way around it, I just had to get it out.

"You're not helping," she said. Now she was just whining.

I wasn't going to repeat what I'd already said.

"I know, I know—but do you agree with Jack? You think you should stop helping me? Stop hanging out with me?"

She was silent.

"Debby, what do you want me to say? You know what I think."

More sniffling.

"I'm sorry Debby, I really am," I said, feeling hopeless. Futile.

"I have to go home now, Kari, I'm sorry. I mean, it is getting late. It's like, 11:30. And I really should check on Rachel."

I nodded. "Don't worry about the wine, I got it."

"You sure?"

"Of course," I said, giving her a side-hug and watching her gather her bag. I only made it worse when I piled on. I had to let her go when it got like this, hope that someday, she'd grow a pair.

"Text me when you get to the Springs," I said.

"Text me tomorrow morning," she answered.

I nodded, and she left.

Listening to the lazy, sad sounds of the saxophone echoing what I felt in my heart, I thought about how I wanted to beat that son of a bitch up. He made her life miserable. He really did. I would never, ever understand her. Close as I was to Debby now, this was something about her that put distance between us. And to threaten her when it came to her kids? That was playing dirty. What hurt me the most for Debby was the fact that he didn't give two shits about the kids. Well, that wasn't exactly right. He did give shits about the kids—but he wasn't threatening to leave her because he was a better parent, or because he worried she was putting them in danger, though I had no doubt that the stories I'd shared with Debby were being communicated directly to Jack, and they were freaking him out. They should. But what wounded me for her was that it was an excuse to try to get her to make her life about him completely. To cut me, and any other person or activity out that meant that she wasn't waiting to do his bidding like a wife-puppy, at all times. Though he disliked me in particular, or rather, was jealous of my relationship with her, he didn't like any of her friends. He'd tried to get her to quit her job once, even though there was no way they could afford their mortgage without it. Shit, he'd stopped her from making a real career for herself after she'd finished her degree in business, because it would take her away from the kids—i.e., him, her biggest, brattiest, kid. It was all so frustrating, and I had little control over the whole thing.

I went out for a smoke, watched the hipsters walk by, the drag queens, the homeless; one of whom had a big, tattered American flag taped to his dirty backpack.

I was at a crossroads. I could let this shit go, or I could try to figure out what had happened to my mother. But how could I do it without hurting Nessie? And driving a further wedge between Jack and Debby?

I stomped my cigarette out, and went back in. I ordered a whiskey and picked my book back up. God, my life was a mess.

That's when I felt her. The electricity in the air. The smell of burning cedar.

Sure enough, when I put the book down, slowly, trying to prepare, and lifted my eyes, there she was, standing in the middle of the tables, the restaurant growing dark around me. People were walking right through her, laughing at her without seeing her there, lifting drinks through her middle, her expression one of pure sorrow. She was mouthing something again, and I squinted, and she began to move forward. I pushed back against the bar.

She kept going, her mouth moving slowly, methodically, and though I could feel the terror coursing through every vein as blood trickled out of her mouth, from her head, further darkening her clothing, I tried to retain control, pay attention.

It was a p-word, I was sure of it as she came so close to me that the smell of cedar was everywhere, overwhelming me. Her eyes were two black tunnels matching mine, portals to another time, another place, somewhere near unknowable.

I gripped my seat hard, sweating, and watched her mouth repeat the same syllables again and again until finally, it came to me.

"Pictures," I whispered to myself, under my breath, and that's when I thought I saw it again—the Lofa, out the window, growling and snarling in the spring rain that had come on so suddenly that I hadn't even noticed it until now.

My mother's ghost turned to look at the Lofa, and then snapped out of this world with the sound of a crack that might've been thunder, and when I looked again, blinking, the beast was gone.

CHAPTER THIRTY-THREE

s this Kari James?"

"Who is this?" I asked. I'd heard the phone ringing in the shower and thought little of it. But when I got out, as I was toweling off, I heard it again, and hurried to wrap a towel around my body. I'd left the phone on my end table, next to the couch.

"This is special agent Cooper Patel."

I froze. Holy. Shit.

"Yes?"

"Is this Kari James? The daughter of Cecilia James?"

I sat down on my couch, hard.

"This is."

"We're calling because you filed a Freedom of Information Act pertaining to your mother."

"I did."

Agent Patel was silent, and I wondered if he'd hung up. Then, "Is there a particular reason you're looking into this matter at this time?"

What should I tell him? Would that affect what they'd tell me? My heart started pounding.

"Well . . . my grandparents, who I've recently come in contact with, tell me that she was involved with protests during her lifetime. With members of the American Indian Movement. And that those folks . . . often appeared on lists."

He was silent.

"And my mother disappeared when I was two days old," I said.

"I see," he responded.

I waited for him to go on, but he was clearly hoping I'd reveal something. What was going on here? Good God, had the FBI been responsible for her death? Or did they just know who had?

"Can you . . . tell me more?" I asked.

He cleared his throat. "We've received your paperwork. And it's going up the proper channels. You will receive a report. But in the meantime, we just wanted to understand better, considering your mother's history, why you were filing—like I said—at this moment in time."

He was clamming up. What did he think I knew? And why was I important enough for a call like this?

"Should I be concerned?" I asked.

He was silent again. "Concerned?" he repeated.

Damn, he was good.

"Never mind," I said.

"You have a good day," he said, and before I could respond, he hung up.

CHAPTER THIRTY-FOUR

By the time I finished Dean Koontz's *The Mask,* I was freaking the full-on fuck out. I hadn't heard from Debby, or Nessie, in days. And that call from the agent was getting to me. He'd told me nothing but stirred up so much.

"Another Bud, Nick," I said, scratching one fingernail distractedly along the wood.

I flipped my hardback, well-worn copy of Stephen King's *The Shining* back open. I'd set it facedown on the bar at the White Horse while I waited for my beer. The orange tabby was on my lap, purring. I was sure she had fleas, but I didn't care.

"That stuff's bad for your head," Nick said, glancing at the cover.

"Yeah? You should live in my head," I responded, taking a drink the minute he set it down, the bitter tang on my tongue more than welcome. I swear there were days I didn't drink before all this shit with my mother went down.

"That stuff's bad for your head," Nick repeated before he left to go sit by the TV again.

"I know, Nick." Poor Nick. That was another thing. The White Horse. Did I want to buy it? I wasn't sure . . .

I hadn't heard from Debby after the night she'd left The Hornet. It was unlike her, but sometimes she forgot, and I thought nothing of it—for a few days. I had some heavy shifts at work—at both the Hangar Bar and Lucille's, and had come home wrecked and tired, and thankfully, I'd slept well three nights in a row, a rarity for me even in normal times. But the fourth day I woke up rested, realizing how long it had been, and shot her a text. Nothing. I spent the day reading, glad my mother's ghost was letting me alone, worrying about her and Nessie, completely spooked by the call from the FBI agent, but able to tune it out enough to focus on the story. I figured she and Jack were busy arguing and then boning, and that maybe they'd work it out that way, and reset, and I'd hear from her when she was ready. But after not hearing from her for a full week, I was getting antsy, and I called. It went to voicemail. I called again, left a message. Then another. Nothing.

We hadn't gone a week without talking to each other since Jaime's death.

I called Aunt Sandy too. She said that she hadn't heard from her either, but that she'd go and check. They weren't home, and the cars were gone. This did not fill me with confidence. Jack was drinking a lot, more than usual—and though he wasn't a real creep, sometimes even average men did terrible things. And it was weird that she wasn't answering my calls, or her own mother's. Sandy told me not to panic yet, reminding me that they had a cabin in the woods, and sometimes they took off to spend some time there to recharge whenever they'd had a particularly ugly spell, and there was pretty much no reception up there. I said that it seemed to me that they would've at least told her that they were going up, so as to not worry folks, but Sandy told me they'd done this before.

I still didn't like it.

As for Nessie, that was more complicated. She'd called me from a landline, and though she might have a cell, I didn't have the number, so it wasn't as if I could send her a text. I just wanted to know she was okay. I'd finally called her too, but the phone just rang and rang, no one picking up.

I felt upside down these days. My life had been so regular, boring really, until all of this. I liked boring. I'd had plenty of not-boring when I'd been young, and I'd left not-boring far behind me, mainly anyway.

When Jaime had died, I'd read *The Shining* over and over again— I'd watched it too, on my father's old TV, when he went to bed. Horror upset him. He only liked his sitcoms.

The Shining was the only thing that distracted me enough from my own pain for any amount of time. I had been, though I'd never told anyone this—suicidal at turns. Debby had known that had been the case for me at first. In fact, she'd been the one to drag me out of the state that I was in, kicking and screaming—but what she didn't know was how much that feeling had come back. Jaime hadn't just been my best friend, the person who had held me like a child when-ever the pain was too unbearable to speak, she was an example of exactly what would've happened to me if I'd kept going along that path, and to be honest, I'd never thought that much about it, nor seen her death coming—at all. Which seemed immeasurably stupid, in retrospect. My survivor's guilt was surfacing with a vengeance. I couldn't understand why she'd died, and I hadn't. We did the same drugs. We were both leading the same kind of lives, maybe one cov-ered in prophylactics, but, nevertheless, full of insane risks. And we'd both lived for that life. But she'd paid for it. I hadn't.

I sighed and drank my Bud. I had been trying to stay away from the hard stuff the last few days. I didn't need to backslide. But that fluttery, terrified feeling wouldn't leave me, and I wasn't sure what my next step was beyond waiting for that report, though I had some ideas.

I pulled out the medicine bag, the one Nessie had sent me. There was no one in here, except for Nick, and I trusted him. And the thing was, I knew what to expect this time. I wasn't, at least I didn't think, going to be falling off my stool.

I touched the bag and closed my eyes. I waited.

My eyes flew open. Nothing. Absolutely nothing.

I scrambled for my bag a second time, fished the bracelet out. Touched it. Closed my eyes. Waited.

Nothing.

Nick was absorbed by the screaming blond anchors on TV.

I couldn't understand it. I'd not even wanted these visions at first, but now that I did, no go? I shook my head. Maybe the bracelet and bag had shown me everything they could? I wasn't sure, and there was something else that kept trying to worm its way to the surface. I was good at puzzles, so the fact that I couldn't figure out what it was that was bothering me, was leading me to believe that my brain just wanted a distraction, or there was some deeper reason my mind wouldn't let whatever it was come to the surface. Of course, there was still so much mystery here.

I touched the bag and then the bracelet again, really laying my hands on them, like a preacher, my head back. I closed my eyes. Thought of my mother. My grandmother. Even of the beast. I mean, for fuck's sake, I was seeing shit now without even touching either one of these things.

Nothing. Still.

I opened my eyes and glanced over where the old Indians had appeared. There was no one there.

"What the fuck am I even doing?" I said out loud, and to myself.

God. For the first time in a long time, I felt lonely. It wasn't an emotion I was accustomed to. I didn't really get lonely, and when I did, Debby was always there when I called, texted, needed someone to vent to. But now that I couldn't get in touch with her, I was left with my own head, and it was nothing but a jumble of confusion and terror. And guilt. The more I thought about Jaime, the more I realized that I could've done something to prevent her death. Told her we both needed to stop. Pulled the shit from her hands. Just not gone to that person's house where she died, for shit's sake. I wondered now if I'd really seen her ghost at all at Roller City. And if the bracelet was what pushed me, opened me up to those things, and I hadn't even touched it then, how had I seen her? Maybe she'd come back in time to push it all into motion, I thought, feeling crazier than ever.

I gave up, put the items away, and drank the rest of my beer, ready to pack it in, catch a cheap burger next door, call an Uber, go home and sleep on all of this, when my phone rang.

It was Nessie.

"Nessie?" I said, picking up, my heart in my throat.

"Kari, I'm so glad to hear your voice." She sounded almost out of breath, and I couldn't help but worry.

"Me too! Or I mean, I'm so glad you called. Are you okay? Where are you?" I knew I was running my words together, but holy shit was I glad to hear from her.

"I'm fine. I'm fine—and I'm at home."

I sighed with relief.

"What happened last time?"

"Michael came home and asked who I was speaking to. Hung up for me. I'm sorry."

"I'm sure he just doesn't want you to get hurt like my mother did," I said, wanting to tell her about the call from the FBI agent, but holding back. Maybe she had something she really wanted to divulge—I needed to give her room to do that.

"I've had a lot of time to think, Kari. I want to meet with you. Tell you what I know. There's so much, Kari, you have no idea." Her voice was trembling, but steady. "I'm glad you came into my life."

I felt my heart surge. "Good for you, Nessie."

"I'm not afraid anymore."

That hit me, hard.

"Good," I said.

"Yes. Michael's out hunting. So, let's plan."

I swung my hand through the air. "Wonderful." I felt strong, determined. Like this was a sign that everything I'd been through with this thing was finally about to pay off. I smiled.

"I just have to hope you don't think I'm crazy," she said, laughing nervously.

I narrowed my eyes in confusion. Why would I think she was crazy? I mean, we'd both had those visions.

"Don't worry about any of that, Nessie. Shoot, you're talking to someone who still wonders if she doesn't have a brain tumor," I said. "Really, let's just figure out when and where you want to meet."

I was dying, fucking dying, to know what she knew, the fuller context of all my visions. If I could just get the Freedom of Information Act back, read what they had to say, and then use the information that Nessie could give me, I just might find out what happened to my mother after all. I thought that even if the FBI wouldn't out-and-out tell me that they'd murdered my mother—or that some men in AIM had—if there was enough evidence that one of them had done it, I'd be able to bring the truth out into the light, and my mother's ghost could finally rest, stop haunting me—pass ownership of the bracelet, and I could go back to my good, old, comfortable, boring life. Maybe I could even heal Daddy, if Squeaker wasn't totally full of shit. Maybe the agent calling was a sign that they were going to send me information that would really fill in the missing blanks.

"It's good to hear you say that," Nessie said. "There's a lot I still have to figure out. But I want you in my life."

"Same here." My heart surged again.

I wished for the millionth time that Nick would let me smoke indoors, city ordinances be damned. My fingers tightened around my pack, and I thought to go outside for a smoke, but this was too important. The phone could accidentally hang up on her as I was shuffling everything around. It would have to wait.

"Anyway, would you like my address?" I asked.

She was silent for a moment. "Let's meet somewhere public, busy."

Boy. That was strange. Was the FBI calling her too? Were they following us?

"How about Union Station? There's a bunch of new restaurants in there now, and I can't think of a busier place," I said.

She was silent for a moment, and I worried that Michael had come home.

"Nessie?"

"I'm here."

I took a deep breath, took a sip of my Bud.

"Union Station. That'll do. I'll walk and take the light rail."

"How about—hold on, let me google."

I looked down at my phone.

"The Mercantile Dining and Provision? Sounds kind of fancy, but what does it matter?"

"Sure," she said. "Tomorrow at five?" She was breathing pretty heavily on the other end, and I thought then about her heart condition. I felt a twist of guilt. I'd already caused one person's death. I certainly didn't want to cause another.

"See you then," I said.

We hung up, and I felt triumphant. I still hadn't heard from Debby, and that was weighing on my mind terribly, but I'd have to put that aside for the moment, focus on Nessie. Not only was this the culmination of everything I'd been working for, but it was also a way to satisfy the ghost.

I shook my head, pet the cat in my lap, who purred loudly in response, her orange fur soft and ratty at the same time. I was glad she hadn't leapt off my legs once I'd picked up the phone.

"Nick? Could I get a whiskey after all?"

It was time to celebrate a little.

CHAPTER THIRTY-FIVE

I woke up to the phone ringing.

"Fuuuck," I said to the walls, and sat up.

I'd been dreaming of my parents as I'd never known them—an intense, vivid dream full of color and light. My father was happy. My mother was wearing a bright yellow sundress, and the whole family was on a hill somewhere in the foothills west of Denver, the wildlife a nearly unspoiled paradise of tall heady-smelling pine trees, the swell of dirt we stood upon covered in bluebells, Indian paintbrushes, purple thistle, sage. I was six years old, my hand on my mother's arm, resting.

The phone rang again, and I blinked, trying to move through the fog, and concentrate. I thought I'd turned the phone off, right after I'd gotten home last night. Jesus, that thing was irritating. Who would be—

Then my heart started pumping, hard. It could be Debby. Or Nessie. Or the goddamn FBI for that matter.

I went to grab the phone, but in my haste, I whacked it right off my nightstand, and behind the bed, though I could hear it ringing insistently.

"Fuuuuck!"

I turned around and started clawing for it. I was sure it was Debby now. I could just feel it. Finally, my hand found the phone, and after several swipes, I was able to grab it, pull it up, and turn back around.

It *was* Debby.

"—Bad reception but I needed to call—"

"Debby, I can barely hear you. Are you okay?"

"—we're—the cabin—but—I—needed to tell you, Jack—"

"Debby, you're scaring me. I can't hear you. What's that? Something about Jack?"

"Trying—Kari, I—Jack, he—"

My heart started really hammering now.

While I was straining to hear what she was saying, all the horror movies I'd seen were moving through my brain. Movies where some psychopath gets a woman alone in the woods, threatens her, tortures her, and finally she finds a way to escape, running through the rain without her shoes, desperate, crying, calling out for her mother, God. Eventually, after hours of wandering—starving, thirsty, she gets to a road, every sound making her scream—thinking that she's lost and will die alone in the woods after all that effort she'd made to escape. The irony. Then she sees a car, and thinks she's saved. The car stops as she limps into the road. The door swings open, and she runs toward the car. Then she stops—and starts screaming. It's the fucking dude who'd imprisoned her, and he drags her into the car while she kicks and screams, right back into the prison she just escaped.

"Jack—threatening—and—scared—"

Then the phone went dead, and I got up, and went over to my couch and sat back down, hard.

I tried calling her back, but all I got was her voicemail, which frightened me even more. How was it that she'd been able to call me, moments ago, and now, suddenly, I couldn't get her back?

It was exactly what I feared.

I went to get a glass of water. I was sweating like hell. I opened the cabinet, turned the tap on, and ran the water, drinking gratefully when I was done. This was not good, and I had to think very clearly—if I didn't, Debby might pay with her life.

I started then to make myself coffee, my hands trembling as I fumbled for the filter, poured the water into the reservoir, shook the Folgers into the basket.

I had to wake up, and fast.

He was up there, with his guns, with the kids, and she'd gotten away and was trying to call me, maybe she'd walked down the mountain with her phone—I didn't know how she still had it, but that wasn't important—and she was in trouble. Jack was threatening her, and she was scared.

I wished I'd let Debby persuade me to get a firearm after all. That was the only thing that shithead, macho guys like Jack paid attention to.

I needed to call Aunt Sandy—I didn't know the address, but I knew she did.

I had to get up there.

CHAPTER THIRTY-SIX

Aunt Sandy, for God's sake, just give me the address," I said, my left hand cradling the side of my head, my coffee resting on the end table beside me, on the couch. I'd downed a full cup already, in the space of less than fifteen minutes.

"Are you sure she's even up there?"

"Yes, she said that she was at the cabin, and she said she was scared."

I'd already told her this. Multiple times.

"But Kari, maybe you misunderstood—I don't think Jack would hurt her or the kids—"

I sighed an exasperated sigh.

"Sandy? This is your daughter. Let's say I'm wrong. They'll tell me to get lost, and I'll get lost, okay? But I'm freaked out. You know how Jack acted the other day when he showed up at the bar. Was that normal? No. It was frightening. He's not himself right now."

I let her mull that over for a minute, then I started in again.

"Has she ever disappeared without telling you first?"

A long sigh. Then, "No, but—"

"Or not answer your calls for days?"

"Well, no—"

"Sandy, I'll call her the whole way there. If she picks up and tells me she's fine, I'll turn right around. If I get there and—"

"Okay, okay. But you didn't get it from me."

I agreed, though of course they would know that I'd gotten it from her. Who else would I have gotten it from?

"Thanks, Sandy," I said, writing it down, and then putting it into my GPS.

I took a quick shower, possibly the quickest of my life, then grabbed my bag, ran out the door, and got in my car, making sure I had enough gas to get all the way to Mount Evans, where the cabin was. I'd known it was in the general area—heck, it'd been in the family for years, I'd even been there. But I couldn't remember the exact address to save my life.

I had just one quick, necessary stop to make at a friend's.

Back on the road, I tried calling Debby again. Maybe I was wrong. Maybe Sandy was right. I hoped so. But no, nothing, straight to voicemail.

My mind was whirling as I got onto I-225, then I-70, the city eventually receding, the mountains appearing in the distance, fields of buffalo on my right. I loved stopping when I had time, hanging behind the fence, watching the old bulls, thinking about the fact that they'd used to cover these plains like a living brown blanket, the very life of a people. Now, they were mainly a tourist attraction en route to Evergreen, a town that had once, like Idaho Springs, been a rough little mountain town containing mainly cowboys and Indians—then hippies, now, mainly yuppies. Idaho Springs had followed, its sort-of-original inhabitants mere interlopers, hangers-on. That always struck me as ironic, considering most of their ancestors had come looking for gold, the driving force behind white settlement of the area. My own actually, on Dad's side.

I took the exit for Evergreen. I'd gone up countless times as a teenager to the Little Bear bar with Jaime. Like the rest of the downtown area, it was old-fashioned, preserved, with plank wooden floors, and an old Colorado feel. Part of downtown was sheer rock face, and you could stroll around—and I had many times, buying overpriced Indian jewelry, or eating at Beau Jo's, an import from Idaho Springs, and then wrap around under the bridge to the water-fall, completing my walk around the lake. Way into the fog of my mind, I distantly remembered my father taking me ice skating there in the winter. There had been a little log cabin where you could rent skates and get hot cocoa. The locals had protested its removal and won—but, its fancier, Aspen-like replacement dwarfed it now, a place where folks with money held their weddings.

The times that Debby and I had gone up to Evergreen were so different than the times Jaime and I had gone up. Jaime and I had hitched, then drove, stuffing drugs into our mouths, laughing around cheap bottles of beer to even cheaper jokes uttered by equally drunk, longhaired men—swirling on barstools, waiting for the band to come on, wondering who deserved a blowie in the bathroom, or if we'd end up partying way up on Fall River Road at home, or somewhere in the neighboring mountain towns after a show.

Debby and I had gone up to walk the lake. Get a mocha or a latte at the restored coffee shop that had been a moldy thrift store during my teen years. It had been returned to its former glory: the wallpa-per and plaster peeled back to reveal the rock walls that were part of a beautiful, brass and wood front lobby of an old, luxurious hotel. We'd sit there for hours on my day off, me telling jokes that would make Debby blush, Debby complaining about Jack and the kids until he'd call, whining about dinner, her eyes dropping. Us getting on the road to race back not long after, so that he wouldn't call her, drunk and yelling.

"That fucking guy," I said to myself, and an electric current of fear ran through me. I tried calling again. Nothing.

I went past the King Soopers, and took a right onto Mount Evans Road, where I'd be for a while. Debby had come from the other side of the mountain, however many days ago. I hadn't gone this direction in years, as generally I kept heading west on I-70 to get to Idaho Springs, instead of taking the turn right after the buffalo, heading into Evergreen.

Though I wasn't much in the mood to take in the sheer drop-offs, the long, wide chunks of rock and gigantic pine and blue spruce trees, the aspens shimmering in-between, the flashes of blue columbines, bright red Indian paintbrushes—I couldn't help it, it was that impressive. I kept glancing in my periphery at the gorges below where I knew the river ran, and imagining Debby's body at the bottom of them, and then shoving that thought out of my head as quickly as possible. I needed to cut that shit out. If I was lucky, Jack was just drunk and raving and I could talk him down, get Debby and the kids out of there.

"Shit," I said, remembering in a flash that I was supposed to meet Nessie at five. It was only noon, but I had no idea what I would find. My hand hovered over the phone. Should I call? What if Michael answered? He'd know something was up, and I didn't want him worrying about Nessie, and convincing her not to meet me. I'd just have to hope I'd get home in time. If I could get Debby away from Jack, then get her back down the Springs, settle her in . . . I tried doing the math in my head, but there were too many factors. I'd just have to see where I was at in a few hours, and I might have to risk a call.

I pulled into a long, dirt drive, my aging Ford hitting each pothole and bump, hard. At the end was Jack's rusty Jeep Cherokee, and Debby's Honda Accord.

I thought about the fact that Jack spent more time fussing over his car than he did his own kids—he was always under that vehicle, his hands covered in grease.

I parked, trying to ready myself for anything.

A scream pierced the air.

Running up to the cabin, I heard another, and my blood ran cold. I put my hand on the handle, and, taking a deep breath, opened it roughly.

Debby was lying on the bed, Jack, nowhere to be found.

The kids were rolling around on the floor, wrestling, and one of them screamed again. I sighed in relief as Debby shot up on the bed, Nosferatu-style, her expression going peaceful when she realized who it was.

"What are you doing here?"

"Your call?" I responded.

She jumped off the bed, told the kids to be good, and walked outside, herding me onto the front steps, and then down them as she shut the door. Right before she did, I could hear Jack, I assumed, rifling in the kitchen.

"I called to tell you that, Kari . . . didn't you listen to a word I was saying?" She pulled on the edge of her pink, long-sleeved T-shirt. This one wasn't bearing any sparkle-messages.

"Of course, I did! You were breaking up, but it was clear you were scared."

"Scared?"

"Yes, you said scared—of Jack."

She blinked a few times. Then, her eyes widened. "No, Kari. I wasn't—I mean, we are fighting. That's why we're up here, but I wasn't calling you to tell you I was scared of Jack. I was calling to say that, Kari, I can't hang for a while."

"What are you talking about?"

"We came up here to talk it out, but look, you're not going to like this but, Kari—he's talked with a lawyer. He's saying," and here she had to blink tears away, "he's going to sue for custody of the kids."

"And you came up here after he threatened you with that?"

I ran my hands through my still-damp hair. Why, why would she go along with this? There were times when she did things that were so beyond my understanding, she might as well have been born on a different planet.

"We came up here so we could get away from—everything, just to talk."

"Do you know how worried I was when I couldn't get ahold of you? When your mom said your cars were gone? When you called and all I heard was 'scared of Jack'?"

"Look, Kari, I'm sorry about that."

I snorted.

"Just listen to me, Kari, would you? He's given me an ultimatum."

My heart started hammering, and I dug in my jeans for my smokes. I pulled the pack out, fingered a cig out, and lit it.

"He's saying it's him or you."

"That's insane."

"It's not insane!" she yelled, throwing her arms out into the air, her hair wild.

I was taken aback. She never yelled.

"Debby, calm down," I said, taking a puff. "He's not going to leave you, and he's not going to take the kids."

Debby looked at me blankly, sadly. "He's talked to a lawyer. I told you that."

"What, for five seconds to some dude who came into the prison where he works? Come on, Debby, you know he's full of shit."

"You don't know that! Goddamnit, Kari, you think you know everything!" Her voice had risen almost to a scream, and she was pounding her fists in the air, her momentary calm gone.

Shock coursed through my body. I didn't even recognize her right now.

"I . . . I don't think I know everything," I said, "I just think that Jack likes to threaten you, that's all."

"Fine. But there's more," she said, tears beginning to stream down her face.

"Okay," I answered slowly, tapping ash onto the forest floor.

"He said that the lawyer told him that he could sue for custody, especially considering that the person I spend my time with, has a record. And is putting me—and potentially my children, in danger."

It was my turn to blink. "That's not fair. My record's old. And minor. And I'm taking care of things—"

"He said that I might never, or rarely, see my babies again," she said, her voice really trembling now.

"That bastard," I said.

I'd known he was a man-baby, I'd known he was selfish, but this? This was cruel. Evil, even.

"He said that if I didn't cut you off right now, he was gonna go live with Carl for a while, and that he'd take the kids, and that there wasn't a goddamn thing I could do about it. And that that's what the lawyer said."

I went quiet. I needed a minute to process everything she was telling me.

"That. That can't be true." I pulled the cigarette to my lips and inhaled deeply. I was worried as hell, sick in my heart. It was clear that Jack had really gotten to Debby this time, that he'd gone straight off the deep end.

"I mean, come on, he's just saying this shit. He lives for you, Debby."

"Kari, don't ask me to choose between you and my babies, cause I know even you would choose my babies over me," she said, wiping at her face and sniffling.

"This ain't a choice between your babies and me, fuck! Jack isn't going to do shit. Debby, he can't take responsibility for them even a little bit. He and Carl gonna raise them? Even gonna feed them?" I laughed, suddenly feeling almost giddy. "Carl is a drunk, and childish as hell. Jack shows with a couple of kids and that fucker's likely to cut himself, and if Jack has to raise them alone? Shit."

As soon as I said it, I knew it was the wrong thing.

"That's exactly right. He's not in his right mind, Kari, you know that. You saw the way he acted last time. But now? Jack is talking like I've never heard him talk. Divorce. Lawyers. I'm not saying he's right, but I'm telling you he's serious." She paused to glance back over her shoulder at the window, her brow furrowing deeply.

Her pain was so visceral, it was like it was coming out of her in a fog, seeping into me. "Can you please understand this? It's not about you, Kari."

Not about me? How was *any* of this about me? What in hell was she talking about?

"Debby, I wouldn't even be dealing with this stuff about my mom if it weren't for you pushing me. Pushing me to see that bracelet in the first place, when you knew goddamn well how I felt about my mother!"

"I—"

I shook my head.

Typical Debby. All hot to have a new adventure, until it inconvenienced Jack one tiny iota. She did everything for him, tolerated his temper tantrums, cooked, cleaned, all so that he could call her up and threaten her with the one thing that he knew he could scare her with. How small. I remembered how he couldn't even be bothered to come to the hospital when her first was being born. But how I'd been there the whole time.

"They're my babies, Kari, please. Please understand," she said, starting to cry again.

I closed my eyes.

"I'm sorry if I pissed you off," I said finally. I knew the deal was done. Jack would do anything to force Debby to cut everything in her life off so that he could be the only thing, and Debby would never challenge him on it.

"Thank you," she said, her tone short.

I smoked the rest of the cigarette while Debby looked down at her feet.

I saw something in my periphery then. Jack in the window, staring at me.

I couldn't help it. I had to try one more time. "I just don't think letting him have his way is smart. I need you on this thing, Debby—"

Her face crumpled. "That's exactly what you would say. It's always about you."

I flinched. That stung to my very core. I loved Debby. I'd do anything for her. *Had* done anything.

"You know what I was just thinking about, Debby? About how your husband, who, as usual, you're dropping everything for, couldn't be bothered to come to the hospital when you were having his kid! You remember that? Or have you forgotten who *was* there for you?"

I paused, taking the last sweet puff of my cigarette. "Because I've always been there for you."

Debby shook her head. "You would say that."

I narrowed my eyes.

"See, for me? I'm stuck between you two, that's how I see it."

I felt like she'd slapped me. "How could you say that?"

I stubbed my cigarette out on the ground, then plucked the box of cigarettes back out of my pocket and started packing them.

She sighed a long, frustrated, sigh. "You want to go to that place in Telluride. Jack wants me to stay home and hang out with him. You start talking about how much fun we'd have. He starts talking about how much he loves me. It's the same damn thing all the time!"

I had never, not once, thought about it this way.

I slid the pack back into my pocket.

"And as far as him not showing up at the hospital? You know what? He was dealing with a prisoner that day who'd shanked another prisoner. That man died, Kari. In his arms. And also, he showed for the next. You didn't. He shows up every day, making sure we have food on the table, making sure I get to my appointments that he drives me to, which you don't. Not that you should, because, Kari, you're not my husband."

"Debby—"

"Don't you Debby me! See, you have nobody because you have me. I love you, Kari, but you treat me like I'm your wife."

"I do *not*," I said, my face growing hot.

"I can't do it all for Jack, and the kids—and you. And for the record? I do love Jack, but if he weren't threatening to take the kids from me, even if he won't or can't, I'd be telling him that I'm going wherever you need me next, to see this thing with your mother through."

She paused to wipe at her eyes. "Because you know damn *well* I've chosen you over him, over my own children," she said, stopping, her voice cracking. "Many times," she said. "Way too many times."

My mind was reeling. I had no idea what to say to her, all I knew was that I felt angry. Angry and betrayed.

She was silent then, and we both went to glance at Jack in the window, who was looking increasingly furious. I wondered if he had his guns with him. He always had guns with him. In fact, I'd assumed that he did.

"Another thing, while I'm at it, is, like, you think you're so independent. But you're not. You rely on me."

"That's not true," I said, knowing it was a lie the minute it left my lips.

Jack opened the door then, coming out onto the steps. He closed the door after him and glared at me. "You need to go, Kari," he said, crossing his arms over his chest.

Damn, motherfucker couldn't help but butt in.

"Jack, let me handle this," Debby said.

"You're not handling it, you're letting her stay. Letting her get between you and me, and I'm not going to stand for it."

"You're such a controlling asshole, Jack," I said.

"Fuck you," he said.

"Both of you! Stop."

"Kari, I'm sorry I laid all of that on you. But . . . you needed to know. I just wish I hadn't had to tell you in the middle of all of this. The thing is, you can do it, Kari. You don't need me. You got your problems, but one thing's for sure," and here she paused to give a weak chuckle, "you're strong."

Jack snorted.

She waited for me to respond. I was keeping my eyes on Jack.

She shrugged. "So stubborn. Maybe you should spend your time thinking about what I said."

It was my turn to snort.

"And also, maybe think about why you won't buy the White Horse? I mean Jesus, Kari, you love that place."

I rolled my eyes. I wasn't about to take advice from a woman who treated her husband like her boss. I was done. I was more than done.

"Fine, Kari," she said.

"Don't be such a bitch, Kari," Jack said, his lips curling up into a snarl.

I started to make a move for him. I was ready to fight this fucker. He'd tormented my best friend for years, and now he was taking her away from me forever.

"Oh, you wanna go?" he asked. He began stalking down the stairs.

"Jack, no!" Debby said, throwing her hands up.

My heart was thudding in my chest.

"She better leave right now then," he said, stopping.

"You tiny dick man," I said.

His face turned bright red.

I laughed.

He began fumbling, his hands moving to the back of his pants, eventually removing a gun from them. "You threatening me? My family?" He began pulling the gun up.

"I thought it might be that way," I said, pulling a gun out from the back of my pants. I'd stopped at my boss's house, telling him that I wanted to borrow a firearm. He'd told me yes, no questions asked.

Jack's expression moved quickly into shock, his arm faltering.

"You're going to put that gun away, then I'm going to put mine away," I said. "Then fine, I'll go."

Debby started wailing.

"Kari, you stupid bitch!" Jack said.

"No, Jack," Debby said.

"For God's sake. Just leave, Kari," Debby said, a note of terror in her voice.

"I will when he puts his gun away."

I wondered if I should make a move for him, fake him out like in my old basketball days, and push or kick the gun out of his hands, or just aim my gun right at his stupid fucking head. But what if it backfired and someone got hurt? What if he or I accidentally killed Debby in front of her kids? I shuddered. There was enough of that kind of shit in my family. I didn't need more. And as fucked up as Jack was, I knew that Debby was right, the best thing for me to do right now was leave, call her tomorrow. I didn't want to make things worse. I wish she'd just confront him, grow a pair, but when it came down to it, this was who Debby was. A girl who still didn't understand her own power, who honestly couldn't imagine that she had more choices than two. And ultimately, she'd chosen him, not me. Though really, she was right: she'd chosen her kids.

Jack set his gun down and backed away, his hands up over his head.

Debby began sobbing hysterically.

"That's good," I said, putting my gun back in my pants. "But if you hurt her or the kids? I will find you, wherever you are, and I will kill you," I said. "Mark my words."

"You're the one who's hurting them, Kari," he said.

I laughed. What a fucking animal.

He walked back up the stairs, his eyes on me the whole time. He opened the door, holding it for Debby as she came up the stairs.

Up at the top, she paused, her back to me. I thought she might tell me she was sorry, or even better, that she was changing her mind.

"Kari," she said, her voice breaking, "I'm sorry, but don't call me." She shut the door, and I was alone.

CHAPTER THIRTY-SEVEN

As I came back down the mountain and turned onto the road that would lead back to the interstate, I wished I could stop at the Little Bear, for old time's sake. I needed a break. Another thing to think about when all of this was over. Honestly, I needed to do a lot of thinking when I'd taken care of the chaos in my life. The tides were shifting—though that kind of thinking made me uneasy.

I sighed. I figured I should call Sandy, let her know Debby was okay. It went to voicemail, and I told her that everything was fine, that I guessed I had been butting in after all.

Back on the highway, I realized that I hadn't put any music on. I clicked around on my Spotify until I found Guns N' Roses' *Appetite for Destruction*, and, knowing exactly what I was doing, started "Sweet Child O' Mine." A lump formed in my throat. It had been Jaime's favorite. Whenever she'd gotten all dolled up to go out, she'd played it, singing and singing in the mirror as she did, pausing to put her eyeliner on Idaho Springs style, which was taking a lighter, melting the black, and applying it to the underside of her lid.

The lump grew into a stone as I thought of her now, vividly, sitting in her trashed-up house. She'd been a foster kid, and every time

I went over, the place was swarming with children of different ages, doing, essentially, whatever they wanted. Whenever "Sweet Child" ended, she'd have me get up from the toilet seat, and go to the stereo, hit rewind until she was done getting ready. It was the opening lyrics that always got to me, and right now, they were slicing keenly into that part I kept tucked neatly away—that part that remembered not only Jaime's death, but her reason for going so hard in this life, the reason why she'd left it.

The opening bars to the song; their nostalgic, hopeful, yet somehow sweetly sad quality ripped into me, and I struggled to retain control.

She was fourteen, not long after we'd first met, when she told me that she'd gone from home to home, that she had no idea who her parents were, beyond their names and ethnic backgrounds—and that almost every place she'd lived, she'd been touched, against her will, by a foster brother, father, or friend of the family. She'd never thought she had a choice.

I remembered her telling this to me the first time, "Sweet Child" playing in the background, one hand artfully applying eyeliner to a lid. I had been looking at her in the mirror, sitting on the toilet seat, listening as her eyes showed no emotion—like it was just part of life. I'd told her that was some serious bullshit, and that she should just come and live with me. She'd smiled the way she did—a big, sweet, shy, sad smile—and said that her foster mom wouldn't allow it. She got a check each month, for each kid. She told me not to worry about it, because the last guy who'd done that to her here was in juvie now. And, she said, applying a long line of maroon blush, she was getting her GED, and that as soon as she did, she was out, and that I should come with her to Denver. Get a house. Never look back. I'd known the minute that she'd said it that, as guilty as I felt at the idea of leaving my dad behind, I was going to do it. I remember feeling like there was so much adventure ahead of me suddenly, that my life finally held some mystery, beauty.

The next few lines of the next verse of the song battered at my heart, badly. We'd had so much in common. Confusion when it came to our parents—almost a complete lack of authority, and mixed heritage—in her case, Black and Mexican. We'd bonded the way children do, without a thought, immediately, by pure instinct, and fiercely, until the day she died.

I started crying hysterically then, with no warning whatsoever, the car swerving and a big, white truck honking at me madly, the gun swinging off the seat and onto the floor. Dear God, I should've put it in the glove compartment—I knew better! But my mind had been such a mess when I'd left Debby and Jack's cabin.

I had to find a place to pull over, get myself together.

I tried blinking through the tears enough to see, and on my right was some space, not far actually, from the field of buffalos, a large, soft shoulder of dirt. I glanced quickly into the mirrors to see if it was safe, and I exited onto the right shoulder. I thought I'd feel calmer then, but as the lyrics finished, a kind of rage overcame me, and I hit the steering wheel with both fists, screaming, angry at Jaime for abandoning me, angry at Debby, angry at my father—and finally, angry at my mother. But after a moment, only guilt remained.

I quieted eventually, my head on the steering wheel, my arms crossed under it. I sighed, heavily. The storm had passed.

I lifted my head, and wiped at my eyes, ashamed I'd lost control.

That's when I saw the red and blue lights in my rearview mirror.

"For fuck's sake!" I said. "Really?"

That's when I remembered the gun.

I hastily threw my jacket over it, waiting for the officer to get out, and around, sweating like I've never sweated in my life.

He asked for my license and registration, and I fumbled for it, my hands moving over the slick plastic like I was in a dream, and while he was gone—for a long while, it seemed, I stared anxiously at the clock. It was now 3:45. I didn't have time to go home first. After this, I'd just have to head to Union Station directly.

That is, unless he found the gun. Then I had no idea what would happen.

When he came back, he questioned me, squinting cynically, as I told him that there was nothing wrong, but that I'd just needed to pull over to check the phone for an important text, and that I didn't like texting and driving. It took every ounce of willpower I had not to glance at my jacket, which felt like it was pulsing like a heart. I was just sure that somehow, the jacket had slid off the gun, and it was only a matter of time before the officer standing stiffly on my left noticed it and pulled his own.

"Do you have any marijuana, any drug paraphernalia of any kind?" he asked, narrowing his eyes slightly. The sun was just behind his shoulder, in the west, and I squinted as it hit me right in the eyes.

"No, sir," I said, blinking.

He was silent.

I could swear he was looking at my jacket. Or that he thought that the reason I was blinking was because my eyes were dry from smoking up—he sure had asked that one without any provocation. It felt like there were insects crawling up and down my arms.

Jesus. What if he took me in, and I missed Nessie? What if I gave Michael just enough time to figure out where she was, get her not to meet me after all? What if the officer shot me?

"Do you have any open containers of alcohol?"

"No, sir."

That last one really pissed me off, but I kept my cool. I couldn't give him any excuse to go off. Not one.

He was silent again. There was no reason for him to give me a ticket, and I could tell he was frustrated. I didn't even have a taillight out, a hangover from my wilder days. I hadn't just done drugs back in the day, I'd sold them for a while, and the last thing you wanted when you were a drug dealer was an excuse for a cop to pull your ass over.

"Have you consumed any alcohol?"

"No, sir. I haven't had one drink today."

"Not one, huh?"

"No, sir. I don't drink and drive."

The irony of this statement was that it was completely true. I hadn't done that since I was twenty-four, to be exact. Not since the day of Jaime's death.

He looked at me, cocking his head. He was white. About mid-forties. And I had no idea what his deal was, but I couldn't help but think if I'd been young and white, he would've asked me a few questions, sure—but mainly, he would've asked if I had a tire out, and could he help. I was ambiguous-looking, but I knew how these things worked. You weren't Indian-looking enough to pass some rando's idea of what an Indian looked like, but if you were brown at all, you were brown enough to have a cop fuck with you.

"You drive safely now," he said finally.

I was so relieved I was afraid I was going to faint. Or at the very least, piss my pants.

"Thank you, sir," I said, the sweat crawling across the small of my back like a living thing.

I waited for him to pull off and onto the road before I took a deep sigh, and did the same, my wheels spinning in the dirt as I moved from shoulder to road.

This was why emotions were bullshit. You couldn't let them have control of you. You had to stuff them deep inside, and leave them there, sealed. I'd turned the music off when I'd seen the officer behind me, and I kept it that way as I drove.

I needed to focus.

Massive shit was at stake, and I had to pull myself together, and get on it. In about an hour and forty-five minutes, my life was about to change.

CHAPTER THIRTY-EIGHT

A new silver hybrid cut me off as I exited onto Wynkoop, and I yelled at the driver. It was 4:40. I had a little time but finding a spot downtown near rush hour to park that was close enough was going to be something. Jesus Christ, this Denver-becomes-LA thing was trying my patience, especially now. I circled Union Station a few times before finally, something became available. I hovered near it, my blinker on, other cars honking at me, sliding my ancient black Ford in, after a few awkward tries, into the vacancy left.

I fed the meter and starting walking, rapidly.

As I came up on Union Station, the bright, new coffee shops that surrounded it, the big, red marquee above, I thought about the fact that even though Union Station was technically over a hundred years old—what I was seeing now hadn't really existed until a few years ago. Now, there was a fancy hotel, a bookstore, bars. The vaultings were high and beautiful, with larger-than-life white, dewdrop-shaped chandeliers lining the ceiling. Every single restaurant was a yuppie's wet dream. And you could catch the light rail, the bus—and go anywhere from here. In some ways, Denver had always been a major hub. But now? It was a nexus, and this spot was the shining nexus of the nexus.

But when I was a kid, you couldn't even catch the train in Union Station. Downtown, in general, had been a dusty, dirty place where bums begged for money. Well, that part hadn't changed—not that I had anything against bums begging for change, I thought guiltily, busting through the front door, and into the fancy lobby. It really was a marvel.

I decided to take the stairs, the Terminal Bar on my left, the letters in gold, the sound of people laughing, clinking long, expensive wineglasses in my periphery. I shook my head and tried to move as quickly as possible as memories of me and Debby sitting in the bar flooded my consciousness. She loved new things, fancy things, and had dragged me to it the second it opened. But I didn't have time for memories now, or regrets. And I figured I had to be at least a few minutes late, and I didn't want to make Nessie nervous. This had to be nerve-wracking as it was.

I took them as speedily as I could, my long legs moving upward easily, and fairly quickly, I could see the sign for the Mercantile Dining and Provision. I glanced down at my phone. I was only ten minutes late. That wasn't so bad. I stopped. Ran my hands through my hair and inhaled. Rubbed under my eyes in case any mascara was still there from my episode in the car. I didn't want to seem any more out of place than I already would in that joint. I approached the large, metal sign with the name etched into the center, and made my way in. There was someone up at the front, and I told them that a "Nessie" should be waiting for me. They told me, after a strange glance that could only be aimed at my tattered gray jeans and Of Feather and Bone T-shirt, to follow them.

The bright light-wood tables, blue chairs, dark wood, and tile floors made me self-conscious—this wasn't exactly the White Horse—but I was beginning to feel that the letdown and shock of this day was at least going to turn around into something better, redeemable. I'd talk to Nessie—

I stopped dead in my tracks.

It wasn't Nessie waiting for me at the table. It was Michael, his legs spread wide, his expression grim, sitting right at the table I'd been led to. No wonder the waiter had given me a look—I'd assumed it had been about my incongruous outfit. But it was because he'd been told to send me over to someone who was clearly not a Nessie. I'd have been curious too.

We both looked deeply out of place in this golden masterpiece of a restaurant, me with my heavy metal getup and him with his pseudo-cowboy one, his big, black hat on the seat next to him, one hand on his shell-button-up shirt.

My stomach hit my socks as the waiter told me to take a seat and I worked like hell to regain my composure. I didn't want Michael to see how uncomfortable he'd made me. I needed to hear what he had to say.

"Bet you didn't expect me," he said soberly, awkwardly. One long, square hand on his shirt lightly fingered a button.

"No, I didn't," I said.

Michael's eyes were hollow like he hadn't really slept, his wrinkles somehow deeper than I remembered.

He took a sip of what appeared to be a beer in a tall glass. It was half full. He'd been here for a while.

The waiter asked me what I wanted, and I told him a Bud, if they had it. He looked like I'd asked him to bring me a pile of shit, but he nodded, and left.

"So, what's up?" I asked, my eyes narrowing in confusion.

Michael deftly struck one long leg over the other, gently pulling the cuff of his Levi's over his boots. "Nessie told me you two were going to meet up."

"She did?" I asked.

"She did. Nessie . . . you don't know my Nessie. She just can't keep a secret."

Suddenly, I worried for Nessie. "But you can?"

I thought he might lose it there, as his face contorted, briefly, into anger, but he pulled himself together and it was as if I'd never seen that expression at all.

"Let's be nice," he said. "No need for accusations." There was a faint edge of distaste to his voice. "I think you've got some ideas in your head that I can help get straight."

"Is that so?" I answered.

"It is. See, you don't know me. And you don't know Nessie."

"You said that."

I was interrupted by the waiter coming back to hand me my beer in a long, tall glass. The beverage sparkled in the golden lighting of the restaurant, the effervescence moving upward as I took a sip.

"Thanks," I said, setting the glass back down. "They say Miller's the champagne of beers," I said to the waiter. "But it's Bud."

"I'll be right back to take your food order," the waiter responded, the corner of his mouth turned up in disgust, his rich, dark hair looking like it'd been lacquered into place.

"I don't think we'll be eating," Michael said.

"Just drinks for you then?"

"Yes," he answered.

I briefly wondered what was in Michael's glass. Nessie had said that he didn't drink anymore, but I figured it could be a non-alcoholic beer. Or not.

Michael watched the waiter leave, and then settled his eyes back on me, his expression belying his irritation, displeasure.

"See, because you didn't grow up with Nessie, you don't know that she suffers from more than a heart condition. Her family," he said, interrupting himself to take a drink, and then continuing, "suffers from delusions."

I blinked, rapidly.

"Delusions?"

"Yes. Nessie ever tell you her grandmother saw things?"

I remembered back to one of our last conversations, when I'd shared that I had visions, that I'd seen the ghost of my mother—she'd told me her grandmother had too.

He was watching me intently. "I see that she has."

I let him speak.

"Her grandmother didn't see into the other world or have *visions*—whatever you want to call them—she ended up in a sanatorium because she was insane," he said, with a flip of his hand. "A state sanatorium, where if you're poor and brown, well, that's where you end up. Very sad," he said, flicking an invisible piece of dust off his jeans.

"Her family tried to care for her. Listened to her about what she was seeing, her sightings, some even took her seriously at first. Your grandmother's people were prone to that sort of thing," he said, sighing deeply, "and she could be quite convincing. But eventually, it all became too much. She was destructive to the people around her." He shook his head sadly. "And her family—well, my family, had to do what was best for everyone."

The place was spinning. I'd remembered when I'd first started having my visions—I thought I'd had a brain tumor. Was it possible that I was just coming into a family inheritance of brain damage, insanity? My God . . . maybe Nessie had been imagining things too, and Michael was just trying to help her. Maybe she'd done this before, and he'd had to have similar meetings with people over the years.

I slid my hands down my glass, feeling the moisture, trying to let the familiarity of the wetness calm me. I took a shaky sip.

"I can see you're thinking about what I'm saying," he said, re-crossing his legs.

The waiter came back and asked if he wanted another.

"I do."

"Another O'Doul's?" he asked.

"If you please," Michael responded smoothly.

A non-alcoholic beer. Shit. He was sober. A good guy who just wanted to protect his wife and the people around her. Maybe I was just causing trouble. A flash of what I'd gone through at the cabin, with Debby and Jack, went through my head. They'd thought I was just causing trouble too. And I'd been wrong. Jack hadn't been holding Debby hostage, she'd gone there willingly.

My stomach began knotting up, and I felt like I was floating.

I took a deep breath, closed my eyes for a minute. I needed to think, and clearly.

"O'Doul's?" I asked.

"Don't drink anymore. Beer, scotch, was my thing." He sat back. "Look. I got to tell you something you won't want to hear." He stopped, tapped his jeans with one long finger. "But you—you've pushed me to the point where I have to. It's why I'm here. For Nessie's good, and for yours."

"Go on," I said.

"Your mother? Like I told you back at the apartment, she liked to hang with the wrong people. But what I didn't tell you, is that sometimes she liked to rile people up. Bad."

The waiter came back with another beer, taking the old glass and sliding the new one across the table. Michael sipped.

The heady, hoppy scent of the drink floated up from the new glass, and I took a sip of my own beer now, my curiosity—and nerves—building.

"Rile people up? My mom was doing good shit with her life. Shit that she hoped would make life better for other Indians. Shit she got in trouble for," I said, thinking of the call from the FBI agent.

He rubbed at his eyes, tiredly. "Yeah. That's what all of them say." His eyes went to his lap, then up at me. "Haven't you ever wondered why your daddy went drinking and driving?"

I sat back like he'd slapped me.

God, I wanted a whiskey.

"What the hell are you talking about? He was just—just—sad about my mother. About her going missing. And how'd you know that?"

"I lied back at the apartment. I knew what happened to your daddy."

I opened my mouth, and then closed it. What was going on?

"Those girls got drunk sometimes. Pushed men. It breaks my heart to say it, but Cecilia—she and your daddy used to argue, hard."

"I don't believe you," I said.

He lifted his hands, put his elbows on the table, and flattened his palms together in a Christian prayer position. "Don't you get it?"

"Get what?"

"Your daddy," he paused to shake his head. "He's the one that killed your momma."

My mouth went dry. I felt like I was going to pass out. And then, I stood straight up, my chair upending behind me, people around us turning around to see what was going on.

"Shut up," I whispered venomously.

"You need to sit down," he said. "Now."

Slowly, I turned around, picked my chair up, and sat.

"You asshole. You lying asshole. My daddy's a good man—"

"He *was* a good man. But your mother was always in trouble. Always dragging him to that political Indian crap—he and I both didn't want her to go to that goddamn Indian Center. To those pro-tests. But she wouldn't listen. And they argued about it most every day. And he put up with it. Until he didn't. Until she took it too far."

I thought about pulling my gun out. Shooting him then and there. God, I hated him.

"Till one night, they got too drunk."

I shook my head silently. "Lies."

"He told me himself. Called me up. I helped him get rid of the body. My own . . ." and here his voice gave out for a moment, "my own child's body."

I looked around at the people in the restaurant. Their white faces. Their mouths, vibrating with laughter. I felt like I was falling down a black hole, one that had no bottom. This man didn't know my father. My father, the one person in the world I knew I could trust. But then I thought about his pain, his guilt, the fact that he'd gone drinking and driving until he destroyed himself. I closed my eyes. I felt like dying.

"No," I said. "No."

I straightened up. "Why wouldn't you let Nessie come, if this is true? Why wouldn't you let Nessie tell me this?"

He sighed heavily. "Because she went crazy when Cecilia died. Retreated into that world of visions, just like her grandmother and mother before her. It pushed my poor Nessie off the edge. She helped me hide her daughter's body. She loved that girl more than anything. I—" he said, his voice breaking again, "I did too."

I shook my head, over and over. "I don't believe you. I want to talk to Nessie."

"Nessie?" he said, recovering. "Nessie would've just told you it was some—some monster. I told you. She suffers from delusions."

I felt blood rushing to my head, and I put my hands down on the table, clasping at the edge, my fingers going white. I thought about how Nessie had worried that I'd think she was crazy over the phone. I felt crazy. The world felt crazy, upside down.

If what he was saying was true? My whole life was a lie.

"You think about what I said." Michael drained his beer in one gulp, slapped a twenty on the table, and stood up. "I don't need you making trouble for Nessie. And you don't need to be doing this to yourself, either. Let it go. Let my daughter rest."

"You . . ." I started but couldn't finish.

"I did everything I could to hide the truth from you. But you just had to know. Well, now you know."

I watched him leave, the sounds of the bar a cacophony, senseless, my mind a morass of pain, confusion. And pure, unadulterated grief.

CHAPTER THIRTY-NINE

am sixteen years old when I break Debby's heart.

I have never forgiven myself.

Jaime and I have been partying on Fall River Road for days, way up the dirt road past town, into the mountains at my friend Sam's house. Sam's house is great, because there's no one around to hear us blast heavy metal, hear us drag kegs up from the trunks of our shitty cars at night, hear us scream and laugh and yell and fight and fuck, hear us go wild in the woods.

I've just done so much crystal I feel like a tiny god, and Jaime is right there with me, lying beside me on one of the couches in the basement. We'd come back from partying at a biker's house a few days ago, another dealer who we'd traded with. He'd given us something new, something so beautiful I feel like I will never come down again. Like I am not only seeing the blue light that surrounds the couches Jaime and I are laying on, but it's now a part of me, like it's coming out of me, out of everything, everywhere. Like it is all made of blue light.

Like I am made of blue light.

I can see it, I have tiny fairies in my lungs, and every time I breathe the light flows out of me in streaming waves. I ask Jaime if she can see the fairies, and she says that she can. I stretch my hand out to hers and she takes it, and there is light in our mutual grasp. I imagine the lights moving out of the room, into the house, blowing like a good, blue wind, out the door and all the way down Fall River Road and into town, into the cracked, uneven sidewalk, past the Victorians and the brick houses that are falling apart, past the grocery stores where people are shopping for Twinkies and potato chips and lunch meat, where the blue light moves into their hands, where it moves into their eyes.

And now they feel holy. And now they feel clean.

We are celebrating the fact that I've just gotten my GED, that I am ready to move out of Idaho Springs, and down into Denver with Jaime and her friends. We have a house on Broadway near everything I love, there is a nurse that can take care of Daddy, and I have a job, and I sell drugs, and I have money, and I feel so good that I don't even notice Debby coming in the door at first.

By the time I do, she's yelling at me, chastising me, asking me if I'm happy like this.

I tell her *I didn't know you cared.*

Jaime laughs.

I laugh too, though I nearly forget what's so funny the minute I make Jaime laugh.

Debby tells me that she'd been downtown and someone had told her that I was here, doing crystal. I feel a pang of guilt, because I am, because somewhere inside of me I know that I am hurting myself in ways I can't undo, but then the lights roll over me and I suddenly can't hear the words she's saying, just her little, pink mouth moving, and I wish that she could see what I see, but she can't.

I know that, and she knows it, and there is nothing more to this moment than that.

When I think about it, which is hard, I wonder, *Why now?* I've been coming up here for years, and she's never showed up, she's never given a damn.

And then I realize I've said that out loud but it's true, the lights tell me so. I let it stand.

Debby's lip trembles and I feel a break in the light and resent her for it so much. I need the light, and she's trying to take it down, take me away from it. What she doesn't understand is that for the first time in my life, I don't hurt, and I plan on keeping it that way.

Debby tells me that she knows I'm leaving the Springs and she knows if I do, I'll die. And that she's not going to let that happen.

The irony is that someone does die, my very heart, my Jaime. Or is it an irony at all? Isn't it just a cold, hard fact? Not that I know that at the time, in fact, I can't even imagine it.

But she does die, and after that, there will never be a time that doesn't hurt, that it doesn't need to be a thing I push down and down and down.

Get lost Jaime tells Debby.

Debby tells her to shut her stupid mouth. That she's not going to let her drag her cousin down with her into the dark, that she's tired of being silent, and that I'm coming with her right now, or she's calling the cops.

There's something about that, that's so funny that I laugh and laugh and laugh, and I laugh so hard, I fall on the floor and roll. God, I feel so much better. The lights are back in control, and they're whispering at me, they're telling me things I can't say out loud because they're not in a language that can exist outside of the light.

You think they care about us? I ask her, once I finally stop laughing. *Because they don't.*

Debby stomps her foot in frustration. She knows I'm right.

I try to get outside of the light enough to reason with her, get her to go away. She doesn't belong here, and she doesn't belong in my life. She hasn't for a long time.

Look, I'll be fine. I'm celebrating.

She tells me to get my things.

I roll over.

She starts searching for my bag, and when she finds it, I ask her if she could hand me my cigarettes.

Jaime laughs again, that rich, musical laugh of hers.

Debby says she will not, in fact, she's going to throw them away.

Don't you dare, Jaime says. *I'm sick of your ass already.*

Debby narrows her eyes, and I can see the red blooming behind them.

Wait—I say.

Shut up, you piece of trash, Debby says.

Jaime's face moves then, into a place of deep hurt. It's that face I've seen when people call her words that are about her Blackness, one of the things that is so beautiful about my best friend. Something that in this town, she has had to fight to value, and I wonder, I wonder if Debby feels that kind of way, and God I am so angry the lights are afraid.

This is when I snap.

Get out of here, I tell Debby.

Her lip trembles.

I don't want you here. You and me? We're nothing but a blood connection. If we weren't related, you wouldn't even talk to me. And if anyone's trash? It's you.

I stare at the walls. The light has fled.

Get out of here before I call my friend Sam, and he and his friends kick you out, I tell her.

I can't look at Debby, but I can feel the pain radiating out of her in waves so thick it's filling the room.

I fear the lights will never come back now, and I am afraid.

Kick your precious ass right out, Jaime says, coughing hard and long after.

I laugh, but I feel like shit. And vaguely, I'm worried about Jaime's cough. She's been coughing a lot lately. But I decide not to worry about it.

Debby's there for a long time, for what feels like an eternity, and

I wait and I wait, and I just want a cigarette now. I tell her again that she needs to leave, that nothing she does is going to stop me from living the life I want.

You're throwing your life away, Debby says, stomping up the stairs.

Thank God. How do you even stand her? Jaime asks.

I don't anymore, I say, feeling like something inside me is breaking. It is.

CHAPTER FORTY

What?" I asked blearily.

"Kari, table number five has been asking for refills for thirty minutes, and you're just standing here in the kitchen, staring at the goddamn wall!"

"I'm sorry, Roger," I said, shaking my head. "I haven't been sleeping—"

"I'm tired of hearing that excuse, Kari! I'm beginning to think that you're backsliding, or—"

"You fucking *dick*," I said. I regretted sharing that particular piece of my childhood with him. We'd bonded one night after closing. I wished we hadn't.

He was silent, and Martín, who'd been tying the trash bag, paused, watching me—his eyes flitting then to Roger, my shift boss.

"You're done. Get your shit and go."

Caroline, who'd been coming up to get an order, had also paused to watch. "Roger, come on. Cut her a break. She's just having a hard time."

"She's been late every day—sometimes as late as an hour—for two weeks straight. I'm fucking pissed at you, Kari, but I gotta be honest," he said, pausing to push his sleeves up, "we've been talking about letting you go for a while now."

"Fine," I said, walking back, "you know where to send my last check."

Caroline argued with him—that one surprised me—but it was too late. I didn't care. He was right. Besides, I had savings. No college debt, plus no kids, plus an almost complete indifference toward expensive clothing or vacations had allowed me to put quite a chunk away for the past twenty years, ever since I got my GED when I was fifteen and moved to Denver. And my boss at The Hangar had been pushing for me to take more shifts anyway.

All of this ran through my head as I pulled my locker door open, got my purse, and walked out—but at the same time, the nervousness spread in my gut. It wasn't just the shit with the ghost, it was the memories of Jaime—I'd spent years pushing my guilt down. I should've done something. She'd looked terrible for a year before she'd ODed. But I'd been too busy getting high, being selfish. And now she was gone. And it was my fault. It was clear to me now. If I had done something, she'd still be alive.

CHAPTER FORTY-ONE

n my dream, I'm walking behind my mother. We're in The Stanley Hotel, in the famous blood-hallway. The smell of rotting meat is everywhere. It's dark, and I can barely see in front of me, the light from the lamps flickering. She's rushing with me, and I am small—maybe six years old—my hand in hers, our footfalls echoing hollowly, passing door after door, each one open slightly until we start to pass it, shutting violently as we do. I can hear the roar of the Lofa in the distance.

Finally, we stop. Room 413. She turns, and the door opens, slowly, creaking. My stomach begins filling with fear, with dread. She shoves me quickly into the room, and I yell in a high, panicked voice for her to join me, to *hurry, Mommy*! She shakes her head and pulls something up in front of her. She plants her feet firmly, her face a mask of determination. In her right hand is an Apache war club. This is when the Lofa roars, moments later appearing around the corner, my mother's arm pulling back.

I wake to my mother in the window, the curtains billowing around her, her eyes white, her hands at her side.

She begins to mouth something. To step closer to me, and though I'm filled with dread, I strain to listen.

"Father," she whispers, full of sadness, and then she's gone.

CHAPTER FORTY-TWO

Daddy, I'm going to go away for a little while. But Camila is going to take good care of you, so don't you worry, okay?" I said, guilt—and confusion—washing over me like a tidal wave.

He watched the TV, the blue light playing over his face. He probably didn't even notice that I was there. He'd been less responsive lately. I rested my hand on his arm, and he seemed, for a moment, to almost turn my way. But perhaps that was just wishful thinking.

"You remember Camila, right, Daddy? Your favorite nurse."

I always say she's his favorite because he seems to fight her the least, when it's time to go to bed, or brush his teeth—really, when it comes to everything. Camila is tall, and brown, and super-smart, and I wonder if she reminds him of Mom, of Cecilia.

I pat his back, hoping he hears me.

It was hard to touch him at first. After what Michael had told me, I'd gone through weeks of denial. I'd stopped visiting. And then when I did, I'd screamed at him like I hadn't since I was a teenager, asking him point-blank if he'd murdered Cecilia. His only response was to moan her name, again and again, my memories of when I'd been young, and he'd first gotten into his accident surfacing in my mind, the images of his head in bandages, my guilt over not wanting to have anything to do with him at first. And then it would all circle back to that question: did my father murder my mother? Or was it something else entirely, and the FBI had been following me—like at Lakeside, where I'd felt eyes on me everywhere. But why would my mother matter so much to them, after all these years?

I was heading to The Stanley Hotel. Though everything that Michael said made terrible sense, the dream I'd had with my mother in The Stanley was powerful. Maybe there was something there for me—a clue, or maybe something that would help me gain closure. Maybe it was just a chance to get the hell away from everything.

"Sandwich, Daddy?" I asked.

Usually, this stirred him. But nothing.

I sighed, deeply.

"Okay, Dad, I'm going to go."

I glanced at my phone. 11:47. I still had plenty of time to make it up the mountain before dark.

He didn't move.

"I love you, Dad," I said, my voice breaking. I did love him, even if I didn't know what I believed anymore.

He seemed to stir a little then.

At the door, I turned around.

He was still staring at the TV as if it was the only thing that existed in the world. There was an episode of *Different Strokes* on, and Willis was strutting around his mansion with his fists at his sides, his mouth puckered. Daddy loved his reruns. I was about to close the door when I heard something, and the hair on the back of my neck spiked.

I turned back, and I saw her, Cecilia. No blood. Eyes dark, and soft. Whispering in Daddy's ear, a smile on her lips, and his.

"My God," I whispered.

She looked up at me then and disappeared.

CHAPTER FORTY-THREE

On I-70, I couldn't help but obsess over what I'd seen at Dad's house. Had she been there, all those years, whispering in his ear? Telling him she forgave him? I vaguely remembered thinking she was a ghost when I was a little girl, before Dad's accident. I shuddered. The way he would talk about her did that to me—always, of course, in the past tense, always with such sadness—such guilt. And every action of his, leading up to and culminating in his accident was in reaction to her disappearance, or so I'd thought.

One thing was definite: after his accident, I hated her.

I took the turn onto I-93, and then I-36, which eventually led to Boulder, and I couldn't help but laugh, despite my sour mood. God, I'd sold so many drugs to the college kids there, and they had been so rich, I'd overcharged time and time again. And then me and my friends would party like rock stars.

I passed Golden on my right, and thoughts of Dad's accident couldn't help but blossom forth in my mind, no matter how hard I tried to push them down, away. How after, he seemed to be in another world. Perhaps he was. Maybe that was when he'd started being able to hear Cecilia. Maybe sometimes he wasn't staring at the TV, but at her. Maybe that accident had damaged his brain but split the border between this world and the next wide open—at least for him. I recalled his leaning in to listen to mom's ghost, her image flickering in and out in that old, sad house. Or maybe it'd just been his guilt.

The sun was just beginning to set, and I hit the accelerator. Those roads up the final stretch were something, with massive, sheer drop-offs on either side at times. I didn't want to drive them in the dark if I didn't have to.

I thought then about my visions—or delusions. The fact that I hadn't been able to see Mom until I'd touched the bracelet. And though I didn't have brain damage—that I knew of anyway—there were things, like Jaime's death, that had changed me, had ripped me open pretty good. And things embedded in me that I didn't know about, things I guessed I'd inherited from my family. Or I was just crazy, like Michael said. It all added up if I took his word as truth. I mean, why *hadn't* Daddy gone further in trying to figure out what happened to my mother, if he hadn't killed her? Why had he gone drinking and driving to die if he wasn't filled with guilt? I'd always thought he'd lived for her. That he couldn't live without her. But maybe he'd just been unable to live with his own sin.

My mind came into bright focus then. Maybe that's why the FBI was calling me. Maybe she had been on lists—then disappeared—and perhaps they'd thought there was something suspicious there, though usually they didn't seem to give two shits if a Native woman disappeared, like Fredrico said. But if they did—maybe they suspected the truth, that my father, I thought, with a lump in my throat, had killed her and my grandfather had helped him to cover it up. And then I had to come along and file a Freedom of Information Act—stirring this whole thing up, and potentially bringing the federal government right to Daddy's door. My stomach twisted.

I focused on the road ahead as the pavement began to really climb, trying to move my head in any other direction than the idea of the police putting my daddy in handcuffs—and failing. Shit. Even

if he had killed her . . . if Michael was telling the truth, I didn't know
the full context. It sounded from what Michael was saying that they
got drunk, argued—maybe it was an accident of sorts?

I shook my head violently.

I thought of one of the opening scenes in *The Shining*. The
family—Jack, his wife Wendy, and their psychic kid were winding up
a highway meant to look like this one—it wasn't though, that highway was in Montana in Glacier National Park. The view had been
bird's-eye, a mass of pine trees on either side. And you just knew,
from the creepy music, that shit was about to go down.

Carefully, I searched for the soundtrack on my phone, and put
it on.

My mind started to move into the space that was *The Shining*;
thoughts of my mother, father, melting away and re-emerging as
the much more manageable ghosts born out of King's imagination.
Though I loved everything by King, I'd always found this particular
book to be spellbinding. I remembered finding it in the library one
day, after wandering the shelves, my fingers brushing the spines, trying to convince myself to check something more realistic out, something more patently educational, and failing—and moving, like I was
haunted, toward the horror aisle. For some reason, I hadn't seen this
book before, and finding it, a King I'd never read, felt like uncovering a magic key, one with infinite potential. One that opened doors
that acted as portals to other worlds. Elated, I brought it to the front
desk, and from the minute I started reading, felt like most people feel
when they're falling in love.

I had my copy packed in my old, brown suitcase.

I was getting closer. On my left were the sheer drop-offs I'd
thought about earlier. I was used to it, growing up in the mountains
as I had, but it was still awe-inspiring. I knew that many people had
lost their lives on mountain roads like this—in fact, a boy a grade
above me in high school had decided it was a good idea to go drinking and driving one night and had missed a turn.

I shuddered.

On my left now was a gigantic lake, and despite myself, I cracked a smile. It was huge, and sparkling in the sun, surrounded by the lush green of the forest.

I was almost there.

A few more turns and I was parking, and dragging my suitcase out of the back, rolling it up to the massive, white hotel. It had been beige in the movie, but that's because in the film, Kubrick had based it off a hotel in Oregon—the whole thing had been filmed in England.

I pulled the suitcase up the steps, and with a deep breath of cool, fresh mountain air, opened the doors, and shut them firmly behind me, taking in the red-carpeted floors, the old-fashioned décor as I stepped into the hotel I'd been reading and re-reading about since I was probably twelve years old.

The line for check-in was long, and there were crowds milling in and out, some of them here for the historic tour offered during the day. A lot of them were wearing American flag T-shirts, leather vests. Then, there were the families in Nikes.

Finally, I was up. "Kari James," I said, walking up to the desk and setting my suitcase to the side, "checking in for room 413."

"Very good," the clerk answered, giving me a little smile. An ex who worked here had fixed me up. I'd told him I wanted 413, as that was the room my mother had brought me to in my dream. He'd said that was the most haunted room—on the most haunted floor—in the hotel. My ex had also gotten me a steep discount. Then asked me to go back out with him. I told him I'd give him a call when I came back.

Behind the clerk was a wall of old-fashioned, metal keys. Leaning in, I noticed that room 217's key was more ornate than the others—and flipped the opposite way, and I felt a brief flash of regret. That had been King's room.

The clerk finished checking me in, and to my disappointment, didn't hand me one of the metal keys—instead, it was your modern standard, a plastic card.

"Thanks," I told him.

I wasn't normally dazzled by splendor, in fact was generally disgusted by things that in any way seemed to cater to the rich, but the lushly carpeted floors that I'd noticed when I first came in, the rich, leather furniture, cozy fireplaces and numerous rooms off to the side—a restaurant, gift shop, and the ballroom—were impressive. There was even a carriage up front, reminding me that for most folks, this place was a cute, cozy, reminder of how they thought the west was won.

As I passed the steps on the way to the elevator where I knew the ghost of the man who'd built the place was often seen, I saw more black-and-white photos—and mirrors, all in ornate, gold frames lining the walls—some of groups of people in various western-style settings, others of singular persons of importance.

The elevator was small, the door ornamented, gold.

I rode next to a family on the way up. The parents were both looking at their phones, the toddler attempting to punch the buttons, over and over, the mother pushing his arms back without even looking up.

On the fourth floor, I got out and looked around. There was something about it. Something heavy. Though I was sure that was just my head playing tricks.

"Here goes," I said at the door.

I slipped the card in.

There was a large, dark-wood sleigh-bed, and a matching desk by the window, where a stand-alone air-conditioning unit sat. There was a gigantic armoire, and, opening it, I found a television. I opened the closet and put my case down on the stand. I sat down on the bed, glancing at the bathroom.

I laid down, sinking into the thick, fluffy mattress.

I looked, briefly, in the corners supposedly haunted by the angry white man. Nothing. I got up, unzipped my suitcase, and put the copy of *The Shining* down on the desk.

I giggled like a kid, my spirits lifting, and started walking over to the bathroom—in 217, it's where the slutty zombie had laid. Who knew what was in this bathroom? But halfway there, I paused.

"Really?" I said out loud, blinking rapidly.

It was astonishing. There was a large, elaborately carved wooden arch between the room and the bathroom—of a Native American scene.

I leaned in.

"What the—"

I would've thought it'd be a battle scene—white settlers fighting bravely against Indians—or at the least Lakota chiefs in headdresses portrayed romantically, stoically. But no. It was Apaches.

There were four men in head scarves, leather vests, blousy shirts, and leather pants. An equal number of women in long, traditional skirts and blouses circled by concho belts, their ears and necks containing silver and turquoise necklaces and earrings. The desert was in the background, with mesas and scrub brush and tall saguaro. The wood was dark, polished, and though it looked old, it was somehow vibrant, as if the tree had been chopped weeks ago, the figures nearly pulsating, their strong limbs almost meaty in the dim light.

"I don't remember this in the book," I said, scanning my memory, thinking about my dream. This had to mean something.

I shook my head. I supposed that not everything in the hotel would've necessarily ended up in the book, but still—considering how obsessed King was with Natives, you would've thought it would've gotten a mention, and if it had, I would've certainly remembered it.

I shrugged and continued my journey over to my original goal— the bathroom. God, that scene—in the book, and the movie, had stuck with me.

The bathroom of course wasn't the green tile I remembered from the film. Instead, there was a creamy white clawfoot in its place—though again, different room. The room my mother had been in, in my dream. I stood over it for a while, recalling the moment in the movie where Jack had gone in, finding a beautiful woman sitting in the bathtub who he, naturally, decided to make out with. Right before she turned into a slutty old zombie. I chuckled.

Really, it was one of my favorite parts.

I pushed the curtain aside, looked out the window, stared in the mirror, and finally sat on the toilet seat.

Disappointing as it was, I felt nothing.

My mind wandered back to my father, my conclusion that the FBI might be mounting evidence against him after all these years—and that it was all my fault, if so. I called his nurse Camila, just to check on him, make sure he was okay. He was. No cops. No agents. Just Daddy and his bologna and lettuce sandwiches, his reruns.

I lay back on the bed. Even if he had killed my mother, I knew in my heart that it had been an accident, and that I didn't want my poor, damaged father to go to jail. It seemed unlikely that after all this time, and just because I'd filed that paperwork, that the feds would be looking into her disappearance. But still. I'd be on edge for a while. And I still felt that there was a reason I was here. The hotel thrummed with something, something I knew pertained to me. Otherwise, why had my mother appeared in my dreams in this hotel, in this very room?

Back downstairs, I wandered until I hit the ballroom—thinking about the scene in the book where Jack hangs with the ghosts from the '20s, then maneuvered around to the main floor, passing the gift shop, the stairs, check in, and a fireplace where I thought I might take a whiskey later. Things had calmed some, and I felt like a drink, so I walked over to The Cascade. Though it was still packed, after a few minutes a couple left, and I took a seat. The bar was long, and wooden—but its surface was a kind of yellow, milky, glassy substance, the shelves behind lit up, the center three tall mirrors, with wooden polls in-between, framing the mirrors. I thought again of the Native carving in my room, thinking that I'd have to re-read, looking to see if there was any description of anything like that. I'd brought the book with me to the bar, as per my usual—and pulled it out of my bag.

I ordered a whiskey and looked around. I had no idea what to look for. If there was anything *to* look for. Maybe that dream had been the result of something I'd remembered from the book, something that hooked into my delusions. Perhaps coming here was the last thing I should've done.

I took a sip, put my head in my book.

There were families, mainly, a few couples, a handful of single men at the bar—and one or two of them didn't look half-bad, though I wasn't here to hook up. I wouldn't mind it, but I wasn't in the place where it'd do me any good, I could feel that.

I glanced at the mirror. I looked tired. Hollow-eyed.

"Another?" the bartender asked.

"Sure," I told her. I hadn't realized I'd drained the first.

She smiled, and brought me another pour, giving me an extra drop or ten—which I appreciated.

"Cheers," I said, lifting my glass. "I'm a bartender."

"Oh?"

"Nowhere fancy as this, but yes."

She seemed nice. Like the kind of bartender you'd have to be at a place like this. My foul-mouthed, super-direct, heavy metal–loving personality wouldn't go over well here.

"I had a feeling," she said, smiling.

I gave her a funny look.

"I mean—that you were a bartender. One gets a sixth sense about these things, after a while."

She went to attend to someone else, and by the time she was back, smoothing her short, brown ponytail with one hand, she could see what I was reading, and smiled.

"I didn't mark you as book person."

"Don't look like a reader?"

She cocked her head. "No."

I liked her. "Something about black jeans and a heavy metal T-shirt doesn't scream nerd?" I said.

She laughed. "Well, if it's any consolation, if I'd known you were a reader, I would've guessed horror. Me too. It's why I started working here. That, and I'd just left my boyfriend."

"See any ghosts?"

"I have," she said, nodding.

"In room 413?" I asked excitedly.

"Not personally."

I leaned back, disappointed.

"But the cleaning lady has. She can tell you all about it, if you can catch her in the hallway tomorrow morning."

I made a mental note.

She attended to another customer, and I put my head back in my book.

"I did see the ghosts on the stairwell," she said.

I hadn't realized she was back and startled.

"Sorry," she said, "didn't mean to freak you out. Happens a lot around here."

"The ghosts?" I asked, to get her going again.

"Nothing special, I'm afraid. But yeah, I've seen one of the women who descend the stairway. Oh. And I've heard the piano. And on the fourth floor, I've had things pull at my clothing—pinch me. One lady who was in 413—that's your room, correct?"

I nodded.

"She woke up to the man in the corner. And a long scratch down her leg," she continued with a smile. "But you'll hear all about that if you're taking the tour tomorrow night—you're doing that, right?"

"Oh yeah," I said, sipping, and making a mental note to thank the ghost in my room for letting me stay there. And I'd get a spirit plate. I mean, it's what Auntie Squeaker would want me to do.

"You like working here?" I asked.

She looked around. She had a cool, calm, peaceful way about her. "I do. I mean, I'd like to own my own place someday but," and here she paused to sigh deeply, "lost most of my money to my shitty boyfriend."

"I'm sorry," I said. Good God. Sometimes it seemed like my dad was the only good man I knew. Or he'd seemed so. Or he was. I wasn't sure about anything anymore.

A couple of guys in greasy-looking T-shirts, one sporting a motorcycle and the other, an angry-looking and comedically patriotic hawk, were waving her down. She nodded at me, and I cheers-ed her with my glass, and she went over to them.

I thought about what she said. What it would be like to come to work not as a worker, but as the boss—as the owner of a bar. When I'd gotten over Jaime's death, or at least, as over it as I was ever going to get—that had become a goal of mine. Owning a bar. But over time, I'd pushed it to the back of my mind, thinking that it would come later. I was happy to have a job, an apartment, happy to be alive, mainly. I liked my life. And when the thought would surface, usually when Debby would push me about it, I thought with a frown, I'd think I wasn't ready. It *was* a huge responsibility. But I had enough in my account to put a down payment on one. And when was later going to come? I was thirty-five.

Specifically, I had money to buy the White Horse. Nick wanted me to buy it. Poor soul was going senile. There was no way he'd hang on to it for much longer. And Debby was an asshole, but she was right about one thing: I did love that joint.

I looked around at this super-fancy bar, at the people happy to be there, sipping their drinks, laughing. The White Horse would never be as opulent as this place, but it could be something.

I ordered another whiskey when the bartender came back, deciding that it had to be my last. I needed rest. I had a lot to do. The tour, maybe a bit of poking around and, I decided with an excited swing in my stomach, calling my bank up, and then Nick. I was going to see what would happen if I tried to buy the White Horse. I mean, I wasn't going to for sure—I needed to really think about it, but just the possibility of something new and good and completely different in my life made me feel marginally better. Even slightly celebratory.

I tipped my drink to the air in front of me and drank the whiskey down.

CHAPTER FORTY-FOUR

The Stanley Hotel—or, the Overlook, in your favorite novel, and mine," the tour guide said, winking at the crowd, "was built in 1909, by Freeland Oscar Stanley."

It was 9 PM—and for the first time in weeks, I'd slept like a baby—though I had peered pretty intently into corners of the room every time I'd woken up, looking for the ghost of the angry old man who might try to scratch me. I'd spent the day reading, then drove up the mountain to take a ride on the Aerial Tramway, which looked down and over the town of Estes Park. At the top, I'd walked around a little, fed the chipmunks, thought more about whether I was insane, and if my father killed my mother—and then I bought a T-shirt.

The Shining Tour had me feeling like a kid in a candy store. The only thing spoiling it was the guy who looked to be in his late teens eyeballing me like I was a hunk of sausage.

"It was mainly a resort for folks like Stanley—as a member of the upper class, and an easterner, he saw this as a retreat for sufferers of tuberculosis like himself. The air, he felt, would help clear them of the symptoms."

"Get *on* with it." It was the kid I'd noticed eyeballing me earlier.

I glanced over, catching sight of a lip ring the size of a small planet in his bottom lip.

"Shut up," I whispered menacingly.

He looked taken aback, but clapped his mouth closed.

"In any case," the guide continued, "today, of course, it's mainly famous for—you guessed it!—the filming of *The Shining*."

A number of us nodded.

"In the book," Dale—according to his name tag—gestured to the short hedge, "this hedge is made into hedge animals, which turn into monsters. But Kubrick changed that into the giant hedge maze scene in the film, where Danny outwits his father. That wasn't the only difference between the two. King placed his ghost in room 217, and Kubrick, in room 237. There were many differences, and King wasn't pleased about any of them—he did his own film, that's much more faithful to the book."

People nodded, and a few of us took pictures.

"Let's move to the Concert Hall, shall we?" he said, gesturing, and the group of around fifteen moved up the stairs, and into the hotel. We'd started in the basement where there'd been a bunch of goofy props, like an ancient, black, Underwood typewriter with a piece a paper with the words "All work and no play makes Jack a dull boy" placed crookedly in the spindles. Someone had wondered aloud if it was the one from the movie. I'd rolled my eyes. There were also posters of the film *Dumb and Dumber*, which apparently had been shot in The Stanley.

Behind me, I could hear the lip ring kid whisper, "God, your ass is hot."

I turned around and looked him dead in the eye. "This ass will cut you if you don't shut the fuck up."

He closed his eyes and bit his lip. I thought I heard a short moan escape.

Jesus Christ.

"The Stanley is on the National Register of Historic Places but," he paused theatrically, "it's known—thank you, Mr. King—for all of its ghost stories. The Concert Hall here," he gestured, "is considered to be the most haunted of all of the properties."

His accent sounded German—maybe Austrian.

"Cool," I said, wondering if we'd see anything creepy, if I'd see anything to indicate that I wasn't insane, that my mother had actually been visiting me, that there was a reason she'd led me here.

"The grounds have a number of ghosts who, if you're lucky, you might see on this very tour! The groundskeeper, Paul. The homeless woman, Lucy, and numerous children. Who might follow you to your rooms."

The big, beefy men in the back laughed nervously.

"Sleep tiiiiight," the guide said, pushing and tapping his spindly fingers together.

I shuddered. Creepy kids were a consistent theme with King. I was creeped out by children even *before* they died.

"Is it true like they said in the movie?" A dude who looked to be in his sixties asked. He was wearing a cowboy getup, and even though he was white, his apparel's resemblance to my creepy grandfather's gave me the heebie-jeebies.

Dale paused, his hand on the staircase. "What part are you referring to, young man?"

"The part where they say that this place is on an Indian burial ground."

The crowd murmured.

Oh God.

"Well, if you know King, you know he sure did love his Indian burial grounds. They're in several of his novels. But as far as I know, The Stanley was not built on an Indian burial ground—nor did they have to repel any warring Indians." He chuckled.

Fuck me. This was the one thing I *knew* had nothing to do with my mother.

"It's all Indian burial grounds," I said, wishing I'd never said it, the minute it came out of my mouth.

Heads turned.

"What's that, young lady?" Dale asked, his expression sweetly inquisitive.

"Never mind," I said, just wanting to get on with the tour, though I did suddenly remember that in the film, the guy who showed Jack around mentioned that the designs were based off Navajo and Apache patterns—which had not been in the book, not to my recollection.

"King was influenced by a number of writers, such as Poe," Dale said, "but these days, most notably Shirley Jackson's *The Haunting of Hill House*."

I hadn't known that.

"However, his biggest influence was his stay here at The Stanley, in room 217," he said, leading us up. "King based his novel—*The Shining*—" he stopped to wink again, "on a real-life ghost encounter. Mainly, it was just a dream. A dream he had about killing his own family—just like in the film," Dale said, moving to a loud whisper, "and in the book—but it's said that King did, indeed, see a ghost. After his encounter, and dream, it's said that he went for a smoke, and by the time he finished, he had the entire plot for *The Shining*."

People muttered.

"Anyone staying in room 217?" Dale asked, arching one thin, brown eyebrow.

A couple raised their hands.

The guide smiled. "Sleep tiiiiiight," he responded in his high-pitched, accented English.

The Concert Hall was empty. The guide told us that ghost children often appeared on the long, wooden stage where all kinds of famous musicians had played. He let us explore before taking us into the basement—into Lucy's room. Lucy had been a young, indigent girl who'd been kicked out into the snow, where she'd died. Many had seen her ghost in the bathroom and by the closet door.

"Yes, that closet right there," Dale said, pointing to an open door that a man was standing in front of.

"That one?" a teenage girl asked.

"Yes, the one that young man is standing in front of," Dale said expectantly.

The tall, burly guy stared, his only response being to blink stupidly.

Several people craned their heads, and aimed their phones for a picture, but the guy in front of the door still didn't get the hint, and Dale moved on, shutting the lights off. He placed lollipops in our palms, invited Lucy to tip them over.

She didn't.

We moved to a room with a long mirror, and a cutout of the infamous twins from the book. People took pictures, sticking their heads into the cutouts, the teenager who was into me asking Dale to take a picture of him with his face in one of the holes, his tongue out and vibrating back and forth, his eyes on me the entire time.

Fucking teenagers, man.

We passed the Lodge, the room built for women to stay in on our way back into the main hotel, where the guide explained that lecherous ghosts supposedly haunted the hallways. One of them supposedly even drank the whiskey out of the glasses of the guests.

Migrating back into the main hotel, and up to the fourth floor, the guide spoke about the infamous scene in the bathtub.

I knew the fourth floor as the infamous "blood hallway"—the hallway where the creepy twins appeared to Danny, the hallway where blood came from seemingly nowhere in a number of shots, flooding the hallways, pushing the chairs aside, splashing the sides of the walls.

"The fourth floor is said to be the most haunted in the hotel—with not only numerous children in the rooms and hallways but," and here Dale paused for theatric effect, "there have also been sightings of furniture moving around. And people have felt ghosts tugging at them."

It was here that I kept my eyes especially peeled, as I'd remembered being in the hallway in my dream.

"Sure, dude," the lip ring kid said.

I turned around and gave him my most intimidating glare.

He responded by moving his tongue up and down, rapidly.

"I'll cut that thing out," I whispered, clearly upsetting a few of the people around me, one older white woman drawing her hand to her chest. I merely twitched my eyebrows, up, then down, in a what-can-you-do gesture.

"And most horrifyingly," the guide continued, "in one room, a cowboy that watches you as you sleep, from the foot of the bed."

I could hear several people murmuring again.

"Could you imagine waking up to that?" the guide asked.

"Who's in that room?" Dale asked.

A father and son combo raised their hands.

The guide smiled. "Sleep tiiiiight."

"Now we'll be moving to the basement," Dale said, gesturing toward the elevator. It took a while for all fifteen of us to get down there, and I made sure not to pile in with the creepy teenager. I wasn't afraid of him. I was afraid I was actually going to cut him somewhere vital and end up in trouble.

Getting out, and joining the rest of the crowd, Dale moved us past numerous boxes of wine and cheese, olives and pickles and other supplies, and at the front of what looked like entrances to a series of large, dark, tunnels.

That was interesting.

"These were the service tunnels that the staff used back in the day, to go from building to building."

Dale paused, allowing folks time to snap pictures with their phones.

"They were haunted by a cat," Dale said.

There was silence. Clearly, this had not had the effect that Dale had been looking for.

"A cat?" a woman asked from the back.

"Yes, a cat," Dale responded petulantly. "It wanders."

"A cat," the woman repeated, derisively.

"It had green eyes that would glow in the dark," Dale finished lamely.

People muttered in disappointment, and that's when Dale pulled the big guns out. Pictures of people on his tour with creepy, glowing-eyed figures behind them. I wasn't sure that I bought it, but the basement was freaky as hell.

We moved on to a room with a gigantic mirror leaning against one of the dirt walls of the tunnel Dale had led us down. Like the ones upstairs, it was ornate and gold. And there was something a little ominous, spooky, about the thing. I had to admit—I was extremely drawn to it. I loved haunted mirrors, and often looked at them on eBay, wondering whether it was stupid to order one or not. Perhaps this was it. Maybe I'd see something in the mirror, something important.

"If you want to take your picture in the mirror, you might be able to see a ghost in it, right beside you. Many have," Dale, said, drawing his fingers up toward his face and twiddling them rapidly together again.

There were murmurs, and I could tell the crowd was impressed.

I glanced over at Dale. He was grinning from ear to ear, and it was clear that he'd redeemed himself.

People began taking turns, and I thought, why not, and took mine. There were noises of disappointment though, as people looked at their phones, and saw nothing but themselves. A couple tried again, and at one point, a girl thought that she could see something in the background. We all looked, and one or two agreed, saying that there did seem to be a white, floating object above her shoulder.

"Maybe it was the cat," I said, and the girl glared at me.

The lip ring kid, however, crowed with laughter.

Shit.

"Moving on," Dale said, this time herding us up the stairs, and, as we got to the first floor, speaking to us about the women some folks saw there, the same story I'd heard from the bartender the night before. He also talked about the piano. I'd wondered what she meant by that— apparently, the man who'd built the hotel had a wife who'd played piano, and supposedly, she haunted The Stanley with piano music.

People took photos, some of them, again, swearing that they saw something in them, the girl who'd seen the object in her photo claiming that she heard faint piano music. We all paused to listen, while the guide checked his phone.

"So," Dale said finally, our last stop is right over here—the ballroom. This is much like the room where Jack speaks to a ghostly bartender," his voice crawled, once again, to an ominous whisper.

"This room used to be where the men, sorry ladies—would play pool. Many ghosts have been sighted here: maids, brides—and more children."

People walked around, snapping pictures.

"This is where the tour ends, but it comes with a complimentary whiskey—so you can be just like Jack. Except, of course, for the murderous obsession," he said, winking a third time, the crowd chuckling appreciatively.

I headed straight for the bar. Just as I'd sat down and ordered, my phone rang.

"Hello?"

"Ms. James?" It was a male voice.

Dear God. Was it the FBI? Were they calling about Daddy? What had I done?

"This is she," I said, feeling sick.

"Wonderful. This is Chris Beauvais."

"Okay," I answered warily.

"From Canvas Credit Union?"

It took me a minute, but then I remembered.

"Right!" I'd made a few calls that morning, first, to my bank, and secondly, to Nick at the White Horse—he was totally down with the idea of me buying the bar and making him part owner. I'd told him we should talk more about it, and then I had to really think it through first, but his enthusiasm had translated.

"I'm calling to let you know that your credit check went through, and all is good. We're emailing you some paperwork right now."

"Sure," I said, feeling nervous. "I really do have to do some more thinking, but I'll get that to you by tonight," I said.

"Wonderful," he responded.

I hung up. Asked for my whiskey.

As I drank, I thought about what I was doing. I should be happy—I was moving forward in my life, I was doing something that would make me more than just someone who went to work every day, though the White Horse did need a lot of work. Nick had really let it go, and not only would I have to put time into the building, but I'd have to put time into the management—and more than that, into advertisement. If I decided to go through with it. But if I did, maybe that was the thing to focus on—not the past.

I sighed. This is where Debby would've come in handy. She'd majored in business and could help me with the books—and knew everything about social media. I felt sad then. I couldn't believe that this was it for us. I lifted my phone. Nothing. I wished I could tell her what Michael had said about my father. About the call from the FBI. I'd always valued her opinion, even if I teased her for it. She'd been right about so much. She'd been trying to tell me I needed to face my shit over Jaime, and I'd brushed that off too. I'd depended on her for far more than I'd realized. I ordered another whiskey and listened to the sounds of the people getting drunk all around me, laughing, telling stories, flirting—connecting with one another in a way that I'd only learned to do with one person, besides Jaime. Now both of them were gone.

CHAPTER FORTY-FIVE

I sat up in bed, and scooted back against the headboard, scrolling through my photos. They were all of Debby. There were countless photos of us in the putt-putt apartment. Funny photos that didn't make sense, like of our feet. Photos of food—Debby loved those. At Lakeside. I moved through each one, struggling to find a photo that wasn't of Debby and me. But there weren't any.

If Debby ever decided it was okay to talk to me again, I'd apologize. I hated the way she let Jack use her as a doormat, but it wasn't helpful for me to judge her, make her feel like shit about being with him, push when he pulled. Maybe I just needed to listen to her—though in all honesty, I wish she would draw some hard boundaries with him. And I probably did need to try to make more friends. It wasn't fair to Debby for me to make her the only person I relied on, socialized with. Other than Debby, the only people I talked to were my dad, Nick at the White Horse, and the little orange tabby that lived there. The prospect filled me with dread, but something about working all of this out left me finally sleepy, and after a few more pages of *The Shining,* I drifted off.

I think I was out for a few hours before I heard something at the edge of my consciousness and stirred.

I sat up abruptly. Someone was in my room.

My breath short, I tried to let my eyes adjust to the moonlight.

I heard a sound. My eyes darted.

The hair on the back of my neck spiked. Was it my mother?

It was coming from the bathroom.

"Oh shit, oh shit," I whispered, thinking about the slutty zombie.

My eyes adjusted.

It wasn't the bathroom, it was the huge, wooden arch in-between the bedroom and the bathroom—the Indian carving, the one I hadn't remembered from the book or movie, the one featuring Apaches. It was moving.

I sat up. The figures—both the male and the female—were looking at me—right at me, and they were gesturing for me to get up, a low whispering in Apache as they did. I'd taken an online course in Chiricahua years ago—and it was close enough to the Navajo I'd heard spoken around me growing up to know what it was, if not exactly what they were saying.

But then I heard it.

They were saying my name, whispering it, among other words.

Kari, they whispered.

"Oh shit," I repeated.

They wanted me to come to them.

My heart thudding, I got up, and started walking toward the wooden figures, praying to Mustaine that whatever they wanted, it wasn't bad. It didn't feel bad.

I stood by the arch, and the minute I stopped, the whispering ceased, and the woman in the forefront of the carving looked right at me and pointed.

I followed her finger, and a beam of moonlight shone directly on a part of the carving. The carving was of a mandala, with the four directions, a star at the top, a symbol for water at the bottom, and on one side, the sun and mountains, the other, the moon and arrows.

Kari, I heard, and looked over. She was still pointing.

Following my instinct, I pushed on the mandala and wood began to separate from wood, the mandala part moving outward. When it stopped, I looked in. There was something in there, in a hollow space that had been carved out of the wood. I couldn't see it though, it was buried in shadows.

I wondered if this shit was like *Dune,* and I'd reach in and there would be pain. Or maybe it'd be spiders, or—

Kari, she whispered.

The oval started to move back in, and quick, I put my hand inside, and felt around. It was an object of some sort, and it was stuck. It was long, whatever it was, and made of stone and wood.

I struggled to get it out as the oval began to close, frustration circling my heart, terror that whatever this was, it was meant for me, and I was going to lose it. I grasped, worried I'd break whatever it was.

Finally, my fingers curved around the object and pulled it out, right as my hand would've been squished under the closing wood.

I stared at what was in my hand.

It was an Apache war club, and it looked identical to the one in my dream.

CHAPTER FORTY-SIX

W hat the . . . fuck?" I said, one hand on the doorsill.

After I'd gotten the war club from the mandala, the figures had stopped moving, as if they'd never started in the first place.

I'd switched the light on, looked at the arch again, placed my hands over the mandala, and, tentatively, over the figures, but nothing. If the war club weren't sitting on the end table, I would've thought I'd dreamt the whole thing. Jesus, I knew more shitty Indian jokes than I knew shit about traditional Apache objects.

I paced my room for what seemed like hours after that, occasionally staring up at the arch, searching my memory—and Google—for everything on Apache war clubs. I'd done some of that when I'd had the dream, but now I was really beating the internet up.

I stopped in my tracks. "I'm so *stupid*," I said. "Auntie Squeaker." She'd at least told me something, though I was hoping for way more now.

I pulled the phone up and stopped. Auntie Squeaker didn't believe in phones. I closed my eyes. "When I get back. I'll bring this to her as soon as I get back."

I'd finally drifted off to sleep, though I don't know how—my phone still in my hands.

But now, in the clear light of day, the wooden arches, the carving of Apaches—was gone. Even though I'd seen it the first time I'd walked in here—in the daylight—it was gone without a trace.

"Michael is right. I'm crazy," I said.

I'd woken up only a few minutes ago and stumbled to the bathroom. It was on the way back, in-between the bathroom and the room that I'd noticed that the entire arch wasn't there anymore.

But was the war club still there?

"Oh *shit*," I said.

I ran over to the bed, stumbling halfway on an abandoned pair of jeans in the middle of the floor, and searched for the war club. If I didn't find it, it was time to fundamentally recognize that my dreams were just the start of what was a slow but inevitable slide into crazy-town.

"Fuck!" I said, tearing through the blankets and sheets, after I'd seen that it wasn't on the end table.

I stopped.

It was right there, right on the end table on the opposite side of where I'd been sleeping.

"I'm not insane," I said, looking at it.

Now that there was daylight, I could see how old it was, though it was in weirdly pristine condition. The club part was stone, and strapped with sinew, to a large, leather-coated stem—made of either bone or wood by the feel of it. At the end of the stem was a long spurt of black horsehair with a pile of black and white feathers tied to it. They looked to be eagle feathers.

"Maybe I have a really huge brain tumor, that's making me hallucinate this whole thing. Maybe I'm in a hospital, dreaming this shit up," I said, genuinely entertaining the possibility. I'd had a friend die of something like this in high school, and she'd been in the hospital, unconscious, for months before she finally left the Earth for good. I'd always wondered what she was dreaming.

Hesitantly, I picked it up, and turned it over in my hands. I started to get a funny, buzzy feeling, and right as I was about to drop it, I entered the tunnel and—

Everywhere around me was blood. Everywhere around me was screaming.

I carried the war club in my hand, and I was running across a field, whacking enemy after enemy as they came for me. I would not go to that place, that San Carlos prison the Americans had designed for our people, to live soft and die.

I slammed my club into another and watched as blood spurted out of his arm. I moved on, not letting his screams deter me, my shotgun also at my side. I led my men closer and closer to the Mexican border, where my relatives were living in boxcars far up in the mountains. They were making the medicine I had known before all this—the medicine I still held—before the Mexicans had killed my wife and children. Before the Americans began hunting my people like game. There was one medicine man living in the mountains reputed to be able to cure the bad, rotting disease. He had cured a Chickasaw, and I had seen it. She had come on a burro; her husband had been one of my men. Her husband had been related to Zapata.

I avoided bullet after bullet, I had only taken one hit, and I could heal myself with the medicine I kept, and my men if they made it. I could bring a storm down if my spirit was strong, and I could see where they were coming from next. The east. I could see them as easily as I'd seen the Americans in my camp all those years ago.

I had powers, and my children would have these powers. And their children.

I looked down at my war club, and it flashed. I smiled.

CHAPTER FORTY-SEVEN

See, this is why I'm very, *very* drunk," I was telling the bartender, who I could sense was seriously considering cutting me off.

"Because of a . . . war club?"

"Yeah, it's in my room through," I said, slapping the wooden bar. "Never mind," I paused, waiving my hands wildly in the air. "I probably shouldn't have told you that."

"Okay."

I sighed. After I'd had the experience with the war club—and I was getting really tired of visions—I'd googled around. The things that I'd found online made me think that I'd seen through Geronimo's eyes, who, apparently, had also had "the shining," to use King's term. In other words, like me, he had visions—and, he had healing powers as well.

What I couldn't understand was what the war club was doing here, in this hotel. I knew that my relatives were Chiricahua Apache—so the Geronimo thing made sense but, how had the club gotten to a resort hotel in the mountains in Colorado? I knew that the Apaches had at times occupied this state, but an archway . . . in a hotel . . . which didn't exist anymore?

I was at a loss. What good was this fucking thing going to do me anyway? It couldn't get me Debby back. It couldn't show me what had happened to my mother, or heal my father's brain enough so that he could either confirm or deny what Michael had said, so why had my ancestors seen fit to give it to me? And why not just make the damn archway appear in my apartment? Did my ancestors know I really, really, loved Stephen King? And was there still a way to heal Daddy?

The bartender brought me a glass of water.

"Thanks," I said.

"Been there," she responded.

I gulped it down gratefully. I'd only had three whiskies, but these days, I was a lightweight.

I'd left the war club in my room; it was way too valuable to be carting around. And I didn't want to be thrust into unexpected visions of my ancestors, anyway. But then again, maybe if I'd brought it, I could've confirmed by showing it to the bartender, that it was real. Maybe I should go get it?

I needed a smoke.

I trundled outside, sat down on one of the white, wicker chairs and lit up, feeling much better as the nicotine hit my veins.

I watched families and couples move in and out and tried to relax. I would be checking out tomorrow morning, and there would be more paperwork, when it came to the transfer of ownership of the White Horse.

That was exciting. Or it should be. If I was going to do this.

I still felt confused, deflated, images of what I'd seen through Geronimo's eyes flashing in front of me as the smoke curled into the cool night air. I'd googled too, about the wife and child. Apparently, he had lost them early on to Mexican soldiers who'd raided his camp while he was gone. How awful.

I took one more puff, stubbed my smoke out, and went back inside.

As I was stuffing my pack back into my bag, my fingers brushed against something unfamiliar.

I settled back in, and opened my bag up, rifling through Chap-Sticks and receipts, to get a better sense of what it was.

"Oh wow," I said. "That's right."

It was the pictures of my mother that Nessie had given me, when I'd knocked on her door, gotten her to let me in.

I started thumbing through them. I guessed I'd left them in there, and just not remembered—so much had been going on.

They were Polaroids, the thick white edges surrounding the images, the saturated colors that spoke to the life of someone who was long gone. It was sad, really. So much waste.

Here was one of my mother at what looked to be maybe six years old, sitting on an old-fashioned, flowered couch, a fat, brown baby at her side.

But wait . . . wait. A baby?

I thumbed to the next. Here was another, my mother looking to be around ten, and there was a girl of about five at her side, who looked a lot like her, standing by The Cyclone at Lakeside. Next to them was Michael, his hands clasping at the gears—perhaps he'd worked there? I flipped the picture over. Sharon and Cecilia, it said, in what I assumed to be Nessie's handwriting. My heart began to hammer.

I moved to the next one. My mother was posing, a corsage pinned into her long, filmy, pink dress, standing at the bottom of stairs, the arm of a young man in a blue tuxedo around her, his smile awkward—I guessed he was Native or Mexican. There was still a hint of sorrow in her eyes, but there was joy too.

In the next picture, my mother, looking to be in her late teens, had her arms around the girl who was most certainly the same girl from the second photo, in almost matching orange and yellow outfits, their arms around each other. Sisters, it stated.

I looked closer. I recognized those chairs, those bookshelves, those vaulted ceilings. This was the old Tattered Cover! On the back it said, "Sharon and Cecilia."

I flipped. The next one was at Orr's, also with her sister. They had been attached at the hip.

I flipped to the last, my hands shaking. If I was right . . . yes. Another picture of the two girls—in The Stanley, right in front of one of the gigantic fireplaces, my mother sitting in an old-fashioned chair, her hair dyed blond, and permed, her sister and parents—Nessie and Michael—standing around her. My God.

Every time my mother had tried to give me a clue, a hint of some kind, either the Lofa—or Jack for that matter, had run interference before I could make any real connection.

But Cecilia had a sister. A sister named Sharon.

Sharon—the name my mother had whispered.

In a flash, I remembered something Michael had said in the restaurant that I had glossed over at the time. He'd said, "they." Girls. Plural.

That thing that had been bothering me almost since this thing had begun came rocketing to the surface. It was almost as if I had known it the whole time on some level, though it astonished me to think about the fact that Nessie had never mentioned her. Or my Aunt Sandy. Maybe my mother hadn't mentioned her for some reason? I shook my head. It was too much.

Why would Michael keep the fact that he had another daughter from me? Unless he were hiding something. Unless he'd been lying to me.

My heart started hammering again. If Sharon was still alive, and I could track her down, *she* could tell me more about what had happened to my mother, if she was willing. Of course, I didn't know for sure that she'd want to help me.

There was only one way to find out.

I pulled my phone up and clicked the calculator. My mom was twenty in 1981. I looked at the pictures again, squinting thoughtfully. Sharon looked to be around five years younger than my mom. That would mean . . . she'd be about fifty years old now. I started with the Denver area. There was no reason to believe that she was still here, but no reason to believe that she wasn't.

Jesus Christ, there it was: Sharon James. 50. Denver, Colorado.

There was even a last-known address.

There was one other thing, something that had been pulling at the edge of my consciousness. I closed my eyes. The smell. The smell of scotch that almost always accompanied my mother's appearances. My eyes flew open. Scotch! That's what Michael had said his drink of choice used to be, when he tried to convince me that it had been my daddy that had murdered Cecilia.

I cashed out and went up to my room, my feet dragging on the carpeted steps, and sat on my bed. I looked at my suitcase, knowing what I had to do. For some reason I'd brought it. I didn't know why then, but I did now.

I pulled the bracelet out of the suitcase, and, sitting back down on the bed, slipped it from the old, gray jewelry sack I'd put it in.

The heat of the metal sinking into my flesh, and then the flash of light—

I was driving somewhere, my heart full of pain and determination.

He won't stop me, my mother said to herself, out loud.

I wondered what she meant, but I didn't have time to ruminate, as we were there only minutes later, parking and walking up the stairs to the apartment, my feet making a determined clanging noise as I went. I was knocking, my mother's dark hand hitting the wood. Finally, Nessie opened the door.

Please. Sharon is going to be fine. Nessie's face was wrinkled with worry, her mouth pulled into a frown.

Was it fine with me? Cecilia asked.

I didn't know, Nessie said, crying. *I swear, I didn't know. He's come to God. He says he won't do it again. He's sober.*

My mother—me—scoffed, and pushed her way in, and Michael was there, sitting on the couch. He turned around, misery in his black eyes, his eyebrows like wild animals above them. The record player was on, the song "Hotel California" floating through the air.

Sharon's staying here. Where she's safe, Michael said, a glass of something yellow in his hand. He sipped.

Safe? How could she be safe with you?

I was drunk! He said, sounding exasperated. *I'm sober now. And you're just going to get her in trouble at those protests! I ain't gonna lose two daughters to that shit. Those men in AIM are trouble.*

Sober? Cecilia asked. *Then what's in that glass, Dad?*

I could hear Nessie shutting the door behind me, begging both of us to calm down.

They're trouble? You have the audacity to say that, after what you did?

He was silent.

You're weak, my mother said. *You're a coward.*

Michael rose from the couch, the scent of rotting meat growing and festering, my mother shrinking back, her father above her, screaming, his face changing, becoming long, otherworldly, his form elongating, his shadow now unnaturally tall, bent over her. He was the Lofa, the beast, his hair long, his teeth nightmarishly longer, his smell like nothing from this Earth, the glass spilling onto the carpet as his fingernails became claws. She—I—was nearly sick, taking the smell of scotch in. He flew toward me in a rage, shaking and shaking me by the arms, roaring, his rotting stench nearly overwhelming— that smell that was like the inside of a cave. Nessie was behind him, begging him to stop, me telling him to let me go, pulling on his paw now, and his arm slapped backward, and Nessie fell to the floor. When he turned around, his arm hit me so hard, I practically flew.

The pain, the regret, built in his animal face the minute his arm drew back, his features moving briefly back to human.

I was swimming through the air, like it was the wide, blue ocean and I was floating, floating, the air far above me, the light dim, my arms growing cold with the seawater, pinwheeling. I tried to stop, but to no avail. I kept floating, sailing through the air like a bird moving backward, a bird whose wings had been broken long ago. I came to a stop, and my head hit something hard, edged, the last sound I hear the rattling sound of the old heater. An audible crack resounded, and then I began to float some more, this time, up. I could see my sister, Sharon, from her bedroom doorway as I did, and her scream blew the night wide open.

I came back for you, I tried to tell her, but it was too late.

Nessie screamed wildly below me, and I wanted to reassure her. I went over to her and put my hand on her shoulder, but it seemed to have no effect. It went right through her as if I wasn't even there. And I began to float again, up, but I stopped when I saw myself in the corner.

My head had hit the side of the radiator, and I was bleeding all over it and myself, my eyes wide and blank.

Nessie had stopped screaming, and had gone over to me, telling Michael that he had to call 9–1–1.

I realized I had to stop floating. I had to stay. I had come back for Sharon. I had to stay, or he would do it to her too. I was sure of it.

And my baby. My poor baby, only two days old. All alone.

It's too late Nessie, my father said. *The girl's dead.* He looked sorrowful, the beast gone, a pitiful, aging man in his place, his eyes closing in shame.

As I—Cecilia—retreated into the ether, the clock flashed, the smell of scotch seeming to fill the room.

11:47.

CHAPTER FORTY-EIGHT

'd driven home, the war club wrapped in a dirty Metallica T-shirt buried at the bottom of my suitcase, the bracelet back in its sack. I'd smoked and looked at the mountains and thought hard about what my next steps were. I also couldn't help but wonder wryly why my mother hadn't given me visions of my own goddamn purse. It would've been really helpful if she had just whispered "purse." Shit. Ghost logic, I guess.

I decided to call Fredrico. I knew he might think I was crazy, but I had to try.

I dug his number out of my bag and dialed as soon as I got home. I'd needed the drive to think, to make sure that this was what I wanted. If I was wrong, and the vision was merely a delusion, I was putting my father in danger of being arrested. But I knew I was right. I knew it in every fiber of my being.

"Fredrico?" I asked.

"This is he."

"It's Kari—Cecilia James's daughter?"

"Oh, hey, Kari. What's going on? Everything okay?"

I told him about my call from the FBI. My meetings with my

grandfather. The fact that I suspected my grandfather of killing my mother and covering it up.

"Kari, the FBI don't usually call just because someone filed a Freedom of Information Act."

My heart started throbbing rapidly.

"It's possible that once you filed, and they looked at the material, they gave your grandfather a call—now that the technology is more sophisticated, maybe they saw something they didn't see before. Or more simply, your call spurred them to look at the file again after all of these years, and the case looked promising—so they decided to reopen it."

I thought about the times I felt like I was being followed at Lakeside. Shit, what if that had been my grandfather—or the FBI?

"I'm scared, Fredrico. I'm scared that my father did this, and I'm wrong, and they're going to arrest him. He's too weak. He'll die in prison."

He sighed. "Don't panic yet. I—I do have one, tiny connection to a friend in the bureau. I didn't mention him before because it's an old connection, and frankly, though I wanted to help you out, I didn't think you had much of a chance in hell. Now I do. And I think you're right about your grandfather. Now that I think about it, there was something about him, he was so willing to blame AIM. And the way his wife kept her mouth shut . . ."

I was breathing heavy and realized it. Tried to take a few breaths.

"I'll get back to you. Don't do anything."

"Okay," I answered. I hung up.

That night, the Hangar Bar was bustling. I was grateful for a little relief from trying to work out the best way to handle this, from the emotional weight I'd taken on, all the stories of not just my immediate family, but my ancestors.

One thing bothered me though—why hadn't my mother told my father about what Michael had been doing to her? Fredrico said my father also thought my mother's disappearance had had something to do with AIM. If my vision was true, and it hadn't been my father who'd killed Cecilia, that meant only one thing: she'd been too humiliated to tell him.

I took my smoke break and fumbled for my phone after lighting up.

I was scrolling when I got a text.

My fingers started trembling, my heart thudding. It was Debby, asking if I was still smoking.

I laughed nervously and texted her back that I was.

She told me she knew it and asked if I wanted to meet at the White Horse around 7 PM. She had stuff she needed to tell me.

I kind of freaked out then. Maybe she wanted to tell me to never contact her again. She was the kind of person who felt that major shit shouldn't happen over the phone, or via text. She'd said that to me many times. But what choice did I have? I would apologize to her and see what she did. Maybe it would change her mind.

Sure, I told her.

At the White Horse, I waited on the stool, a Bud in front of me, *The Shining* open on the wooden bar, the orange tabby purring, also on the bar. I looked at her, and she half-closed her eyes while I pet her. I was almost done with the book—I'd forgotten how different from the movie it was.

The door opened, and I turned, the slight smell of spring rain coming in with Debby as she smiled and sat down next to me. Her T-shirt was plain, no sparkle-message to convey her mood.

I wasn't sure if I should hug her, but Debby made that easy. She leaned over, and embraced me, hard. I wasn't much for those, but this time, I was grateful for it.

She ordered a Corona, drank a little, and sat it down. Turned to me.

"I think you'll be proud of me," she said.

"Oh yeah?"

"Yeah. In fact, I know you will."

I nodded.

"But first, did you think about what I said?"

It all came out in a rush. My apologies for taking her for granted, for not just listening, for judging her. The fact that I was thinking about buying the White Horse. What had happened to me at The Stanley. The FBI. Fredrico. My father. My grandfather.

"Holy moly," she said, after. Debby was good at not interrupting, even when she should.

"I want to see that club," she said, shaking her head. "And before we do anything, we need to get you to Auntie Squeaker, pronto. She'll know more about it."

I nodded. She was right.

She finished. "First things first. You really are going to be *so* proud of me. I'm proud of myself," she said, straightening in her seat. "So, first of all, thank you for apologizing. I know I had my part in this, and you were right—Jack was awful. When you left, he just kept ranting and ranting about you, and at first I agreed."

"Okay," I said, ordering another.

"But on the way down the mountain, I kept thinking, is this the rest of my life? No Kari, forever? And I knew it wouldn't stop there. Jack, as you well know—" she said, pausing as Nick brought my drink, "is jealous of all of my friends. All of my time."

She sipped at her beer and sighed.

"I told him when we got down the mountain—after dropping the girls off at Mom's—that I was done. That he had two options."

I raised my eyebrows. This was getting good.

"I could leave him, or he could go to therapy. That this stuff wasn't good for us, or the girls. That if he was a good guy, that he'd learn to act like one."

"Did he shit?" I asked.

She laughed. "Yes. I told him that until he showed me that he was willing to make some real changes, I was gone. Then I left. I went to Mom's. I didn't answer one phone call or respond to one drunken text."

I lifted my eyebrows.

"I didn't. I was done. And let me tell you, Kari," she said, pausing, "he texted *a lot*. And a lot of crazy stuff. But I stayed strong."

I *was* proud of her. This kind of thing was hard for Debby.

"I stayed up all night, sure that this was the end. But, Kari? He texted the next morning that he was willing to go to therapy. And that he knew that he had a drinking problem."

"You believe him?"

She shrugged. "Well, we'll see. We've already gone to our first session, and it was good. He was honest, and I think we're getting somewhere. But life isn't any happily ever after, it's work every single day for what you want."

I had to admit, I was shocked.

"Anyway, you got time to see Squeaker tomorrow?"

I did.

"And after that, want to find your mother's sister?"

I laughed, a short, ecstatic laugh. I sure did. God did I *ever*. Pure joy shot straight through to the heart of me.

"Show me the address you found—the one for Sharon."

I pulled my phone out. I'd missed Debby's industriousness. God, I'd missed *Debby*.

Debby plugged it into her GPS. "Shoot, Kari—she's about twenty minutes from here."

I lifted my Bud and Debby her Corona, and we clanked.

I was happy as hell. So happy that, at first, I didn't realize that Nick was standing in front of us, his hands twisting at a rag. "Kari?"

"Yeah, Nick?"

"I gotta tell you something."

He looked nervous, upset.

"What's wrong?"

"I guess I forgot to pay my mortgage this month."

My stomach dropped. I did want to buy the White Horse. But it was a lot. So much paperwork, commitment—there were so many steps, including inspection, which I had no idea how the White Horse had passed in years. And though I was technically in the process of buying it, what would happen now? How would this affect that process?

"What if they take it from me, Kari? What if they take the White Horse?"

CHAPTER FORTY-NINE

'd been on the phone for hours with the bank about the White Horse. Though I had enough for the deposit, I didn't know if I had enough for all the other fees—inspection, for one, just to start, though it looked like I could just take over the mortgage for Nick—if I was approved. I'd never had a credit card, something I thought would be in my favor—but it was the opposite. And there was so much going on in my life right now. Maybe I needed to put this on pause, deal with my grandfather first.

"You okay?" Debby asked.

I nodded. Then shook my head.

"Don't worry about the White Horse. There are going to be a lot of steps, but I'll help you take them. You'll get it. But right now? Let's focus on the task at hand."

We were on our way to Squeaker's.

Pulling up to her trailer, my nerves ran like an electric current.

She was outside in her garden, cutting herbs. She stood up, put her hand over her eyes, smiled. "Thought you'd be coming by today," she said, pulling her blue gardening gloves off, and smacking her hands against her thighs to rid herself of the dirt. "Had some dreams that told me so.

"Come on in," she said, and we followed.

She pulled her apron off and handed it and the gloves to one of her men.

She sat down at the table, and we sat opposite.

"I got something to show you, Auntie."

She nodded.

I pulled the war club out of my bag and handed it over.

She sucked air in through her teeth. "Hot damn. I never thought I'd see this in my life," she said, her voice moving to a reverential whisper.

I told her then how I acquired it at The Stanley, and the call I'd gotten from the FBI. The dreams I'd had after I'd gotten the club.

"You need to be prepared. This is Geronimo's. After his family was killed—like in your dream—Ussen gave him the gift of being invulnerable to bullets. I always suspected the gift resided in this— his war club."

Debby gasped.

"You're saying this club is Geronimo's?" I asked.

"It is. I know it's his. His spirit is here. And I believe you're right about your grandfather. Why else would your mother's spirit be unable to rest? It takes a big thing like that to keep a spirit in this realm."

"But Auntie, what do I do with this club?"

"It will protect you. You need to bring it with you when you confront your grandfather."

I nodded. "But why was it in The Stanley?"

She laughed. "It wasn't. Not until you went there. With the bracelet."

"Okay . . ." Debby said.

"It followed you. On your journey. This path was the one you needed to go on. To heal. To help your mother rest. To face your guilt."

I turned red.

"I know about your guilt. It's all over you."

"Guilt?" Debby asked. "About who? What? I'm confused."

"It should've been me."

"Wait, what?" Debby asked.

"She thinks it's her fault that Jaime died," Squeaker said.

Debby knit her brows together. Put her hand on mine. "You can't believe that."

Squeaker sighed. "Only she can get to the other side with that one."

"It's not your fault, Kari—you didn't put those drugs in her mouth."

I was silent for a time.

"About my grandfather though," I said. "So, when I get him—when I find Sharon, and if she's willing to testify, put my grandfather in jail, and my mother is able to rest—then the bracelet's mine? And I can heal Daddy with it?"

Squeaker sighed and sat back.

"You gotta tell me how I do that."

"You can't. I lied. Well, I didn't lie. I let you believe what you wanted."

I blinked, rapidly, my mind reeling with this betrayal. "What the fuck, Squeaker? You lied about the bracelet healing Daddy? Why would you do that?" I stood up, and some of her men came closer. She shooed them away.

"I said the bracelet heals. You assumed that meant it could heal your daddy's brain. It don't work that way. But I couldn't tell you that, could I?"

"I'm sick of people lying to me!" I said, slamming my fist down on the table. "My father. Michael. You!"

She let me rant, and when I was done, and panting heavily, she sat up. "The bracelet can heal your spirit. You're helping it to heal your mother's. And then, it will help to heal yours. It already is."

"Let's go, Debby. I don't want to hear this shit anymore," I said, and Debby scrambled up, apologizing, her face red.

"It's okay, honey," Squeaker said.

Just as I was about to slam the trailer door, Squeaker told me to bring that club. And to be prepared.

"I heard you the first time," I said, slamming.

CHAPTER FIFTY

My phone warbled with a text. I used a T-shirt to pluck the war club off my desk and stuck it in my bag, pushing it all the way underneath my wallet, receipts, lip balms. It made me nervous, the idea of taking it anywhere, but I had a feeling that Sharon would need to see it. I'd decided that even if Squeaker had lied to me to put me on this journey, I was on it. And I was going to see it through to the end.

"Are you ready?" Debby asked.

I got in, slamming the car door hard.

"I think so," I said, running my hands down my favorite pair of black jeans. I'd worn my warrior outfit today—black jeans, short, black rock-star boots with silver buckles, the Megadeth T-shirt I'd had on the day Jaime had died. That shirt had power.

"You okay?" she asked, sensing my mood.

"I'm mad at Squeaker."

Debby sighed.

"Just say it," I said, scooting further into my seat.

"I don't know anything, or like, very little about Indian stuff. Beyond what I've learned from you, or from other Natives in town. But like. What Squeaker did? I know it's kinda tricky of her, but it seems like an Indian thing to do. And especially a Squeaker thing to do. I'm not sure you would've gone on this journey if you didn't think it could help your dad."

"She should've just told me the truth. Let me decide."

"But you're—" she interrupted herself to honk at a man cutting her off in an old Cutlass. "You're stubborn, Kari. You hated your mom. Nothing I ever said, or my mom ever said—or what Squeaker ever said made a difference. You decided that she was to blame for your dad's condition, and that was that."

I was silent.

"Just think about it."

We drove in silence for a while, the squawk of Debby's GPS guiding us the only sound.

"I hope Sharon listens to us," Debby said, breaking the quiet.

I shrugged.

"The worst thing that could happen is she turns us away at the door—or that she's not the right Sharon after all. Then maybe I can work on Nessie. She was ready to see it my way. Michael probably just scared the shit out of her," I said, blowing smoke out of the window, but inadequately, as Debby fanned the air.

"What a mean old man," Debby said. If there was one thing Debby didn't abide, it was cruelty. She didn't mind my edgy sense of humor because she knew my heart was good. But true cruelty—that made her angry as hell.

"I can tell he feels bad about killing my mom. I think he did love her, and in his way, I guess he was trying to protect Cecilia and Sharon. Those dudes from AIM really could do nasty shit, not to mention the way the government would disappear activists. But to not own up to it?"

"Right?" Debby answered. "And God, people who molest children, teenagers." She shuddered. "I just can't understand it. I can't."

"I know. It's unthinkable."

"When it really comes down to it, he just doesn't want to go to jail. And he was cool with trying to make me think my daddy killed her, to save his own ass."

"I—" Debby started, but she was interrupted by my phone.

My heart began thumping.

"Ms. James?"

"This is she."

"This is Chris Beauvais—from Canvas Credit Union?"

"Right, Chris. Good to hear from you." My heart slowed to its normal speed.

"Well, I have good news. I'm calling to let you know that your loan's been approved, pending a few more steps."

Relief flooded through me. "That's great," I said, though it was hard to feel excitement, considering where we were headed.

"Congratulations!"

"Thanks," I responded. "How long do I have to decide?" I really didn't have the money for anything beyond the deposit. But if I didn't do this, the White Horse would probably move into bankruptcy, and I'd lose it forever. And one of the few places that was old Denver—old Indian Denver—would be lost to time, forever.

"You have a few weeks, if you need it."

I took a long drag.

"You know, I pulled your app out of the pile myself," he said.

"Really?"

"Yes. I'm quite familiar with the White Horse."

"You are?" I asked, incredulous.

He laughed. "I'm Sicangu—my dad's from Rosebud. I know all about that bar. You're Indian, right? I just can't see a reason that a white person would buy that bar, unless they had clear plans to bulldoze it, and put a set of condos up—and I just didn't get that sense, talking to you."

I laughed. "I am. I'm . . . Chickasaw and Apache, actually. Well, sort of, you know. I'm urban."

"I'll come on by sometime. I had a time or two, back in the day.

My dad, he *lived* in that bar. Sometimes Dad would take me when I was little. I'd sit in the car with a Pepsi and a book, waiting for him. Then, when I was old enough, he got me in there a time or two. But then he passed on, and well . . . I guess I forgot about it until now."

"Oh wow," I said, wondering if his dad and my mom had ever crossed paths. It was possible. The Indian world was so small. "And sorry to hear about your dad."

"It's okay. It was a long time ago," he said. Then, "Is that bartender still alive?"

"Nick?" I asked.

"That's right, Nick—that was his name."

"He's still kicking."

"Wow," he said, sighing.

Memories rang in that sigh.

"He seemed ancient to me when I was first going there on my own. He okay?"

"He's getting up there. Repeating stories. He's ready to retire. But I'm gonna keep him around," I said.

"Glad to hear that," he said. "Well, anyway—Ms.—okay if I call you Kari?"

"Of course."

"Well, Kari, like I said, I'll drop on by sometime."

"I'd like that."

"Who was *that*?" Debby said, taking one arm off the wheel to elbow me in the side, auntie style.

"It's just the guy from the bank. I've been approved."

Debby squealed so loudly I thought she was going to go off the road.

"When this is over, we need to celebrate!" she said.

I nodded. "I'm still not sure it's going to go through, so, let's hold off on the champagne.

"Also . . ." I took a deep breath. I wanted to ask her something that I'd been meaning to ever since I'd thought about actually doing this.

"I was thinking, you know maybe, you could work with me?" I said. "If I even do this. Which I might not."

She went silent.

"But if I did, you'd be part owner, and neither of us could quit our jobs at first, I know that—but um, you could do the books, and the social media, which a lot of that could be done from home—" I cut myself off, looked over at her, cringing. I was waiting for her to tell me no, that Jack wouldn't like that, that it would take time away from her kids.

She was smiling, tears running down her cheeks.

"I'd love that," she said, wiping at tears. "*If* you decide to this," she finished slyly.

I laughed. We both knew that this was almost certainly a done deal.

"I want to be able to do something for you, for a change."

She cried harder, and I patted her awkwardly on the back until she quit. Debby was so comfortable with crying. In a way, I envied that.

"Okay," she said, "I'm so excited. But we have to put all this away for a bit."

I nodded.

Twenty minutes later, we were outside of a large, sprawling apartment complex. It was attractive, one of the new ones, the kinds that looked almost industrial. Debby hated them, but though they were evidence of a gentrifying Denver, I thought they were pretty cool-looking. The landscaping was smooth too, simple, with white flowers of various kinds—petunias, daisies, orchids—scattered throughout, and well-kept shrubs at the front of each yellow, maroon, or navy complex. There were also trees—redbud and catalpa by the look of them—their green leaves and white blossoms shimmering in the sun, rippling in the light, spring breeze.

We walked up three flights of stairs and stopped at 248. I knocked, wondering if she'd be home. We'd picked early evening, but that didn't mean—

Footsteps shuffled to the door.

It opened, and a woman's face appeared. I couldn't help it, I gasped. There was no doubt that it was Sharon James, my mother's sister. Although she was shorter, her nose smaller, wider—she looked so much like her, like me.

"Can I . . . can I help you?" she asked, her eyes narrowing inquisitively. It was clear I was familiar somehow.

She blinked a few times, "Do I know you? You look . . ."

"I'm Cecilia's girl," I said. "This is my cousin, Debby."

She went pale. "Oh," she said, shaking her head. "You know, you're nearly the spitting image of her."

"So I've been told," I said.

She went from pale to greenish.

"I need to sit down," she said, "but come in."

We followed her inside, her apartment nicely decorated with dark gray couches and framed pictures of different Native figures, prints of Monet, small white and gray figures of cats, and little glass jars—and a small, dark gray cat to match, sitting on her couch.

"Can I get you a glass of water?" Debby asked.

Sharon put her hand to her face, rubbed her temples.

It was a pleasant face, heart-shaped, lightly freckled, and brown— one that said she'd had a rough go of it at first but had quit whatever had started to etch those wrinkles in early enough. She had crow's feet around her eyes, and stronger lines around her mouth, but though her expression carried something I wouldn't quite characterize as bitterness, but perhaps a seasoned wisdom, she looked younger than her years.

"Yes," she said. "Thank you."

Debby rifled around in the kitchen. When she got back, she handed Sharon a tall blue glass full of water, and sat.

I had been sitting not too far from the cat, who'd sniffed at me suspiciously at first, but had decided my presence was acceptable, and stayed.

She drank and sat the glass down on the coffee table in front of her. "I'm sorry. It's just—I try not to think about my sister, or my family at all," she said. Then, "What do you know about them?"

I took a deep breath and told her everything. Even the things that might make her think I was insane, about the bracelet, and the war club. The FBI. But all she did was listen patiently, and nod.

"My family has always had visions, other things," Sharon said. "Do you mind if I smoke, out on the patio?"

"I'll join you," I said. "I recently started up again."

"I bet," she said, chuckling lightly. She seemed better, less pale at least.

We walked out onto a little deck. It was covered in plants, ivy, succulents, mainly green but a few flowers too, hanging from pots from the ceiling.

"I've quit everything else," she said, "even alcohol. Tried to quit this but," she said, turning the cigarette up in her hand then lighting up and handing me the lighter once she'd finished, "it never takes. And I only smoke two or three a day," she finished, inhaling.

"That's not bad," I said, "I'd been quit for years. I'll quit again."

Debby snorted and settled into a chair.

"So, you're here because you want something of me. I can sense that. That was always my thing," she said, smiling slightly. "Your mother didn't have visions, or anything—nor did—does, my mother—Nessie," she said, pausing to grimace. "But I was always a little like Grandmother. She had true visions, like Geronimo. But me, just—I can feel someone's emotional agenda, if that makes any sense."

I took a deep breath and told her about the vision I'd had about her father.

"I was there. He did molest her. He did murder her. And that's just like him to try to convince you he's the hero in this situation. Your father loved your mother. He supported everything she was doing. She didn't push him—in any way, and certainly not to murder her. They supported each other. Cecila was trying to get me away from him. I wish Nessie had stepped in, or just left him," she said, bitterness edging her voice.

I breathed a sigh of relief so visceral, I thought I might be choking for a moment. I didn't realize how badly I'd needed that confirmed. Confirmed for me in the flesh, in this world.

"I wish I hadn't been too scared to do anything but run away," she said. "I wish I hadn't taken my dad's threats to heart so seriously. Let him get away with so much."

"It's okay—you were just a kid!" Debby said.

Sharon hung her head.

"Sharon . . . I know it's hard, but—thank you. I honestly thought I was losing my mind. Or had a brain tumor. And of course, Michael was more than happy to push me to thinking that I was losing my mind." I put a hand out, patted her awkwardly on the shoulder, her cigarette smoldering between her fingers.

She nodded, her head still down.

I let her process for a moment, and when she brought her head up and smiled weakly, took a drag off her smoke, I knew it was time to tell her what I thought we should do next.

"I'm hoping you'll testify against him—Michael, your father. I wish there was a way to know where my mother's body is buried, but, barring that, if you saw him killing my mother, you could testify in court. I want him in jail. I think that's what Cecilia wants as well. I think, well—I'm pretty sure anyway, that that's why she began appearing."

She nodded. She'd listened intently when I'd told her that I'd hated my mother, that my father had gotten into an accident a few years after Cecilia disappeared.

"I don't know, Kari," she said.

My heart dropped.

"I'm not saying no—but when I ran away? I was with a rough crowd for a long time. I'd found a group of men at Bar Bar—they took me in. I was maybe fifteen, sixteen," she said, squinting. "And I got on H, and anything else I could get my hands on. A man in that group who always felt sorry for me helped me get out—earn my GED—set me up in an apartment. It took me years to get where I am now. I'm an accountant. And my father? He's a good liar."

I was quiet.

"I mean," she continued, "I should have done something then. But now? I just . . . maybe it's too late."

"I'm so sorry," Debby said.

I nodded.

I reached out to the cat, let it sniff my outstretched fingers a few times, before trying to pet it. Eventually, he let me.

I looked out. The sun was setting over the mountains. I felt a stinging, unexpected stab of inexplicable fear, tried to push it away.

Sharon smiled. "Mousy's better than a German Shepard, isn't he?" She reached out, and pet him, and he purred under her hand. "He knows when bad people—and spirits—are around. I could tell when I picked him out at the pound."

It made me happy to hear how much she loved cats. Briefly, I thought about the little, orange kitty at the White Horse. Shit, I loved cats.

"So anyway, Kari—and Debby, let me just think about it. I know you're right. I don't want to be a coward like my mother. I just . . . need a minute."

My phone began ringing. It was Fredrico.

"I'm so sorry," I said. "Let me take this—it's my cop friend. The one I was telling you about."

I picked up, Debby and Sharon's faces looking anxiously on.

"Kari! So glad you picked up. I'm not supposed to tell you this. But when you filed, the FBI did reopen the case. They've been watching your grandfather."

"You're telling me they're going to arrest him?"

"They're on their way to his apartment now."

CHAPTER FIFTY-ONE

I am twenty-four when Debby saves my life.

I am sitting alone in Daddy's house and I am staring at the small white pills that I have lifted from the medicine cabinet and the pills that I had already had before Jaime died and the coke I'd scored about twenty minutes ago, in Tommyknocker's, a miracle, as usually that place isn't about the fancy drugs.

I snort the coke and snort more, my hand lifting to my nose, feeling the acrid, racing burn on the tender part of my flesh—and then I duck back down to the mirror, the new white line, making another line, again, again, and finally I feel like I'm floating up to the ceiling and I briefly wonder what it will do to Daddy when he finally wakes up and comes down to my body on the couch, staring up.

But it's hard to care about things like that when you're high like I'm high.

And I'm so high I barely know my own name right now.

I'm looking at the pills and they're all lined up on the coffee table, the same coffee table that my mom set her coffee on twenty-four years ago, but I don't want to think about that because she's a horrible bitch who abandoned me, left me to care for Daddy and I hate her.

And without Jaime I am totally alone, and I know it.

I pull one of the bottles up and shake the pills onto my palm and sift through them with a finger and I think about Jaime's beautiful, heartbreaking face, right after I found her. That's what comes to me, again and again and again, in my dreams and in my nightmares and in my waking life, a distinction I no longer really feel exists.

The door bursts open as I start to shovel the pills down my throat, one after another after another in the most satisfying and pitiful motion, Jaime's face floating in front of me like a good and lovely dream, but it isn't Jaime's face in front of me, it's Debby's—and she says *I knew it! Dammit, Kari!*

Leave me alone, I tell her. *Let me do this.*

Leave you alone until I have to find your body, you mean, she says, and if I could cry, I would.

She comes charging at me like a bull and for the first time in my life I am afraid of Debby instead of the other way around, but she just pulls the pills from my hand and hits me on the back of the head. I cough the little white pills out onto her waiting palm, strings of saliva following. Then she yanks the pills from the table and sifts through the ones that are Daddy's, and shoves those in her bag, and goes to the toilet with the other ones, and I can hear her flushing, I can hear her muttering, angry.

God, I had hope a minute ago, but now I feel so empty.

When she comes out she takes me in her arms, and she holds me, and again I wish I could cry, but I can't, I'm broken that way. Just fucking broken, like the clock on the wall. Stopped in time. But she rocks me and rocks me like a sleepy child and I let her.

After a while she takes me outside, into the good, cold night, and tells me to look up at the stars.

To just look up at the stars.

At first it is only black but then after a minute I see light, I see formation, I see structure and beauty and life and Debby tells me *see? See?*

I do see.

A year goes by.

Debby feeds me like a baby bird, and I am weak for a long time, living at my father's house and taking care of him because that way, I have something to do. That way, I don't have to think about the next step and for a long time, that's all I need.

I take Debby to the graveyard on the edge of town near the old high school, where Jaime and I used to go to get drunk, to get high, where Jaime is buried. Now all I drink is cold air.

All night, laying by the headstones of the long dead, I tell her about Jaime, about everything we'd done, and she doesn't judge. I show her the constellations we had considered ours, the ones we'd watched whenever we were too high, or the men we were partying with too rough, the stars that reminded us that no matter what happened, we were so small, and that was a good, right, thing. All of that eternity.

I ask Debby to forgive me for what I said when I was sixteen and she says it's okay, but I tell her what I thought she'd meant, that maybe she'd meant something ugly about Jaime's Blackness and she gets very red and says that I should've known her better than that.

And she's right.

I feel strong by the end of that year, I am healed. But I don't realize that healing requires scars, and I am still rough beneath them, I still have pain locked behind that ropy skin. And there is weakness there, there is vulnerability, a thing I have always been terrified of. A thing that has festered. A thing that can take me down into the dark. And feed. And feed.

CHAPTER FIFTY-TWO

There was a hard rapping at Sharon's door, and the cat jumped out of my lap with a shrill meow and ran into the living room.

"Oh my God," Debby said, a nervous trill to her voice.

I laughed. "Chill, Debby."

Sharon stubbed her cigarette out, twisting it hard in the glass. "That's weird." She laughed anxiously.

And suddenly, I felt nervous, that seemingly irrational spike of fear I'd felt a moment ago returning, doubling.

"If you'll excuse me," Sharon said, standing up, clearing her throat.

Debby and I went silent, both of our heads cocked toward the living room.

I couldn't help it, I knew—with everything I was, that it was Michael at the door. That somehow, he'd become aware that the FBI were coming for him. And now he was coming for us.

"Dad," Sharon said, and I felt shock hit me, hard.

I stood up, after putting my smoke out. "How could he . . . ?"

"I don't know," Debby whispered.

"Let's go," I said, getting up, Debby following.

Michael stood in the doorway, looking abashed, one arm pushed up against the frame.

"You," he said, seeing me come in, his eyes narrowing. He sighed heavily, his eyes carrying more shadows than I remembered from the restaurant. "Somehow, I'm not surprised. Better this way, actually."

I wondered what he meant by that.

"Hi, Michael."

"Dad—" Sharon started.

"Can I just come in? I only want to talk."

"I don't think so, Dad," Sharon responded.

"I ain't here to make excuses. I just . . . want to give you my side of the story."

Sharon was quiet. Then, "Dad, I know what you did. I was there. And everything you did to cover it up. There's nothing else to say."

I wondered if I should excuse myself, text Fredrico. Tell him Michael was here. Michael might really just want to talk. But why was he here now? When I knew the feds were on their way to his place? And would Debby and Sharon be okay if I left them alone with him? I didn't trust this guy, not after Sharon confirmed what I saw in my vision.

"Go away, Dad," she said, and began closing the door.

He put his hand out, stopping it.

"You get your ass out of here! I'm going to say something to the police, Dad, I'm not afraid of you anymore, you molesting, murdering—"

He pushed the door open, violently. "Stop!"

I realized that maybe opening the door to this fucker was our first mistake.

"I . . . I was drunk! I used to drink, I don't anymore. It was a mistake, I . . ." and here he trailed off, his voice breaking. "I loved you girls. I loved Cecilia. But she used to make me so mad! Going to those damn protests—I told her it was going to land her in jail, or get her raped, or worse!"

"That's goddamn ironic, Dad!" Sharon said, and he seemed to wilt. But then he walked in, slammed the door behind him.

"You got to listen to me! This one—" he said, pointing to me with his lips and finger, "stirred things up. And there's cop cars outside my place. If they take me to jail—and I'm not saying what I did was right—who'll be there to take care of Nessie? She needs me. She's not right in the head."

I laughed. "She's not the sick one."

He narrowed his eyes. "I came to God. I quit drinking. I've spent the rest of my life caring for Nessie," he said, his voice a low growl.

"But what you did was wrong, Dad," Sharon said, her voice trembling.

All I could think was, how in *hell* had he gotten past the cops?

He hung his head, wiped at his eyes. "I really did love her, you know. It sounds wrong, but when I was drinking, it . . . would come over me. Like I wasn't myself."

I sighed.

"That's the thing," he said, reaching behind his back and pulling out a .44. "Sometimes you have to do things that you normally would never do." He began screwing a silencer onto it.

We all backed up, quick.

"Oh my God, oh my *God*," Debby squealed.

He aimed the gun at me, determination lining his eyes.

Sharon gasped, and he swung it over to her.

I pushed Debby behind me.

"Stop it, Kari!" she said, trying to get back out in front of me. But she was small, and I was strong.

"Debby, you have kids. Just *think*. Stay behind me," I said.

"Don't do this, Dad," Sharon said, her voice trembling.

Tears streamed down his face. "I didn't mean to! I loved her!" He beat his fist against his chest with every word.

"Just turn yourself in, Dad. That's the right thing to do," Sharon said once he'd finished.

"Nessie, she won't make it without me. She needs me."

"You gonna kill us all?" I asked, and he moved the pistol in my direction. "You might be able to. But then, you'll have more bodies. More guilt. And where you gonna hide those bodies—or yourself? Let it go. You've been caught."

He was silent, his eyes darting as if he was thinking through what I was saying.

I took a shuddering breath. Maybe he was listening.

"I can't!" he said, raising the gun at Sharon, his voice rising to a hysterical scream. "I can't go to jail! Nessie needs me!"

"Dad," Sharon said, wailing. "Come on, Dad, stop this. Don't do this!"

He began crying hysterically, and I hoped that maybe he'd lower the gun, but he didn't. He kept it trained on Sharon, though his hand trembled while he was wracked with sobs. One hand covered his eyes for a moment. I darted my eyes over to Sharon, both of us clearly thinking the same thing: get the gun while he was distracted.

Sharon went for it, and for a moment, I thought she had him. She was quick. She was halfway there, one hand on his arm, when he realized what she was doing.

He screamed, yanking her hand off his arm, pulling the gun straight, his eyes filled with terror. He fired.

Debby ran out from behind me, slamming Sharon into the ground.

Her face crumpled as the bullet hit her instead. She fell to the floor and pushed herself slowly back against the wall.

"I'm sorry!" Michael said, but he kept the gun trained on us.

Debby was moaning, bleeding from the wound in her side.

Sharon's eyes streamed tears. "Daddy, no!"

"I can't go! I can't!" he said, his voice almost inhuman now with grief and rage.

I edged over to Debby and sat by her side, cradling her head. What had I done? Was I going to lose my best friend? Again?

I looked over at Michael, who was pointing the gun at me, and then at Sharon.

Sharon kept her eyes trained on Michael. "Dad. You need to stop and think. There's still time to call the hospital. This woman," she said, gesturing to Debby, who was turning alarmingly pale, "has two small children."

I stood up. "She's a good person. I know you're a good person," I said.

He cried harder and aimed the gun at me. He squinted, and his face, in that moment, seemed to take on the shape of something else, something determined, something monstrous. A smell began to fill the room. A smell I knew well, of rotting meat.

I knew he was about to squeeze the trigger.

I pulled the war club out from the back of my pants where I'd shoved it when I first stood up, after hearing the doorbell—regretting not bringing my gun like *hell*—and ran. Ran like I hadn't since I was a child. Since I'd seen Daddy in the hospital. Since the day Jaime had died, when they'd pulled me away from her body while I screamed and screamed, asking God to take me because I couldn't live with the pain. Ran like I had from my mother's ghost, like I'd been doing my whole life, except the wrong way. Like I'd been running from my own guilt, my own pain. I ran toward my grandfather and with a leap and a yell like my ancestors, I lunged back to crack him on the skull, even if it meant my death. At least Sharon and Debby might survive.

The gun went off.

And that's when it happened.

Shit froze.

It was like the club had cracked open an invisible chasm in time, in space. There was a thunderclap, and fissures all along the air where I'd begun to move forward, like there had been an invisible blue pane of glass in the air, and the club had found it. I saw through the pane a bullet—one meant for me. It froze inches from my face.

There was a flash of light, and I was somewhere else, somewhere strange and beautiful and yet somehow so sweetly familiar.

Red Desert—but with waving lines of fluorescent light in the dirt moving beneath my feet. Brightly lit pink saguaro cactus—the lights of the needles flashing like something from Vegas, but the lights looked contradictorily natural. Tumbleweed rolled through, but up and down, backward, then forward again, or in circles. Sometimes they'd dance with one another and cackle with the voices of tiny children. A dry, sandy wind filled with the smell of sage. Mesas in the distance—some of them floating in the air, some of them upside down. And strangest of all, Johnny Cash's "I Walk the Line" was everywhere, in fits and starts.

"What the . . . hell?" I said. "Where am I?"

"This is your people's homeland, not mine," Michael said, behind me. "Figures you'd fight me on your own turf."

I turned around.

He was there, standing feet from me. "Course," he said, lifting his head like he was smelling something, "I got my music here. That came with me. Always loved Cash."

The world I was in was surreal, strange—not exactly my ancestor's homeland, but at the same time, it fit. It was as if we had entered an alternate dimension, somewhere the club had brought us—maybe somewhere that Geronimo had had access to, somewhere he'd drawn his power from.

As I listened to the lyrics, trying to process what was happening to me, Michael standing there awkwardly in his black, tooled-leather cowboy boots, tight Levi's, and black hat contrasting his look of shame and sadness, something came over me then. I thought of the way his voice, in the other world—my world—had pitched into a growl, into something not quite human back in Sharon's apartment.

"You're it, aren't you? The monster from my dreams. The Lofa."

I thought about my vision, how I hadn't even had time to process the fact that Michael had become the beast when he killed his own daughter. It hadn't been some metaphor my brain had come up with to cope, it was my mother trying to tell me that Michael was capable of transforming into a literal monster.

I felt sick.

"That's what I become when I drink. Or when I can't . . . help myself. When I need to protect myself."

I didn't know what to say. It was awful, it was frightening, and worst of all, I knew now why we were here, in this other world: Geronimo had brought me here, or at least, his medicine had, to fight Michael—and he was here to kill me. He was going to become the thing that he hated in order to prevent me from holding him accountable for his sins.

He looked sad then, shifting from foot to foot, the sand pooling heavily around each boot. "Your grandmother. She used to take Cecilia down to New Mexico to see the Crown Dancers. You know that?"

I hadn't.

"She used to ask me why I didn't take the girls to stomp dance, in Oklahoma."

"Why didn't you?" I asked, my hand over my eyes, wondering when it would happen. Wondering just what he was up to. He was standing directly in front of the sun, and in-between two mesas. His image was shimmering in the desert heat, almost shifting.

He plucked a leaf of desert sage, rubbed it between his fingers. "My family gave all that up long ago. Was illegal anyway for a long time, you know that?"

I dimly recollected something about that from one of my visions.

"My connection was lost. And besides. We'd gone Christian. And there's good there too."

"You can get that shit back."

"Some things, Kari," he said, a small break in his voice, "are gone forever. You do things, or people before you do things—even if they're forced to, and a line is drawn. A border, a boundary that cannot be crossed."

I was silent then, listening to the sound of a coyote howl mournfully in the distance. What was he telling me this for? And would a little war club be enough to fight off a literal monster? That thing in my visions, in my dreams, it was huge, a predator the likes hadn't walked the earth since time immemorial.

He laughed at the sound of the coyote singing, breaking the tension a little. "Shoot. This place is like a regular Road Runner cartoon."

He looked more like a little boy then, not the man who could turn into a beast of epic proportions, the man who'd molested then murdered his daughter when she confronted him, the man who'd been chasing me just as the FBI was chasing him. If I hadn't been at Sharon's, he would've shot her, come for me next. He looked sad and vulnerable—and he flickered then, the dust shimmering in the air behind him, the pink saguaro lighting his face up like a dream— and he became a little boy, a toy car clutched in one hand. He was skinny, clothed in old jeans and a beat-up white T-shirt. There was a shadow at his back, something much larger than he was, one hand on his shoulder, stretching long into the desert behind him. A low, warbling moan emanated from it. Something came to me, a memory of part of a dream that I'd had when this first started up, the dream I'd had of a child. It had been this child in front of me now. It had been Michael.

My throat closed up, and my eyes began to water.

The boy looked at me, his eyes haunted.

"You were touched when you were young."

He nodded.

"My father."

"I'm sorry."

We were quiet then, and the wind picked up, a hollow whistle.

Then, "What about Jaime?" He wasn't smiling when he said it. He wasn't mocking. But he knew what he was doing.

My body coursed with shock. "How did you . . . ?"

"I know about everything, in here. I know about Jaime. About how much pain I put my daughter through when I was blackout drunk. About her not being able to walk on."

"What does she have to do with any of this?" I asked.

"Everything. It's why you never could heal when it came to your mother. And your wounds around your mother are why you became friends with Jaime in the first place. It's a big, dang, ugly, circle, girl. And the thing is, you got just about as much guilt as I do."

I thought of Jaime then, her smile, her lovely black eyes, so like my own, but different, almond to my slant. Her unexpected gentleness. The way she'd held me so many times, my body curled up into a ball of pain. The way she wouldn't let go until I was ready. The fact that she partied harder than anyone I knew but had the softest voice. Child-like. Not doll-like, no. But soft, kind.

I felt like dying then. Why hadn't I done more? My shame quickly turned to anger.

"How dare you bring her up, you pedophile!"

His lip curled, and he became the man, Michael. His eyebrows knit into one furious line.

"What I did, I admit. I just don't want to go to jail. You—you want to bury it, bury Jaime. Bury everything you done to her."

"You piece of shit!" I screamed, feeling the guilt crawl through me like a thousand cockroaches. "You molested your own daughter! That ain't the same."

He snarled, and I smelled the scent of dead meat on the air.

"I know who I am! You—you, you fool yourself thinking you're so tough—so pure. When you're just like me," he said, laughing then.

"I'm nothing like you! I fucked up. But you—you say you've come to God, that you know who you are, but you're too much of a coward to face up to your sins, pay for them like a man. Nessie, my ass! You're not willing to kill three more women to protect Nessie, you're doing it to protect yourself."

"You bitch," he said, his voice moving into sharp, jagged, animalistic syllables.

He began to vibrate then, the particles beneath his feet dancing, the smell emanating off him visceral: rotten meat, bones, and misery. Cruelty. Long hair sprouting greasily from its height—which looked to be over seven feet. Teeth the size of a bear's, nails curving yellow and almost down into the ground. The Lofa, the monster from my nightmares, the one who had been chasing me, all this time, had been thwarting my mother.

It roared and went for me.

In both realities, I—

Yanked the club up and yelled with rage, with grief, and went toward the beast. Pulling back my arm, I tried to bury the weapon in his furry skull. It threw my arm off as if it were nothing, air. It roared and I pulled my arm back again and I yelled as the muscle tore. It pushed me to the ground and pulled a strip of my skin off and brought it to its lips, the blood still slicking the skin. I kicked with both legs right into its testicles. It curled into a ball, twisted, and came for me again.

Debby cried in the background, and Sharon screamed for her father to stop, to leave me alone.

I was in the desert.

Then the apartment, watching Sharon hit her father in the arm, the gun wavering her way, the powder in the air as it went off, Sharon falling to the ground.

Now in the desert, the beast tried again to tear at me with his claws. I swung to the side to avoid them. In the apartment, Sharon got back up and pounded at her dad's fist, the one that had the gun.

It fell to the floor. Bullets rained around me. They had not touched me.

In the desert, the Lofa pounced and flattened me to the dirt. It ripped at my flesh, and I screamed. It pulled the meat to its mouth again, and fed.

I dropped the club.

My grip on reality loosened. I worried that Debby had died, and I was alone, and that Sharon was gone too, and what would it matter then? It began to pull at my flesh again, laughing like a mad gibbon, and blood pooled under me, my eyes fluttering. Desert. Apartment. Desert.

The scent of Jaime's perfume came over me then, like a dream. It had been a soft jasmine, something she bought in the drugstore. At least once a day, I smelled that heady scent, as if it arose out of nothingness, out of the well of grief I kept locked away, a secret pool that lay stark in the heart of me. I thought of her smile, and in the desert, I grasped for the club. I felt like fainting, my eyes rolling back. I bit down on my lip, hard.

It ripped. I screamed. But it woke me fully.

I ground my hips into the dirt then maneuvered to my left by swinging, hard as I could, my hand feeling for the club. I saw it not far from me. But the Lofa pinned me again, pushing the part of me I'd worked free back into the dust. I gathered everything I had inside, and pushed down, and then up, sharply, into the Lofa with my hips, popping it off of me for a moment.

I turned over and grasped the club. Finally.

It took everything I had not to fade, to allow myself to be carried off into the tide. I bit my lip once more as the Lofa moved to pin me again and thought about how Jaime wouldn't want me to die, or carry the guilt of her death like this, how wrong it was that my guilt was the same size as Michael's. About my mother, who I sensed was holding me like she never could when I was a child and so alone.

I clasped the club hard, despite the blood, and brought it down in the apartment on the side of Michael's head. His face crumpled, blood spurting out of the side.

I kicked the gun, and in my periphery, I could see Sharon picking it up.

I kept my eyes trained on him while I pushed the club back into my pants. I pulled my phone out, first calling 9–1–1, then Fredrico.

I moved a few steps backward, watching him. He was still breathing. But he was out, and the blood was pooling rapidly onto the floor.

I turned and sat down next to Debby.

She'd pulled her jacket off and had managed to push it over the wound, but her hands were growing weak now. I took over for her.

Michael groaned, one hand reaching into the air. The hair on the back of my neck spiked, and the blood from where the Lofa had torn increased. A roar came from the other world. He turned over and sat up, his knees folding under him.

I scrambled to pick the club out from the back of my jeans as he began getting up, stumbling, and Sharon hit him in the head with the gun, hard. He fell. Lay still.

I wondered if he'd survive this. He shouldn't, I knew, but some small part of me felt sorry for him.

"I'm so sorry," I said to Debby, my voice breaking. I was. I would take all of this back if I could. I needed her. Her children needed her. And she deserved so much, just for herself.

"It's okay, Kari," she said, faintly, and then passed out, the sound of sirens everywhere.

As I waited, my hands pushing a lavender sweatshirt we'd bought together at the mall last year over her wound, I thought about all the years I'd had with Debby, about all of the ways she'd made me feel less alone. It was so unfair. She'd saved my life, and now I was responsible for this? I couldn't live with more guilt. I just couldn't. I couldn't lose her and keep walking forward. The other world parted into ours once more, and I could see the desert, a place, I knew, I would visit with Debby if she survived this.

I looked up to the blue sky, the sound of the sirens close now, and blending with the howls of wolves on the mesas mournful in their cacophony, the scent of sweetgrass and sage in the wind, the feel of the dust on my legs, and waited. And waited.

CHAPTER FIFTY-THREE

On the way to the hospital, they tried to staunch Debby's wound. She was out cold, gray-skinned, and bleeding profusely by the time the EMTs got to Sharon's apartment. They'd lifted my cousin onto a stretcher and gotten her as quickly as they could to the ambulance, the sirens going the minute they took off.

One of them inserted an IV into her, flooding blood back into her body. It could've been my imagination, but after they did, she looked warmer.

As they worked, I listened to the heart monitor beep out a reassurance that my cousin was still with us, wishing to God that I'd never pursued this thing with my mother. I had the truth now, but if I lost Debby, it wouldn't be worth it.

The cops had taken Michael in a separate ambulance. He didn't require sirens. Fredrico reassured me, as I rushed out the door at Debby's side, that he'd be taken into custody, and tried for his crimes—of which there was now plenty of evidence for—as soon as he got well enough to leave the hospital.

I stared down at Debby's sweet, doll-like face. One of the EMTs pulled her eyelid up, flashed a light into it, and her pupil dilated, then contracted. He did the same with the other.

"That's good," one of them said, her face a placid mask of focus.

"She going to be okay?" I asked.

"I don't want to promise you anything," she said, adjusting the IV, and supervising the other EMT while he packed her wound further. "But the shot's exactly where it should be."

"Where it should be?"

"If one has to be shot, you want it here," she said, pointing to Debby's side. "No organs, no major arteries. That's good. But I'm not gonna lie. She's bleeding a lot. Luckily, we're close to the hospital. Should be there in three minutes."

I felt my heart thundering, and since they'd finished doing what they could for her, I held her hand. I wanted it to be warmer than it was, it felt cold to me, and I thrummed with fear.

At the emergency entrance, I moved out of the way as they rolled her in, got to work on her somewhere I couldn't see.

I sat on one of the rough hospital seats, Sharon joining me not long after, and waited.

Sharon held my hand. She said nothing. She knew there wasn't a damn thing I could hear that would comfort me now. And there was something I had to do, and goddamn, how I didn't want to. I had to call Jack.

After what seemed like eons, but was probably an hour or two, a surgeon came out, called first Jack's name, then mine. He'd blown up at me on the phone like I'd never heard, hung up, and, presumably after taking the kids to Debby's mom, got here not long after. He didn't yell at me though, just looked at me with abject sorrow in his eyes and sat down a few seats away. I glanced up at the surgeon, ready to hear the worst, praying, though I didn't know what I believed, for the best.

"She lost a lot of blood, but she's going to be fine," the doctor said, and Jack sobbed sharply, and sagged, grabbing my arm. I held him up, and he let me.

We were allowed to go in to see her, told that she was conscious, but weak. To make it brief, and to keep it cool.

"Hi," she said softly, and both Jack and I rushed to her.

Jack caressed her hair, leaned down into her, and took her hand.

"I don't know what I'd do without you," he said, sobbing again, this time uncontrollably.

"It's okay, sweetie, I love you. I'm okay."

She let him get it all out, and then looked up at him, then me. "Here's what I want," she said, "I want you two to get along from here on out."

"But you could've died because of her," he said.

"He's right," I said, and Jack's face contorted in surprise.

"No. I want both of you to get something straight. I make my own choices. I'm my own person. I love you both, and I listen to you *both*, but I made my choices here. And I want this shit to end. Now. Forever."

I'd literally, never in my life, heard her cuss.

"Say it. I want to hear it from both of you," she said.

"Okay," I said.

I thought for a minute Jack wouldn't do it. He seemed to be battling something in there, something big. But after a minute or so, his face went slack, and he sighed, heavily.

"Okay," he said. "Alright, Debby," he said, his voice gentler than I'd remembered in forever. Since he'd been a child, since we'd all been children, really.

CHAPTER FIFTY-FOUR

As the buzzer sounded to let me in, Debby's words echoed throughout my brain. "You don't have to do this," she'd said. And she was right. But I'd thought about it, long and hard. I'd asked Squeaker about it, who I'd forgiven, and most of all, I thought about what my mother would've wanted. I was visiting my grandfather in jail.

He'd been tried, and convicted, both Nessie and Sharon testifying, and sentenced to life without parole. He'd pleaded guilty—which surprised me.

I picked up the phone.

He picked up on the other side.

"Hello, Kari," he said. "Surprised to see you."

He looked deflated, tired, his thick, gray, hair cut even shorter than I remembered.

"I thought you might be," I said, settling in the chair. It was hard, and plastic. Unforgiving.

"I think I know why you're here," he said.

I smiled grimly.

"It's . . ." he said, his voice breaking, "by a plateau. In Evergreen West. Where I used to go hunting. I buried her there."

He'd known I was going to ask where my mother was. He'd just known. I was grateful he hadn't drawn it out.

"It's so beautiful in the mountains, I just . . . thought she'd like it. I'd taken her there, as a girl. We'd gone hiking. I'd bought her these boots, you see. God, they were heavy. She was so skinny as a child." His eyes moved out of focus for a moment, and I could see the mountains, the vibrant red Indian paintbrushes, the pine, the purple and white columbine.

"It's funny, she was always special. I remember on that hike we were sitting there, taking a break, eating some trail mix when a deer—it came right up to her. She stretched out her hand to that tiny little god . . . and just stroked it. The doe, she closed her eyes. It was beautiful."

"I bet, Michael."

"I can tell Nessie the specific spot," he said, gathering himself. "Took her there too, once."

I nodded.

"I'll come by again," I said, gathering my bag.

He looked surprised. "You will?"

"I know that's what she would've wanted," I said.

He sat there with his mouth agape for a moment, and then shook his head.

"Doing sweats in here, you know," he said. I'd just gotten up, turned around.

"That's good, Michael. I'm glad to hear that." We had that in common. I'd promised Squeaker I'd let her do a ceremony for me. One to heal my heart.

I held Sharon's hand in my left, Nessie's in my right as they pulled my mother's body from the rocky soil. Nessie turned her head, weeping as it came out; bones and some bits of faded red fabric, tattered shreds of jeans. But Sharon and I watched, and I felt, for the first time in forever, at peace.

EPILOGUE

Tell me a story, Nick. Tell me a story about back in the day when my mom used to come here," I said, sitting at my favorite barstool, the little orange tabby purring beside me on the long, wooden bar.

It was the night of the soft reopening for the White Horse.

I knew Nick didn't remember Cecilia specifically, but he practically lived, in his mind, during the White Horse's heyday—when I knew my mother and father had frequented it.

"There were so many Indians. I knew the Beauvaises from Rosebud, I knew the Two Bulls from Pine Ridge, the Bitsuis from the Navajo Rez—and there were Indians in big, silver and gold belt buckles sometimes, dancing to Dolly Parton and Glen Campbell some days, and Indians listening to CCR other days. There were fights," he said, chuckling. "But there were so many good days too, and all of the romances that started here—"

The door swung open, and Sandy, Jack, and Carl came in . . . and a couple of folks I realized were from my high school days in Idaho Springs, behind them.

Debby clapped her hands like a little girl and gestured for them to join us at the bar. She'd been running around like it was her kids' birthday parties all day with last-minute errands.

"Shoot. I remember this place!" Carl said, coming up and standing next me. "I got so drunk here once."

"You got drunk in every bar in Denver, once," Jack said, and Carl told him to fuck off—in a friendly way.

"So. Where's all this fancy champagne I heard about?" Jack said, smiling at me tentatively. I smiled back.

I retrieved the champagne, and, as I was pouring everyone a glass, a few more folks came in, including my boss at The Hangar, and my old pals from Lucille's, Rafael and Martín—and even Caroline.

"Kari?"

I turned around at the sound of the voice, and in front of me was a tall Lakota, by the looks of him, in black skinny jeans with short, wavy, dark hair. He had a Metallica T-shirt on.

"Hey," I said.

"Hi," he said, holding his hand out.

"I'm Chris."

He saw my look of confusion.

"Chris Beauvais."

It took a minute, but I finally was able to put it together. "You're the one who I talked to on the phone! Who approved my loan."

"I know half your family," Nick said reverentially.

I hadn't realized Nick was behind me.

I smiled at Chris.

He smiled back. It was a warm smile, full of generosity.

"Could I get some of that champagne?"

"Sure," I said, pouring him a glass.

Auntie Squeaker and her entourage came in, and then Dr. Goodbear. One of Auntie's people requested "I'm Every Woman," and the bar flooded with the sweet, dulcet sounds of Whitney Houston. I offered Auntie some champagne. She asked for tequila.

"Tequila is medicine," she said, and I laughed.

I supposed that was sort of true though—our ancestors had been taking mezcal since time immemorial.

Fredrico was there, and he had an envelope from the FBI. It was my mom's file, with a few things redacted, of course.

My mother had led a full, and brave, life. She was also funny. She'd gotten a friend with a dump truck to back a ton of earth onto the Columbus statue in front of the Denver Civic Center.

She'd also masterminded the release of a herd of wild horses onto the front lawn of the capitol.

Inside the file was part of a statement she'd made during an arrest:

"I believe in the full return of all so-called American lands to its original peoples. Let us be the stewards of the earth that holds the bones of our ancestors, and the seeds of our future ancestors."

I loved reading her words, but it hurt that her life was cut so short. However, it made me feel better to contemplate how much she'd love the idea of my buying the White Horse with her sister. Turns out, Sharon had always wanted to buy a bar, and between me and her, we'd been able to make the down payment, and deal with the fees. And now, it was ours. And Nick's—we were keeping him on as part owner.

The White Horse, with its white plastic horse in the gold and black framed background, the PLEASE PAY WHEN SERVED sign above it. The print of the white and gray horse on the wooden walls, the multicolored lights strung up above the booths with the Miller Genuine Draft sign above them, the pool tables in the back where thousands of Indians had played, and lost, their sticks sliding against the aging green velvet. The old, brown speakers set in the corners in the walls, the windows with bars crisscrossed over them, the LADIES and GENTLEMEN signs painted in old-fashioned white script on the doors to the restrooms leading to toilets that barely worked anymore. The American flags, the prints of idealized Indians on white horses hunting buffalo, the NO ID NO SERVICE sign, sitting under the wooden YOU

MUST BE 21 TO BE AT THIS BAR sign, the wooden feathers tacked above
the gold-etched mirrors that looked like they'd been teleported directly from the '70s, the paper signs hanging from string tacked to
the ceiling that told the price of Corona, and of course, the ancient
jukebox, that had sung whole generations of Indians to sleep, their
heads spinning after a dance with a stranger.

"I hope you don't mind," Chris said, smiling and gesturing at the
newest group. "I called my dad up, and he called some folks, and we
just got the word out that the White Horse was where all the Indians
left in this town needed to be tonight."

"I don't mind," I said, and Debby squealed behind me. She hit my
arm. "Ouch," I said. "What was that for!"

"Thank the man, Kari!"

"Oh, of course. I'm sorry. Not so good at this kind of thing," I
said, my throat going tight. More Indians poured in, Okie mixes,
Diné, and Lakota, all kinds of Indians, all kinds of tribes, folks that
looked like they worked in a law office and folks that looked like
they drove trucks, and young Indians with nose rings and dyed red
and blue hair, young, hipster Indians that looked like they were
from Santa Fe. They were laughing and Nick was staring at them
and shaking his head, and I was getting as many people as I could a
glass of champagne, and then I asked if we could all cheers together
and the crowd roared, and Debby clapped her hands like a little girl.

"You'll never guess," Debby said.

"What?" I answered.

"That old cabin of Jack's? It finally fell over."

"Sad," I said. "End of an era."

"Don't be sad. Now we can build something new," Debby said.
I smiled.

"Oh!" Debby said, reaching into her bag. "I forgot. I got you a
little present!"

I smiled wider. Debby loved to buy the people in her life little
presents, randomly. Jaime had been like that too. My grief, after all

these years, seemed smaller—less tumescent. I'd pulled a picture of us that I'd kept tucked away in the back of my closet and framed it and put it by my bed. I talked to her almost every morning while I played Guns N' Roses for her, told her I was sorry, that I missed her.

"What? Whiskey?"

She rolled her eyes and continued digging. "Here it is!"

It was a black mug with the phrase INDIGENOUS BOSS BITCH emblazoned on the front.

I took it and thanked her.

Nessie even came at one point, though she didn't stay long. She and Sharon were slowly coming back around to a friendship, and hopefully to a place of forgiveness. Nessie had confessed that the reason she hadn't met me that day at Union Station was because Michael had threatened to kill Sharon too. He'd told her he had her address.

"Oh. Hello, you," I said, feeling something soft curl around my ankle, a little, furry tail. It was my favorite orange tabby. She jumped up on the bar, and I pet her, and she purred.

"Okay if I bring this one home, Nick? I've always liked her," I said, watching the kitty shut her eyes, as I moved my long, brown hand across her fur.

"Oh, sure," Nick said.

We closed up. I got the kitty kennel I'd brought. Debby hugged me and told me she loved me, helped me get the kitty into the cage. I told Nick I'd see him tomorrow and got myself an Uber.

In the seat, I looked over at the cat. "I think I'm gonna name you Cecilia," I said, softly. She looked up at me and yawned.

The next morning, I promised Debby I'd visit her. After, I walked the few blocks down to my father's house from Debby's, enjoying the golden rays of the sunset on the mountainside, the wind blowing through the grasses, the hiss of it through the pine trees.

I stood in front of the old, peeling door for a few minutes before I opened it, the blue sound of the television greeting me.

"Dad," I said, and he looked up, then back, squinting.

I sat down next to him, the laugh track from *The Jeffersons* echoing throughout the room, and I wondered what he would do if I told him where I'd been, what I had come to know. If he could even understand. If he wanted to.

I leaned into him, and his soft, white arm came around me, and I rested, closed my eyes.

I thought of my mother, her life taken by a man who, if not a literal beast, was a beast nonetheless, someone shaped by the shape of someone else's pain, who only knew to take that pain and try to give it to someone else, thinking that it would take the pain away from himself.

What I knew: once, I'd had a mother who had loved me, and who was gone. I had women who loved me, and I was always welcome with them. And now, I knew a little more about where my mom had come from. And where she'd ended up.

As to the war club, we were making plans to return it to the Chiricahua, where it belonged.

With my father's arm around me, I thought about the fact that I'd spent my life hating someone who'd loved me. And though she had died days after I'd been born, I felt like I knew her, at least a little bit, and could finally love her back.

Tears formed in my eyes, and it was okay, for the first time in my life I didn't feel like punching something because I felt sad. I was ready to just feel it, and I nestled into my father's shoulder, his hand going up to my hair. It was fine. And that anger I'd felt under my heart, it was gone.

I felt my mother's ghost then, a strong presence in the room. Dad felt it too. He lifted his hands into the air and closed his eyes, like he was remembering a tune he couldn't quite get clear in his mind. And then just as quickly as she came, she blew out like a wind and we were left, just the two of us, his hand back on my shoulder, my tears dry now, the blue light of the TV covering us both like a blanket, one that my mother had left behind, just for us. And as I drifted off, my head on his shoulder, we became one.

ACKNOWLEDGMENTS

Boy. It's so hard to write these things. Mainly because when you've been writing for long enough, there are so many people to thank—and deeply. First of all, I want to thank my editors at Flatiron, Zack Wagman and Maxine Charles. They have gone through countless rounds of this book with me, sticking through my stubbornness and my many, many questions. I can't describe how much I appreciate their insight and intelligence.

My agent, Rebecca Friedman, is a jewel—she's funny, and she's kind, and she always listens, really listens. Not to mention that she's smart as hell, and a brilliant editor in her own right. I could thank her a thousand times, and it wouldn't be enough.

Let's all take a moment to thank editors at independent presses: personally, without Jacob Knabb and Duncan Barlow, who took small resources and used them as hard as they could to support me and my work, I wouldn't be where I'm at, and they worked tirelessly, like so many editors, to help me realize my dreams. And they're good people. That matters.

I also want to thank Helen O'Hare, whose insight really mattered—whoever works with her is working with a dream.

Without my friend Bob Johnson, this book wouldn't exist. He's one of the most brilliant, sharp-edged short story writers I've ever had the privilege of reading, and someone who knows how to cut to the chase without sounding like a jerk when giving feedback. He read my novel twice—twice, without committing any crimes. I also have to thank my student-turned-friend Christine Kuster, who looked at chunks and gave me the fresh insight I needed, long after the brain had gone horribly numb to the words on the page.

Wow. The Native fiction writing community is one of the best. Brandon Hobson. Kelli Jo Ford. Stephen Graham Jones. Daniel H. Wilson. Rebecca Roanhorse. Chip Livingston. Morgan Talty. Theodore Van Alst. Shane Hawk. Margaret Verble. My partner David Heska Wanbil Weiden. These are the folks that I could email/text/call who made all the difference. And there are so many more, and more to follow at long last.

I also want, as always, to thank my family, who come from a long line of criminals, thieves, whorehouse owners, gangsters, and on the other side of things, teachers and dancers and singers—all stubborn, independent thinkers.

On the heels of the last sentiment, I have to thank the community that formed me—Denver, and the two small towns I grew up in-between, Evergreen and Idaho Springs. The mix of poverty and middle-class life, white, Indian, Black and Indigenous Mexican-American and/or Chicanx/e cultures came the strange and unique mix of culture that has forever been my muse.

I want to thank the horror community: I loved horror as a young girl and coming back to it has been a gift. I'm especially thankful for the work of Silvia Moreno-Garcia—a writer who took the time to answer my questions, even when her star was wildly on the rise—and whose novel re-arranged my head.

Thanks, also, to the Kenyon Review and Tin House community for letting me into your worlds.

I want, lastly, to thank my boyfriend, my partner in life, a phenomenal writer and person—who listens to me complain, who reads my work—over and over—and who is just there. That came to me later in life, and it's been a gift.

ABOUT THE AUTHOR

Erika T. Wurth's work has appeared in numerous publications, including *BuzzFeed* and the *Kenyon Review*. She is a Kenyon and Sewanee fellow and a narrative artist for the Meow Wolf Denver installation. She is an urban Native of Apache, Chickasaw, and Cherokee descent.